An Unexpected Governess to Tame his Wild Heart

STAND-ALONE NOVEL

A Western Historical Romance Book

by

Ava Winters

Disclaimer & Copyright

This is a work of fiction. Names, characters, places and incidents either are products of the author's imagination or are used fictitiously. Any resemblance to actual events or locales or persons, living or dead, is entirely coincidental.

Copyright© 2023 by Ava Winters

All Rights Reserved.

This book may not be reproduced or transmitted in any form without the written permission of the publisher.

In no way is it legal to reproduce, duplicate, or transmit any part of this document in either electronic means or in printed format. Recording of this publication is strictly prohibited and any storage of this document is not allowed unless with written permission from the publisher

Table of Contents

An Unexpected Governess to Tame his Wild Heart 1
   Disclaimer & Copyright 2
   Table of Contents 3
   Let's connect! 5
   Letter from Ava Winters 6
Prologue 7
Chapter One 13
Chapter Two 19
Chapter Three 27
Chapter Four 34
Chapter Five 42
Chapter Six 51
Chapter Seven 66
Chapter Eight 73
Chapter Nine 82
Chapter Ten 92
Chapter Eleven 100
Chapter Twelve 107
Chapter Thirteen 115
Chapter Fourteen 120
Chapter Fifteen 125
Chapter Sixteen 132
Chapter Seventeen 142
Chapter Eighteen 152

Chapter Nineteen 158
Chapter Twenty 168
Chapter Twenty-One.. 173
Chapter Twenty-Two.. 179
Chapter Twenty-Three 187
Chapter Twenty-Four 199
Chapter Twenty-Five.. 207
Chapter Twenty-Six 216
Chapter Twenty-Seven... 225
Chapter Twenty-Eight.. 229
Chapter Twenty-Nine... 238
Chapter Thirty.. 245
Chapter Thirty-One 259
Epilogue 277
  Also by Ava Winters 294

Let's connect!

Impact my upcoming stories!

My passionate readers influenced the core soul of the book you are holding in your hands! The title, the cover, the essence of the book as a whole was affected by them!

Their support on my publishing journey is paramount! I devote this book to them!

If you are not a member yet, join now! As an added BONUS, you will receive my Novella "**The Cowboys' Wounded Lady**":

FREE EXCLUSIVE GIFT
(available only to my subscribers)

Go to the link:
https://avawinters.com/novella-amazon

Letter from Ava Winters

"Here is a lifelong bookworm, a devoted teacher and a mother of two boys. I also make mean sandwiches."

If someone wanted to describe me in one sentence, that would be it. There has never been a greater joy in my life than spending time with children and seeing them grow up - all my children, including the 23 little 9-year-olds that I currently teach. And I have not known such bliss than that of reading a good book.

As a Western Historical Romance writer, my passion has always been reading and writing romance novels. The historical part came after my studies as a teacher - I was mesmerized by the stories I heard, so much that I wanted to visit every place I learned about. And so, I did, finding the love of my life along the way as I walked the paths of my characters.

Now, I'm a full-time elementary school teacher, a full-time mother of two wonderful boys and a full-time writer. Wondering how I manage all of them? I did too, at first, but then I realized it's because everything I do I love, and I have the chance to share it with all of you.

And I would love to see you again in this small adventure of mine!

Until next time,

Ava Winters

Prologue

Atlanta, Georgia

10th April 1885

Arch Sutton sat at his large desk, bent over a piece of paper as he carefully penned a letter to his estranged brother, Thomas Sutton. They didn't speak much, and so each letter that Arch wrote to him took far too long to compose.

They sent letters back and forth and had done so for a few years, but Arch's own awkwardness meant that he often took months to reply - which was precisely what happened this time. It had been four months since he had received the letter from his brother. He kept meaning to write back. It was just that he was never sure what the right thing to say was, or how many questions to ask about his wife Sylvie and their little family.

He felt that asking too much would make Thomas resent him for not visiting, but asking too little felt inconsiderate. He did want to visit, it was just hard. Things were complicated.

He put his fountain pen down on the mahogany desk and flung his head back with a sigh, his sandy blonde hair quivering slightly with the motion — he wasn't getting anywhere with the letter, and it was driving him insane. How was it that he could run an entire accounting firm but writing one measly letter to his brother was this difficult?

Don't be ridiculous, Arch thought to himself, pulling his head back forward. He took a large sip from the glass of scotch on the table and sighed. *It's just a letter,* he reminded himself. *He's not going to overthink anything you say,* he continued. With a slow and steady breath out, he picked his pen back up and put it to paper.

Dearest Thomas,

I am sorry to hear that you are having trouble getting both your boys to behave — but I imagine that this is an age-old quarrel between fathers and their sons. We were not much interested in what our father had to say at that age ...

Arch breathed out shakily; he didn't really think back to their childhood often. Every time he did, a small shiver traveled down the back of his neck, and his palms began to sweat profusely. He grumbled under his breath and put his pen down once again, scratching at his beard. He stared at the paper, reading over what he'd written again and again, before shaking his head and crumpling it up, chucking it across the room into the large fireplace on the far wall. Standing up, he stretched his lean form, then stalked around his desk and perched himself on the edge.

"Get it together, Sutton," he whispered to himself.

Before he could shake off the ridiculousness of his struggle to write a simple letter, there was a small knock on his office door.

"Sir, there's a telegram for you," the voice of Arch's polite, timid secretary Miriam Hall barely made it through the thick door.

"Bring it in, Miriam." He plastered a small smile on his face and straightened himself up off of the desk. The large door creaked open and a small, middle-aged woman wandered in. Her hair was brown but peppered with gray and white around the temples, and she wore a peach-colored dress that covered her from the neck down. She nodded politely at Arch as she entered and strode over to hand him the telegram.

"Here you go," she said politely, placing the envelope in his hand and turning on her heel to exit.

"Thank you, Miriam," he replied, watching her leave and close the door behind her before opening the envelope in his hands. Once she was gone and the door had fallen shut, he stared at the note in his hands. He was not expecting news of any kind- after all, none of his accountants were out of town. He frowned at the envelope and walked back to his desk, leaning slightly on the front of it as he turned the telegram over in his slender hands, pondering for a moment what it could be before opening it and pulling the card out.

To: ARCHIBALD SUTTON, SUTTON ACCOUNTING

I REGRET TO INFORM YOU THAT THOMAS SUTTON, 29, AND HIS WIFE, SYLVIE SUTTON, 33, HAVE PASSED AWAY. THEY LEAVE BEHIND THREE YOUNG CHILDREN AND A RANCH, WHICH YOU ARE TO RECEIVE RESPONSIBILITY FOR.

PLEASE RETURN TO PADDINGTON, TEXAS, AS SOON AS POSSIBLE.

SHERIFF RUDY PARKER

Archie's hands began to shake, and he looked over his shoulder at the desk and the letter he had been writing. He had just been writing to his brother — how could he now be dead? How long ago did it happen? *If I'd replied to his letter sooner ...* Arch found himself thinking as tears began to sting his eyes. He reread the telegram and ran his fingers over the grooves of the letters left by the typewriter.

Shaking his head, he placed the telegram down on the desk and covered his face with his hands. Taking a deep breath, he tried to calm himself down, only to find that his despair and anxiety worsened. He reached behind him for the scotch and poured it down his throat in one go.

The burn of the alcohol helped to distract him for a moment, and he let out a long deep breath. Squeezing his eyelids shut, he counted to five in his head, trying again to let go of his emotions and calm down.

Once he'd reached five, his hands had just about stopped shaking, though he could still feel the sting in his eyes.

Arch reached for the telegram and read it aloud. He paused when he reached the second paragraph, swallowing harshly at the very idea of returning to Sutton Ranch, let alone to return as a guardian of three young children whom he had never met.

"No," he repeated yet again. "How did this happen?"

How could he just leave the life he'd built himself in Atlanta for the ranch life that he had run away from as a young man? He had no idea how to run a ranch; his father had neglected to teach him that. And he *definitely* didn't know how to look after three children.

But he knew that even thinking like that was selfish - his niece and nephews had just lost their parents. He was all they had. He walked around and took a seat at his desk, and, taking a deep breath, put his letter-writing tools away.

There's not much of a choice, he sighed. He wasn't going to just leave the children with no guardian, nor would he let the ranch fall into someone else's hands. If he tried, he could make it work; he'd have to run the office from Texas somehow, and let the building in Georgia go. He was sure he would be able to sort something out in the coming weeks.

Assuming that Thomas had employed some ranch hands, he wouldn't have to do too much work when in Texas — he hoped not, anyway. There was just the matter of the children to worry about, now. But he'd have to deal with that when he got there.

His hand wandered to his beard again, tugging at the straw-colored hairs. It was getting a bit long, and too unruly for his tastes — he would need to trim it before he left. Arch took pride in his beard, and he didn't want to appear scruffy the first time he met his brother's children.

Packing his desk up neatly, he paused at the photograph of himself opening up the Sutton Accounting building. He looked at it and sighed - he'd left his family for this life, and that picture of the cheery blonde man with a straw-colored beard had been the result. The epitome of his dreams come true.

Yet here he was, heading back to Texas. He turned the photo away, continued to gather the most important files into a briefcase, then walked over to the door. He turned around and took one final look around his office. Sadly, he admired the large, ornate fireplace and elegant wooden desk. He looked down at the patterned carpet and nodded forlornly before stepping out of the door.

He was going to have to man up and go back to Texas - no matter how much it frightened him.

"Miriam, I need you to find me a seat on a train to Texas," he stated as he stepped into the hallway where Miriam's small wooden desk sat. "And extinguish the fireplace, please," he gestured behind him at the office. "I will be back in an hour or so, I just need to gather some belongings."

"Texas, sir?" Miriam raised an eyebrow. "What's in Texas?"

"Family," Arch sighed. *Or there used to be, anyway,* he thought to himself.

Miriam nodded curtly and smiled at Arch. "Very well, then, I shall see you soon."

Arch nodded back and headed out of the office and back home.

Chapter One

Atlanta Station, Georgia

10th April 1885

Looking down at the ticket that Miriam had obtained for him, Arch chewed the inside of his lip. The train was in an hour, and there was very little near the station that he could do to keep himself occupied. His entire body was full of nervous energy which fizzled away beneath the surface, making him unable to stay still for longer than a few moments. He dreaded the long, grueling train journey ahead of him almost as much as he dreaded reaching Texas. Even now that his father, Simon Sutton, was long gone, the very idea of Texas made Arch's skin crawl.

Standing just outside the station, he turned and looked around, considering what there was to do. After a brief evaluation, he resigned himself to heading onto the platform and taking a seat on an old, rickety bench.

There were few people on the platform - it was an odd time to catch a train. The long platform ended with a small ticket office right at one end, on his left. To his right, there were more benches, and then the built-up, raised platform faded away into the dirt.

He held his bag between his legs and sat, leaning forward with his elbows on his knees. Taking a deep breath, he tried to fill the time by thinking about the logistics of keeping Sutton Accounting alive. He considered ending the contract on the office, moving the entire business to Texas, or possibly trying to use this as an opportunity to open another branch.

But without the figures in front of him, he could not determine which idea was the best and ended up overthinking again. It seemed that his mind was adamant that he dwell on his brother and sister-in-law's passing, the new responsibilities that had fallen on him, and the intricate situation that surrounded it all.

It was all made a thousand times worse by Arch's own guilt. He had been putting off visiting for years, and he'd even put off replying to Thomas' letters, too. If he'd have been a good brother, this wouldn't be as daunting a task. In fact, if he'd been a good enough brother, maybe he'd have been able to care for Thomas and Sylvie when they had fallen ill.

Or at least, he assumed that's what had taken them. From all accounts, Thomas seemed to be a healthy man with no enemies — so he couldn't imagine it being anything else. He tapped his foot on the platform anxiously and continued to wait, trying — but failing — to keep his mind empty.

The hour passed slowly, and Arch felt every single second of it. He spent each minute fighting off the guilt, the fear, and the sadness, and when that didn't work, fighting off tears.

He and his brother had been far from close in recent years, but as children, they'd been one another's anchors in the midst of a poor childhood with a strict father and intense ranch life. He would sincerely miss exchanging letters with Thomas, and hearing all about Sylvie and their lives.

It was far too late to do anything about it now. They were gone. And he, in their place, had a ranch to run and children to raise, despite never having met them, nor having any practice with children. *I'll manage*, he tried to tell himself, again and again. It was the same thing he'd told himself when setting up Sutton Accounting, and that had done him well. He just had to hope it'd have the same effect now.

Eventually, the train pulled up alongside the platform. Arch shot up from his seat and almost ran to the door. Climbing aboard, he found himself a seat away from other people and tried to get comfortable. He closed his eyes, hoping that sleep would make the journey pass quicker.

The second his eyes closed, he fell into a long, restless sleep. His dreams were full of oddities; children running amok and chasing him over hills, bankruptcy leading him to become a monk, and a field so empty that his whispers echoed.

By the time his eyelids fluttered open, the train was halfway between Georgia and Texas, and he felt more tired than he had when he fell asleep.

Arch filled the rest of his journey with watching trees and landscapes change out of the window, reading over some of the documents he had bought with him, and dining on smoked haddock and potato in the dining car. He felt his emotions fizzling beneath his skin and struggled to remain still, so found himself shifting position countless times before they reached Texas.

Once in his home state, Arch got off the train and hailed a hansom cab. Standing on the sidewalk, the intense Texas sun made him sweat profusely. He still wore a suit on his slim body, not having had the time to change, and the material clung to him.

The cab driver, sitting atop a small seat behind the square carriage, pulled the reins of the two horses attached to the front, pulling them around toward Arch and to a halt in front of him. The carriage had two small windows on either side and was open to the front. The reins of the two large mares leading it went up and over the top of the wooden carriage, held in place with small eyelets.

Arch directed the driver and climbed aboard, bobbing his leg up and down as the driver moved the horses forward. It was not a long journey from the town to the ranch, and for this, Arch was incredibly grateful. After a half-day's journey on a train, the last thing he needed was a long drive.

Once the horses started moving, he tried his best to ignore his surroundings, for he was well aware that focusing on them would just send his mind reeling back to his childhood. In the small amount he did see, not much had changed since he'd left. A few buildings had been made taller and longer, and there were several homes where trees used to be, but that was about all.

Soon enough, the cab pulled up outside the house that Arch had grown up in. It seemed not to have changed since he left. It was large, and the porch attached to it went around from the front of the house all the way around the left side of the building.

There were a couple of differences, though; there were two benches along the wall of the house that hadn't been there when he had lived in Paddington, and a woman that he did not recognize sat on one of them. She was gentle looking, with a small, plump face and wide, kind eyes.

She wore a large pink dress which only made her pink-tinted skin stand out more. From what Arch could tell, she seemed to be around his age. Arch stepped out of his cab, paid the driver quickly, and walked toward the house.

"Can I help you?" The woman asked.

"I was wondering the same thing; this is my ranch," Arch replied. "Who are you?"

"Oh! You must be Arch!" The woman's voice rose in pitch and her small smile got much bigger. "It is lovely to finally meet you, albeit in horrible circumstances." She shook her head sadly.

"And you are?" Arch asked again.

"Oh, right, yes! I am Angela Parker. I'm the neighbor. I've been looking after the children and the house whilst we awaited your arrival," she explained, walking toward Arch.

"Ah, Angela." He nodded, rummaging through the names that Thomas had mentioned in their letters. He was sure there had been an Angela. From what he could remember, they were friendly with one another. "Hello." He offered her his hand, and she took it swiftly, shaking it.

"Let's get you to meet the children," Angela said, still smiling. She preceded him into the house, and Arch couldn't help but feel a bit uneasy at being shown into his own childhood home, but he ignored it. Angela led him into the dining room, where a large man sat holding a young girl — *must be Pauline,* Arch thought to himself. On the other side of the table sat two young boys who looked exactly like Thomas as a young man. The three children all had noticeably bright green eyes, which must have come from their mother; they weren't traits Arch had ever seen within his own family. Their skin was light and freckled, like his and Thomas', and their hair seemed to all be almost exactly the same color. Arch cleared his throat.

"This is my husband, Sheriff Rudy Parker." Angela gestured to the man. "And that is Pauline." She pointed to the young girl. Arch knew her to be his two-year-old niece. "This is Fred." She pointed to the eldest and largest of the two boys. "And David." She gestured finally to the other son.

"Hi, Fred, David," he nodded and waved. "I'm, well, I'm uh, I'm your uncle Arch," he said awkwardly. Fred and David looked at one another and then shook their heads, their blonde hair moving as their heads moved. The two of them wore casual shirts that were too big for them, and Arch wondered if the shirts were their father's.

"We don't need an uncle," Fred said simply, standing up from the table. "Come on, David." He walked around the table and out of the doorway that Arch had just entered through, and David followed close behind. Arch turned and watched the two boys storm away upstairs and into their rooms, the doors shutting harshly.

"Well, that ... Didn't go to plan," the sheriff said quietly.

"I'm sure they'll warm up to you," Angela tried to reassure Arch, placing a hand on his shoulder. "They've just lost their parents — and, if you ask me, it wasn't exactly natural."

Arch turned his head to face Angela and furrowed his brows.

"What do you mean?" He asked. He still had not been told the cause of death. It was not in the telegram, and nobody had mentioned it yet.

The sheriff shot her a warning glare, but she rolled her eyes and turned to face Arch.

"Well, the day before they died, I happened to catch a suspicious-looking gentleman on our ranch, sneaking out of Sutton Ranch. He was wearing a lot of baggy clothes and looked too skinny to be a ranch hand. Had pale skin, dark hair, and a beard that I'd recognize anywhere." She shook her head.

"It was just a traveler," the sheriff sighed. "Ignore her; she likes all these conspiracies. Unfortunately, your brother's passing was simply horrible luck," he looked up at Arch apologetically.

Arch hummed in acknowledgment. He was sure it was nothing — Thomas had never really mentioned anyone not liking them or having any quarrels with the neighboring ranches. It was probably simply poor luck that they both fell ill at the same time. Regardless, he was much more focused on the fact that both of his nephews just dismissed him in one fell swoop. It seemed all of his anxieties about coming back to Texas were entirely valid.

Chapter Two

St. John, Kansas

7th May 1885

Bridget Edwards walked quickly through the town of St. John, her head bowed and eyes on the ground to avoid the glances of others. She'd grown accustomed to walking in such a way; people had always looked at her, for as long as she could remember.

She walked through the main street, occasionally glancing up at the stores to see if there was anything new, or if there was anything in them that piqued her interest, but for the most part, the small storefronts held in them the same that they always did; the butchers had no new exciting meat that she could use for dinner, the bakers had no new recipes, and the tiny haberdashery seemed to have had the same fabric in its store window for months now.

So she continued on her walk home, a small woven basket in her hand that was full of fresh vegetables and fruit, a small cob of bread, and some jerky.

The streets in St. John were wide and, despite being lined on both sides with various stores, they felt very open, as the buildings were all only a story or two high. Many of the busiest streets gave way to smaller, quiet streets that led away from the town and toward the residential areas.

Bridget knew that as soon as she'd passed St. John Town Square with its large open space, she was almost home. The town was small, and not well populated, so by the time she'd journeyed most of the way home, Bridget was entirely alone on the sidewalk.

Now that she was alone, she lifted her head and looked around as she walked, feeling much more at home in her own company than she'd ever felt around those who lived in the town. Since she was a child, they had made it clear, in small ways, that she was not a wanted part of the community.

That was precisely why she wanted to leave Kansas. Her grandmother had always told her she was being ridiculous for thinking so; after all, the townspeople were never *mean*, they were just cold. There'd been sideways glances, and whispers in church, just enough to make a young girl feel very certain about being unwanted. It started as soon as she moved in with her grandmother when her entire family fell sick.

She'd just managed to survive it, as a babe, and from that moment on, people seemed to act as if she were cursed, as if she was the cause of her family's undoing. None of them would ever admit that to her face, of course. They were nice enough in person.

Bridget reached the end of the town square and turned left, walking down a small street. Eventually, she reached the small home that she shared with her grandmother and walked up onto the porch. She paused outside the front door, shifting her weight from one foot to another. Before she'd left the house, she'd received a letter in reply to an application she had made on a whim.

She'd applied for the role of a governess in Texas after discussing her unhappiness in St. John with her grandmother. They'd spoken about ways that Bridget could change how she felt, and the idea of becoming a governess had come up. She did love children and was very good at keeping a household, so it made sense. Evangeline had suggested it to Bridget, saying that she'd once been a governess and it had changed her life.

It may have been her grandmother's own suggestion, but Bridget was certain that it had only been said in an attempt to placate her. Shaking her head to wash the nerves away, she pushed the door open.

"Meemaw," she called affectionately as she stepped into the house. She stood in the hallway for a moment, listening for a response.

"In here, Biddie!" Evangeline called from the living room. Bridget smiled — her Meemaw had always called her Biddie. It was what Biddie's older brother had called her when she was born. He couldn't quite handle the 'r' or the 't' in her name, and so 'Biddie' was born. Evangeline used it so much that others picked up on it, and eventually, people tended to call her that more than her actual name, at this point.

Biddie nodded to herself and took the basket with her through to the living room on the right side of the house. She beamed down at her grandmother, who sat peacefully on a large armchair, a pool of wool in her lap, her knitting needles clicking away.

She looked up at Biddie with sparkling, happy eyes and a warm look of appreciation. Her face was wrinkled with age, but she still had her beauty. Her eyes were a warm green color and she wore her dark hair in gentle curls that fell around her face, though the bulk of it was tied back into tight waves on the top of her head.

"That basket looks awful full." Evangeline eyed the basket in Biddie's hands, grinning.

"It is quite full; the store had plenty in today," Biddie replied, setting it down on a small table in the center of the room. She opened the lid of the basket and began to pull out items, holding them out to display to her grandmother. "Apples, plums, yams, and some bread," Biddie explained each item as she pulled it from the basket. Evangeline nodded, approving each item as it came. "And finally, some jerky." Biddie placed everything out on the table, and her grandmother scanned the produce briefly.

"Great job, love," she approved. "Did they say when they'd next have some chicken in?"

"Tomorrow, Meemaw," Biddie replied. Her grandmother loved chicken more than any other meat, but there weren't too many ranches around St. John that raised them, or who didn't keep them alive for their eggs rather than slaughter them for their meat.

"Ah, wonderful! A chicken pie for supper tomorrow, then." Evangeline grinned from ear to ear, and Biddie's heart sank. How was she supposed to tell her grandmother the news when she was so chipper? She nodded cheerfully along with her grandmother's joy and began to pile the shopping back into the basket.

"Sounds perfect," she said simply, picking the basket up and heading toward the door. She'd tell her grandmother later, she decided. As she walked away from where Evangeline sat, she felt her grandmother's eyes on her, and before she could step out of the door, her grandmother spoke.

"Biddie," she said softly. "There's something on your mind, isn't there, child?"

Biddie stopped in her tracks. Her heart felt as if it were in her throat, and she felt herself begin to sweat profusely from her hands.

"No, Meemaw, I'm fine," she answered weakly. This woman had raised her, she should have known that she'd pick up on something.

"Now, Bridget Edwards," her grandmother's voice turned stern. "Do not deceive me, please, I raised you better than to lie to an old woman." She raised an eyebrow, and Biddie could see it from where she stood. She let out a small sigh and turned to face her grandmother.

"There's nothing wrong, as such," Biddie began. "It's just ... well ... " she looked down at her feet. She'd never liked upsetting her grandmother, and she was sure that this would. Her heart remained firmly seated in her throat as she continued. "I applied for a role as a governess, Meemaw," she began to explain.

"Well, good," Evangeline nodded firmly in response, but her face seemed to disagree with her words. "Well, we'll just have to wait for the response."

"That's the thing," Biddie replied. "I got a response. They accepted me. I am to move there in a week," she said quickly.

Evangeline's eyebrows dropped, and her brow furrowed into an inexplicable knot across her forehead.

"Oh. Right," she said simply. "Well, I suppose you're moving to Stafford or Macksville?" She asked.

"A little bit further, actually," Biddie replied gently. Stafford and Macksville were the neighboring towns, but she was going all the way to Paddington, Texas.

"How much further?" Evangeline stopped knitting, placing her project in her lap.

"A bit," Biddie replied, clearing her throat. *Why is this so hard?!* She asked herself.

"Bridget," her grandmother warned.

"Texas," Biddie replied.

There was silence. Evangeline's eyes met Biddie's, and their usual emerald sparkle had been replaced with a murky, sad green. Biddie's heart finally left her throat and sank, and she felt tears sting in her eyes. She knew her grandmother would be sad, but she didn't expect to get so affected by it.

"Texas?" Her grandmother asked weakly.

"Mmhm," she replied. "The family has suffered two losses — both parents. It's just the uncle, two nephews, and a niece now. The advertisement said that they need someone to help the family adjust." She looked at her grandmother with wide eyes. "They've lost their parents, Meemaw."

Her grandmother sighed and smiled sadly; Biddie knew that expression well and knew that her grandmother had no intention of stopping her from going to Texas. She just wasn't happy that it was happening.

"I understand," Evangeline eventually said. "I'm proud of you for helping them," she said gently. "I will miss you, child, more than anything."

Biddie felt a tear fall from her stinging eyes. She'd waited a long, long time for an opportunity like this, but she would miss her grandmother an incredible amount. She had never known any other company, really. It would be bizarre not to have Evangeline around. Wiping the tear away briskly, she nodded.

"I know, Meemaw," she sniffed. "But, we have a few days until I need to leave. So chicken pie for supper tomorrow, yes?" She forced a smile onto her face, and her grandmother nodded gently. "Wonderful. I'll go and put these in the pantry," Biddie stated, leaving the room.

She walked through the house, into the kitchen, and placed the groceries in the pantry. On the counter next to the pantry was a jug of fresh lemonade that her grandmother had made that morning. She poured herself a large glass of it and leaned against the counter, taking small sips.

On the wall opposite was a small looking glass, and she caught her own reflection. Her wild, curly hair was pinned back, the dark waves framing her face and making the singular white streak stand out as clear as day. Her glasses perched precariously on her large nose, and she could see how little she fit in here.

Even her appearance made her stand out — a pale woman with bright green eyes, dark, unruly hair and a slim figure ... She understood why people stared. But still, she hoped that would not be the case in Texas.

Looking away from her reflection, she lost herself in thought. Her mind wandered to whether her grandmother would be able to survive here on her own, and when that thought became too worrying and too upsetting, she instead thought about what might await her in Texas.

There had not been a whole lot of information in the advertisement, nor in the letter that she had received back from Mr. A. Sutton. All she knew was that the three children, aged two, eight, and nine, had lost their parents and that their uncle had moved from Georgia back to Texas to care for them. But, being a busy man, he was unable to provide proper care for them and needed an extra pair of hands.

That was where she came in. She wondered whether the children were kind and sweet or stroppy and spoiled — she hoped for the former, obviously — and whether their uncle would be a gentle boss. She pictured what she imagined a family house on a ranch to be like, and excitedly fantasized about how the ranch might look, with rolling fields and crops, animals, and plenty of workers, all chatting away as they worked.

A small wave of joy flooded through her mind; leaving her grandmother was hard, but this was the most excitement she'd felt in a long time.

With a newfound skip in her step, she placed her glass down on the counter and went through the house and up to her room. She opened her wardrobe and began to pick out the items she wished to pack for her move. Mostly, she picked out square-necked dresses in rich colors like plum, brown, and indigo.

As her complexion was fair and her hair dark with unruly curls, she favored dark colors. Lighter dresses always seemed to make her look unbalanced — there was too much dark on top to be light on the bottom. Once she'd pulled out all of the dresses she wished to take, she picked out some books from her shelves, a couple of pairs of shoes, and some accessories. Neatly, she began to fold and stack the items into a large case.

She had to fight with the case in order to get it shut, but once it was latched, she propped it up in the corner of her childhood bedroom and took a seat on her bed. She stared at the case, a whirlwind of excitement, nervousness, and sadness wreaking havoc within her mind.

Moving to Texas was a big decision. But she'd been desperate to leave St. John for years. *Texas cannot possibly be worse than Kansas,* she thought to herself.

Chapter Three

Sutton Ranch, Paddington, Texas

10th May 1885

Arch walked over to the crib where Pauline lay, sobbing loudly. She writhed around on her back, wrinkling her soft nightgown, and slowly freeing her wispy young hair that had been swept away from her face and held firmly in place with bandoline. She seemed deeply unsettled, and had been since Arch had arrived.

He was unsure whether she had picked up on the lack of her parents, or if it was simply his presence that had caused her foul moods. She certainly seemed far from fond of him. He reached down into the crib and hooked his hands into her armpits, pulling her up onto his chest.

As soon as his hands reached the threshold of the crib, her sobbing worsened, and Arch grumbled under his breath.

The entire month that he had been back in Paddington had been nothing short of a nightmare. Pauline seemed adamant that the best response to Arch in any situation was to cry, or in this case, cry harder. The two boys, Fred and David, were relentlessly playing pranks on him.

They had unscrewed his bed legs but left the bed balanced together, meaning that Arch fell into a heap of wood on the floor that night. They had knotted all of Arch's ties together in a heap that took him almost an hour to undo, and they kept hiding his belongings from him — first his briefcase, and then his suits, then his shoes … They were little devils, and Arch could not figure out what he had done to make them act like this.

He bounced Pauline up and down on his chest, holding her close to him. He'd seen mothers and fathers do the same, and assumed that it was the correct way to handle a screaming child — and yet, it seemed to do nothing.

Every now and then she would take a breath, and Arch would sigh in relief, only for her to look at him and then continue crying. He could feel his spirit being chipped away bit by bit and prayed that the governess he'd hired from Kansas would bond with the children better than he had. He wasn't sure how much more of this he could take without consistent support.

Angela had visited every day or every other day to help him cook or to allow him time to bathe, but it just wasn't enough. He was, for the first time in a very long time, struggling.

With Pauline still held against his chest, he left the bedroom and wandered downstairs toward the playroom. It had once been a living room, way back when he lived in the house, but it had long since been taken over by rocking horses and wooden toys.

He knelt down on the floor and placed Pauline down. She wobbled on her legs for a second, the sobs making her slightly unsteady, but soon found her feet and toddled away from Arch.

The second that she was a few inches away, the crying stopped. Arch sighed deeply and stayed where he was, watching as the young girl teetered around the playroom, grabbing random stuffed animals and wooden blocks and giggling away to herself. *She's sweet when she's not screaming at me*, Arch thought to himself.

She began to build a small tower, and he watched with curiosity as she tried to figure out which blocks of wood would best hold other pieces up. She managed to get four pieces, one atop the other, and stood over the tower triumphantly.

Arch smiled to himself, only to then see her jump at the sound of a knock on the door. Her small hand jumped away from her body, knocking her tower down to the floor.

Arch froze.

Please don't cry, he begged in his head. But it was no use. The sobbing started up again and he let out a long, frustrated sigh. Standing up from the floor, he swooped Pauline up into his arms again and carried her, still crying, to answer the door. Pulling it open, he relaxed a little at the sight of Angela.

"Morning, Arch." She smiled warmly, but her eyes locked onto the clearly very unhappy Pauline. "Need me to take her?" She asked. Arch's sad eyes looked from the toddler in his arms and his friendly neighbor, and he nodded. Angela held her hands out, and Arch handed Pauline over to her. To nobody's surprise, the crying began to subside almost instantly.

"I don't know how Thomas did this," he said gently, moving to allow Angela into the house.

"Well, it is easier when they're your children," Angela explained. "But just give them time, they'll warm up to you." She gazed up at him, her eyes full of reassurances that Arch couldn't help but doubt.

"I'm not sure they will." He shook his head, following her as she led the way to the dining room. "But that's fine. As long as they warm up to the governess that I've sent for."

Angela laughed heartily as she pulled a seat out at the dining room table.

"You'll need more than just a governess to keep this house and ranch afloat, Arch," she said through her laughter.

Arch frowned, his eyebrows coming together across his forehead as he pulled out his own chair.

"What do you mean?" He asked.

"A governess won't be able to keep on top of the housework, the children, the kitchen … Just you wait; you'll still be short-handed, I'm afraid," Angela explained. "This is a big house, and these little ones take a lot of work. That's without even considering the work on the ranch …" She looked at Arch with wide, sad eyes. "I'm afraid Thomas and Sylvie haven't left you in much of a desirable position."

"You don't need to tell me that," Arch sighed. He looked at Pauline, who was sitting upright on Angela's lap, playing idly with the hem of her skirt. "I went from a big city accountant to a guardian of three children who hate me and a ranch that seems to be barely afloat …" He shook his head.

"It will get easier, Arch," Angela tried to reassure him, and her kind eyes helped a little, but he just could not see his life on this ranch ever being enjoyable.

"That's not even to mention the fact that my brother's death seems to not be as simple as I thought." He rubbed his eyes with the heel of his hand and slumped back into his chair. He'd been thinking about what Angela had said the day that he arrived, and couldn't help but wonder if maybe there was something more there. His brother had not, as far as he was aware, reported any illness. Neither had Sylvie. Unexpected deaths happened, of course, but something felt inherently off about this situation. "Would you be able to explain a bit more about what you saw, and what you think happened?"

"I really shouldn't, Rudy says it's just a flight of fancy," Angela said uncomfortably and darted her eyes away from Arch.

"Please, Angela. If there's even a piece of you that believes my brother's death was unconventional, I need to know," he begged. "We weren't close in life, and I spent far too long away from him. All I have now, all I can do now, to make up for it, is to do good by him," he spoke softly, and tried, despite what he was saying, to keep the tone of his voice cheerful so that Pauline stayed ignorant of what they were discussing. She seemed blissfully unaware as Angela bounced her on her knee.

Angela's eyes slowly made their way back to Arch, meeting his. He stared at her for a moment, his brows furrowed in concern, and she eventually nodded, her lips pulled tightly across her face.

"Alright, alright," she said. "All I know is that Thomas and Sylvie were in a bit of a standoff with another resident — a Mr. Wellington. He wanted to buy their land and their water rights from them. But they wouldn't give it up. No matter what was offered, Thomas remained firm — this was his family's land. It was not to be passed to anybody else." Angela smiled as she spoke of Thomas, and Arch felt a small smile appear on his own face. It was nice to know that Thomas wouldn't just hand over their family legacy, even if Arch wasn't a part of that legacy. "They also didn't want to give up the water rights. The man who was after them, Mr. Wellington, isn't a nice man, they didn't trust him."

"I'm glad that he continued to be a kind man," Arch said. "He was always such a sweet boy. I worried that he'd pick up traits of our father when I left." He shook his head. "I'm really very glad to hear that wasn't the case."

"Not at all. Your brother was an impeccable gentleman," Angela agreed. "Anyway, this feud had been going on for quite some time, and Mr. Wellington seemed to be getting increasingly frustrated with Thomas and Sylvie. Rumor has it that he had tried to ask for Sylvie's hand in marriage before she met Thomas, and he was furious when she turned him down." She sighed. "Men and their egos."

"Indeed," Arch chuckled gently. "By the sounds of it, she made the right choice, though."

"Undoubtedly."

"So this feud, do you think it is connected to the gentleman you saw exiting the ranch the day of Thomas' death?" Arch asked.

Angela inhaled sharply, as if she were anxious to respond, and took a moment to look down at little Pauline, who had, in the time they had been talking, drifted off to sleep in her lap.

"I can't say for definite. I didn't recognize the man, but I'm sure it can't be purely coincidental ... An old, tall man in all black with a hood and no bag, no gun?" She eventually responded. "I don't know, Arch, it's just all a little suspicious. But Rudy says there's no evidence of foul play. So nobody can investigate it." She shrugged and shook her head.

Nobody official, Arch found himself thinking.

"I see," he replied. "Thank you for being honest with me, Angela."

"Of course." She nodded. "You've got enough going on, I'm not going to add to that someone lying to you," she said sincerely and stroked Pauline's hair gently. "I meant what I said, by the way. They will warm up to you, just give them time."

"I'm not so sure," he replied again.

"They've just lost both of their parents, and a man who they've never met before turned up and started telling them what to do. Would you have taken well to that as a boy?" Angela replied, her tone verging on frustrated. Arch felt a pang of guilt — she was right. They'd lost Thomas and Sylvie too, and they were all the children really had. Maybe if Arch had listened to his brother's pleas to come and meet them ... Maybe things would be easier then.

"I definitely wouldn't have, no," Arch replied.

"Just give them time. Be gentle with them. You'll see. They're just testing you right now. Making sure that you're here to stay — I don't think they know that it's what they're doing, but I can see it clear as day." She raised a brow at Arch and smiled.

"Well, I'm definitely here to stay. I guess I just need to make that clear to them," he said simply. "I think once the new governess is here, it'll really help. At least then you won't have to traipse all the way over here whenever madam is having a tantrum!" He chuckled gently and looked down at Pauline asleep against Angela's chest.

"I still reckon you're going to need much more than just a governess." She shook her head humorously. "Thomas and Sylvie barely managed with the two of them — and they were experienced home runners," she teased.

"I'm sure we'll manage just fine." He rolled his eyes jovially. "I just hope this governess is competent. Otherwise, I'm at a loss." He made an exaggerated gesture of crossing his fingers, and Angela chuckled again quietly, careful not to wake the tired tot in her lap.

Chapter Four

On the train to Paddington, Texas

14th May 1885

The train sped through the state of Texas, and Biddie watched outside as the scenery passed by her window. She was nearing her destination now, and despite it only having been a matter of hours, Biddie felt that the small town of St. John and the life she had lived within it were worlds away.

She'd spent the train journey people-watching, intrigued by the different groups that made their way on and off of the carriage at each stop. There had been businessmen, most of whom had got on the train in Oklahoma, and had left the train in Dallas.

There were a few families, and Biddie had enjoyed pulling little faces at the children and hearing them giggle excitedly in response. The mothers would notice and smile at her — it was a nice change from the way most of the mothers in St. John had reacted to her.

Her mind was awash with fantasies about the world she was about to step into, so much so that she had yet to really think much about the life she had left behind. Her leaving St. John had been a long time coming, and she would not really miss anything other than her grandmother.

The few times that she had thought back to the start of the journey, her heart ached with longing for her meemaw; they had never spent longer than a couple of days apart, and now Biddie was uncertain when she'd even see her grandmother next. The idea made her feel queasy.

So instead, she continued to indulge in her fantasies about the ranch, the children, and her new life. This was easily the most exciting thing to ever have happened to her.

The train began to slow, and her heart sped up in her chest. Sweat began to bead on her forehead and her hands became damp and clammy. She reached for the handle of her bag, which she had placed on the seat next to her, and bounced her legs to remove the sudden excess energy she seemed to be experiencing.

Her eyes flickered between the slowing scenery outside the window and the other people on the train who were all gathering up their bags and belongings in anticipation of the train pulling to a halt. The scenery outside began to change from rural grassy plains to more city-like streets.

There were rows of buildings, houses, and railworks, and Biddie definitely felt like she had come a long way from the small Main Street of St. John. The train ground to a halt, and Biddie peered out of the window one final time at the train station before standing up and carrying her belongings out onto the platform.

She walked across the small platform, looking around at all of the other travelers as they dashed and darted around, running for the train or out of the station. To her left, she saw a sign screwed onto the side of a small brick building that read "EXIT".

She took a small breath before heading straight for it. Carrying her bag in her right hand, Biddie walked through the entrance to the small building. There was a small office on one side of the building, and then a small store on the other side.

Opposite the entrance, there was an equally-sized exit. She wandered over and through the exit, taking herself out onto Paddington's main street.

***

Paddington, Texas

Biddie took a moment to push her spectacles up on her nose, standing still outside of the ticket office. Around her were things she was largely unfamiliar with. There were more people walking in and out of the station than she had ever really seen walking around St. John. From what she could see of the street leading away from the station, there were more than just the usual handful of stores.

She could see at least two haberdasheries, a handful of saloons, and even a barbershop. Her eyes widened, and a grin began to form across her face. She stepped away from the entrance to the ticket office to ensure that she was not in the way and rested her bag on the floor. She straightened the bodice of her emerald-colored dress and patted the skirt flat, waiting for her new boss to arrive and collect her.

They had arranged all of this in their letters — he was to come and pick her up from just outside of the station and take her back to the ranch. There, she would meet the children and settle in, and her work would start officially tomorrow. In exchange for governessing, she would be given room and board, as well as a small weekly allowance of $2.

It was better than many of the deals closer to home and provided her with the opportunity to escape. She was glad she'd taken the plunge.

As she stood waiting, though, she thought about her grandmother again and her eyes stung with tears that she quickly blinked away. They were states apart for the first time in her life, and no matter how excited she was for her new adventure, she would always miss her meemaw.

Interrupting her thoughts, a tall and strong-looking man approached her. He walked over from a medium-sized buggy parked on the corner. He wore a well-chosen casual suit that made him stand out against the other men around the station in denim slacks or overalls. His hair was a light blonde with speckles of a darker, straw color, which also happened to be the color of his well-groomed beard and mustache.

As he walked toward her, the light hit his skin and Biddie could make out that he was uniquely pale. His light skin was dotted with freckles that were as light as his hair — he was very clearly an attractive man, Biddie noticed, and he seemed to hold himself in a confident, yet gentle way that suggested he was not one of those men who knew how good he looked. He approached her tentatively, one golden-sandy brow arched.

"Miss Edwards?" he asked. His voice was distinctly not Texan. It had an undertone of the usual Texan drawl, but there were other, more formal tones within his voice too. It suited him, though, Biddie thought. The way he spoke matched everything else about him. It continued to provide him with a subtle air of confidence combined with a gentle warmth that Biddie found herself wanting to feel more of. Suddenly, she realized she had yet to reply.

"Yes, hello!" Biddie beamed excitedly. The man's eyebrow dropped and a smile took residency on his face. His teeth were white, and as he smiled Biddie noticed that his blue eyes sparkled. "Are you Mr. Sutton?" she asked.

"The very same," he replied. "But please, Mr. Sutton was my father. We will be working closely together, so call me Arch."

Biddie nodded gently, a small heat spreading across her cheeks. *He may not have the Texan drawl, but he definitely has the southern charm*, she thought to herself.

"And Arch is short for Archibald, I assume?" she asked, bending at the knees to collect her bag from the floor, one hand on her glasses to keep them from sliding off as she glanced down.

Arch nodded and took the bag from her hand. She blinked rapidly to process the movement and then smiled politely in thanks.

"It is indeed," Arch replied. "Follow me, Miss Edwards," he said, carrying her bag and leading her away from the station and toward the buggy on the corner.

"Alright then," she said simply. "Well in which case, please call me Bridget. Or Biddie. Usually, people call me Biddie," she rambled as she tried her best to keep up with his long-paced steps.

"Okay, Biddie," Arch replied as they reached a buggy with two seats. There were two horses attached to the front, one a slender black-coated mare and the other a slightly bulkier palomino gelding. He placed her bag up in the buggy and then offered her a hand as she climbed in. His hand was much softer than she'd expected a ranch owner's to be, and somehow, despite the Texas heat, the warmth of his hand on hers did not unsettle her. It all felt very natural. She'd not been in Texas even an hour yet, and Biddie felt as if she'd certainly made the right decision. She sat on the small plush seat of the buggy and waited for Arch to climb up next to her, and soon the two of them were on their way.

Biddie found herself staring at their surroundings as they traveled, too amazed by the change in scenery from her hometown to engage her new boss and landlord in conversation. It wasn't until about fifteen minutes into their journey, when Arch cleared his throat, that she began to pay attention.

"So, you know a little of my family's situation," Arch said. Biddie nodded — he had explained some of the family's story in their letters prior to her moving.

"Mmhm, you mentioned that you are the children's uncle, I believe? And that they lost their parents? Poor babies." She shook her head sadly.

"Yes, that's right," he nodded, staring straight ahead. "Their parents — my brother and his wife — passed recently. They died of a gastric flu of some sort and left me the sole guardian of the children as well as the owner of the estate. I moved back from Georgia to handle the responsibilities, but it seems that the children are more of a handful than I had first anticipated," he spoke calmly, with an eloquence that she had not been expecting.

"Children can be surprising like that," she remarked, and a small smile appeared on Arch's face.

"Indeed," he replied, a small hint of laughter in his voice. "Luckily, it seems that my brother was friendly with the neighbors, the sheriff, and his wife Angela. Whilst I have been adapting and waiting for your arrival, Angela has been primarily caring for the children. They know her and seem to take her caring for them much better than they have been responding to my attempts at the same."

He let out a small, sad sigh, and Biddie felt a wave of sympathy wash over her. This was a man who had not had any children, but had now been forced into a life of parenthood and was seemingly at a loss for how to handle it. She was glad she was there to help, and that this Angela woman was easing the transition at least a little.

"Children can be slow to win over." She nodded in reply. She thought back to the stories that her grandmother had told her about when she moved in. She'd apparently cried for two whole weeks, getting louder each time her grandmother picked her up or came near her. She'd only been very young, but she still felt a small pang of guilt about treating her meemaw in such a way. She imagined that Arch was likely going through something similar with his niece and nephews.

"So I have learned," Arch replied as they pulled into a small side road that led through a grassy field and onto a medium-sized ranch. From where Biddie sat, she could see most of the property. There was a large house in the far left corner of the ranch, surrounded by a wooden porch and with a small flower garden to one side of it. The fields that spread across the space between where Arch was maneuvering the buggy and the house were filled with crops. From what Biddie knew, one seemed to be full of budding corn, and the other appeared to be full of wheat, or possibly barley — she wasn't quite sure. Opposite the home, on the far right of the ranch, there was a medium-sized wooden barn and something that looked like a chicken coop but that had clearly not been built by an expert. Next to the coop was another large field full of cattle, all of whom seemed to be mindlessly grazing on the plush grass beneath them. Dotted around the ranch were men in overalls and large boots doing various work in the fields with the crops and the animals.

"Wow," Biddie said quietly. "This is really quite something."

"It's just a ranch," Arch replied quietly.

"It's much bigger than the ranches back home," Biddie replied. St. John had its fair share of ranches, and there were a couple of larger plantations that she knew of, but she'd never actually seen a ranch this size.

"I'm glad you're impressed," Arch stated with a nod before clambering down from the buggy. He offered Biddie his hand again and she took it, a small blush covering her cheeks again as she again felt the warmth of his skin on hers.

"Very." She grinned at him as he grabbed her bag.

"Let's get you settled and introduced to the children," Arch said politely, holding her bag. "Are you ready?"

More ready than I've ever been for anything, Biddie thought to herself. Each second that passed just got her more excited for her new life.

Chapter Five

The Sutton Ranch, Paddington, Texas

14th May 1885

Arch walked beside Biddie, leading the way between the corn and wheat fields to the house. He held her bag in his hand as they walked along the dusty path. Looking to his left slightly, he glanced at her. He'd been shocked when he'd seen her at the station.

His assumptions had led him to create an image of a governess in his mind, and Biddie very definitely did not align with that image. Where he had thought of someone older, wrinkled, perhaps lacking in beauty, she was young, and she certainly did not lack beauty. She was tall and slender, and her pale skin made her emerald green eyes shine.

Her skin was smooth and clear, save for a few freckles and a light pink color across her cheeks. Her hair, pinned back behind her head, was long and unruly, with curls and waves flowing like waves across her head. It was incredibly dark, the darkest hair he'd ever seen, but had a singular white streak at the front which was tucked loosely behind her ear.

She wore round wire spectacles that sat delicately on a shapely and elegant aquiline nose. A sage-green dress with a square neck and a sharp dip at the waist emphasized her petite size, and a slight silver fringe necklace with stones that bore resemblance to pearls, but were slightly transparent, decorated her neck. He'd had to fight to keep from staring at her.

Not only were her looks surprising, but he had assumed that a governess would be a relatively ordinary woman. And yet, Biddie was anything but ordinary. From the small conversations they had already had, Biddie seemed to be intelligent and kind, and it struck him as odd that someone so beautiful, so intelligent and so sweet would choose to move across the country to become a governess.

Surely she could have settled down in her hometown with someone wealthy who could provide for her? It baffled him that she would need to work at all. All the same, he was glad that she did, for from what he had seen of her so far, she seemed like someone who would truly be able to make his new living situation much, much easier.

Part of him also reveled in the idea of having someone so beautiful around, but he tried to ignore that thought.

"So the children, what're their names?" Biddie asked after walking in silence for a while.

"Pauline is the youngest; she's two years old. Then the two boys are David and Fred. They're both handfuls — David is eight and his brother is nine, but they seem determined to be the heads of the house." Arch chuckled slightly, though exasperation was evident in his short laugh.

"Ah yes, they always talk about how difficult babies are, but from what I've heard, young boys are by far the hardest to handle," Biddie said sweetly. "I'm sure they'll grow out of it soon enough, though."

"Perhaps. I hope so," Arch replied solemnly. "Angela tells me that they were sweet boys — well, actually, she uses the present tense," he snorted. "I think I've yet to see that side of them, but I understand that the circumstances … Well, they don't make for the happiest of children." He sighed as they neared the house.

"I understand," Biddie replied, her voice soft and gentle. Arch had known her all of a few hours, but he already felt comfortable in her company. He found himself thanking God for sending such a gentle woman — he needed someone like her.

At last, the two of them reached the house and they walked up the wooden steps of the old rickety porch that Arch's father had built when he was a boy. The wood creaked under two pairs of feet, and Arch watched as Biddie jumped slightly at the noise.

"Don't worry, the porch may seem close to the end of its life, but it's been sounding like that since the day it was built twenty years ago," Arch reassured her. Biddie nodded gently, pushing her spectacles up on the bridge of her nose.

Once they were up the stairs, Arch led the way into the house. He opened the large wooden door and stepped in, making room for Biddie. Placing her bag on the floor to the right of the door, he ushered her in. She stood just inside the door and looked around.

The house would be quite beautiful, Arch supposed, to anyone who didn't grow up in it. It was a large square building, with a mezzanine balcony around the top floor connecting the master bedroom, the office, and the two children's rooms.

On the ground floor, where the two of them were standing, there were four rooms — the kitchen and dining room, which ran along the left side of the building, the playroom directly opposite, and then the spare room at the back right and a room that was currently used for storage.

"This is lovely," Biddie commented, her eyes taking in the high ceiling, wooden stairs, and ornate oil lamps which hung from the ceiling.

"Thank you, I'm glad you like it. Your room is just through here," Arch said, gazing at her warmly. He collected her bag from the floor and led her through the large open hallway into the medium-sized room in the back of the house. There was a wooden framed bed in the corner of the room beside a large wardrobe. In the opposite corner, there was a small table with a bowl and a jug of water, and next to it, directly beside the bedroom door, was a small dressing table and desk. He placed the bag on the bed and turned to look at Biddie for approval. She looked around the room tentatively and then smiled a wide, toothy smile that offset her natural beauty, making her look rather sweet.

"It's wonderful, thank you," she said softly, stepping into the room. She plopped herself down on the bed with a satisfied hum. "This will be just fine."

"I'll go and get the children; just settle in for a few minutes and come out to meet them when you're ready," Arch replied as he turned and walked to the doorway. He stood there for a moment. "Thank you for applying for this role," he said simply. "I think you'll do well."

"I hope so," she replied, and with that, Arch left the room. Searching for Angela and the children, he walked through the house and out of the front door. Wandering down the wooden steps, he walked around to the back of the house and found them sitting on the ground. Angela had Pauline in her lap and the two boys were running around her in circles playing tag. As Arch approached, Angela looked up.

"Hello, Arch," she smiled warmly.

"Angela." He nodded. "Bridget is here, the new governess. I'd like the kids to come in and meet her," he said simply. Angela nodded, the smile on her face widening.

"Oh goodie!" She grinned. "What's she like?" She asked, collecting Pauline from her lap and standing up off of the ground.

"She seems nice — very kind-hearted." He nodded. "Boys! Can you come in with Angela and I, please?" Arch called to the two young boys. They stopped in their step and Fred rolled his eyes. Arch tensed in frustration but tried his hardest not to react.

"Why should we?" Fred asked. David laughed and Angela shot him a warning glare.

"Because I asked you to," Arch replied. Fred seemed to consistently see issues with his demands, regardless of what they were. Every time he had asked Fred to do anything since moving back to Texas, he'd been met with a "why" at the very least, if not a plain "no". It was beginning to grate on him.

"And?" Fred asked again.

Arch exhaled slowly through his nose.

"Fred, please," he begged. Angela looked from him to Fred with sad eyes, and Arch caught her stare. "I'll see you all inside," he said simply.

He turned on his heel and walked back into the house quickly. He could not lose his temper with the boys. He was adamant that he would not be anything like his father, but it was getting increasingly harder to maintain his composure.

He pushed open the front door and walked in, taking a seat on the stairs. He propped his elbows on his knees and buried his head in his hands. *It'll be alright*, he told himself as he waited for the children to come back in.

A few moments passed, and he heard a door creak open. He raised his head from his hands and looked around. The front door remained unmoved, and he furrowed his brows in confusion. He heard a few steps behind him and bent his neck to look.

Approaching him was Biddie, her curly hair neater than before, and in a different dress than when he had picked her up from the station. Before he could say anything to her, the front door flung open and David and Fred darted in, followed by Angela, who held Pauline closely to her chest.

The two boys ran into the house, skidding to a halt right in front of Biddie. She looked down at them with a small smile and waved, and they darted their heads toward Angela and Arch for an explanation.

"Boys, this is Miss Edwards," Arch said, standing up from the stairs. "She will be looking after you from now on. She'll be teaching you how to help around the house and will give you lessons in basic arithmetic and reading," he explained.

"Hello boys," Biddie said, her voice as sweet as it had been when she'd spoken to Arch earlier that day. "I look forward to getting to know you both." She bent down and offered her hand to Fred to shake. Arch watched and he tensed up again — he thought back to his own introduction to the children and panicked that the two boys would react the same way to her. He watched with nervous anticipation as Fred looked at her hand and laughed boisterously. He looked at David and slapped his arm aggressively before running away.

"TAG!" He yelled as he darted away from a bewildered-looking Biddie who stood up straight.

"Oh dear," Angela sighed. "Please excuse them, they are rather excitable today," Angela said. "It's nice to meet you," she said softly, approaching Biddie and taking the hand that she had offered Fred. Biddie smiled back, her bewilderment not wholly gone, and Angela directed Pauline to look at her. "This is Pauline, the easiest to handle of the Sutton children."She chuckled.

Biddie looked around at the two young boys who were now doing laps of the hallway. Her eyes followed them for a second and then looked up at Pauline and Angela.

"So I can see," she said gently. "And you are Angela, I presume."

Angela nodded in response.

"Pleasure to meet you both." Biddie offered her hand to Pauline who took her index finger in her tiny fist and grinned. Biddie giggled and took a deep breath in.

At least one of them is behaving, Arch thought to himself. Biddie pulled her hand away from the little girl and turned to look at the boys. She took another long breath.

"Boys, if you stop playing tag right now, I'll let you off a week of arithmetic lessons," she said sternly. Her voice somehow had a sternness that was still gentle and warm, and it froze both the boys in their tracks. They both shared a glance, and Arch watched them with confusion. A few seconds passed and then the two of them slowly walked toward Biddie.

"Promise?" Fred asked.

"Yeah, do you promise, Miss? No arithmetic?" David followed his brother.

Biddie smirked and nodded. "I promise, boys," she said. "Now, will you introduce yourselves to me, please?"

The two boys looked at one another and then Fred nodded once in response. He offered his little hand out to Biddie and smiled politely. Arch's eyes widened. He'd never seen Fred be so polite before. Biddie took his hand and shook it firmly.

"Hello, Miss, I am Fred. Fred Sutton. I am nine years old," he said, his voice formal and squeaky.

"Hello, Fred, lovely to meet you," Biddie replied and let go of his hand. She turned slightly to David. From where she stood, Arch could only see her back, and he caught himself staring at her shiny ringlets tucked and pinned into a beautiful coil on the back of her head. He quickly darted his eyes away.

"I'm David," David said simply, not offering his hand. "I'm eight."

"Hi David," Biddie replied. "Lovely to meet you, too."

Arch watched both boys and Biddie carefully, waiting to see the boys react and act out again, but neither of them moved. They simply stood calmly in front of her. A wave of relief and confusion washed over him — how had she gotten them to behave so easily? With one sentence? He shook his head in disbelief. She was perfect for the job.

"Boys, can you go and wash up for dinner?" Angela asked, taking their and Arch's attention away from Biddie.

The boys nodded quickly and sprinted out of the hallway and up the stairs to their bedroom. Biddie turned to face Angela and Arch and smiled delicately.

"I think we'll be okay," she said softly.

"I think you will, too," Angela nodded. "I've not seen them act so politely before!" She giggled. "But nevertheless, if you need me to, I am happy to stay here for a few days. My husband's away, so I can help to show you the way the children like things until he comes home. I get awful lonely at home without him anyway." She looked to Arch for confirmation, and he nodded in response. Having the two of them around would make his life *so* much easier, and it would be nice to have someone to show Biddie the ropes.

"That would be wonderful." Biddie nodded excitedly. "It'd be really nice to have a friend around."

"I'll get you all caught up with how this house runs in no time." Angela beamed.

Arch watched the two women chat with each other. Between the two of them, the children would have plenty of care and education, and he could get on with moving the business over and running the ranch.

Maybe moving back to Texas isn't all bad, Arch found himself thinking, his gaze locked firmly on Biddie.

Chapter Six

The Sutton Ranch, Paddington, Texas

14th May 1885

Biddie and Angela stood in the kitchen. Angela leaned on one of the counters, holding Pauline close to her chest. Biddie could hear the boys upstairs getting ready for dinner, and wondered what Arch was doing up in his office. The kitchen was full of wonderful scents, from rich, meaty smells to something sweeter and exciting — it was clear that this kitchen was well used.

She took a deep breath in, embracing the smells and the atmosphere that spread out from the room and into the rest of the home. The scents were simultaneously familiar and all brand new, and they brought a warm smile to her face.

This was her life now — family kitchens, children running laps around her. It was much more exciting than the life she was used to.

"So, I've already started supper for the night," Angela said, turning to her left and gesturing at a large stove. Sitting atop it was a large metal pot. Biddie walked toward the pot and lifted the lid, sniffing the contents. She was instantly hit with a rich, overwhelming scent of corn and pork.

"This smells amazing," she said, looking back over her shoulder at Angela.

"Thanks, love. It's a recipe my mother taught me many moons ago." She sighed fondly. "I can finish it up if you want to spend some time with Pauline?"

Biddie looked at the young girl nestled against Angela's chest. Pauline had a small amount of hair on her head, all of it a light blonde much like her uncle's. She was small for her age and had wide blue eyes that took over much of her face.

She seemed to constantly look curious, and her eyes were often following someone around the room or watching someone intently. Currently, they were locked onto Biddie. Arch and Angela had said that Pauline was two, but she had yet to hear the young girl speak, or see her walk. She wondered if there was a reason — it was unusual for a child of such an age to be held all the time.

"Of course," Biddie said gently. She held her hands out to Angela, and Angela handed the young girl over. Biddie took her happily and held her against her own chest. "May I ask, is there a reason you hold her? Surely she can walk?" Biddie asked.

Angela nodded. "She can walk, but we've found that since her parents ... Well, she cries a lot when left alone. She enjoys the comfort of being held," Angela explained. "She also stopped speaking shortly after her parents' passing." She sighed as she picked up a large spoon and began to stir the soup.

"So she can speak?" Biddie said softly, trying to make sure that if Pauline could follow their conversation, she wasn't upset by anything she heard.

"Very well for a 2-year-old, actually," Angela replied, adding ingredients into the pot. "She's just become very quiet since. I think she feels lost or maybe abandoned. That's one of the reasons I've stuck around." She continued to fuss over the pot on the stove. "I hope that having another woman in the house will help to bring her back out of her shell."

Biddie's heart ached. Losing people was awful, she knew that better than many people, but she'd presumed that being as young as she was would keep Pauline at least a little protected from the grief and emotional turmoil. The more she found out about the Sutton family, the more she was glad that she had taken the job.

They needed someone to help them, and she needed an escape from St. John — she only hoped that they were well-matched. From what little she had seen of her dashing employer, the house and the children, it felt like she could make herself happy here.

It was beginning to seem that God had brought them together, and she was going to do everything in her power to make it work.

"It's so sad, what happened to them," Biddie replied.

"So very sad," Angela nodded. "And Arch is not handling having three children very well. I think the concept of being fatherly is alien to him. From what I gather, he and Thomas didn't have the best example set them." She looked over at Biddie with a sad smile and then returned her attention to the pot of soup.

"It is a lot to adapt to, I suppose," Biddie replied, bouncing Pauline in her arms. She had yet to see Arch really interact with the children, but he sounded as if he cared for them on their journey from the station. He'd struck her as a gentle, caring man; it had warmed her heart. Being a parent was hard work, and must be especially difficult when one was just thrown into it. She could see why he might be struggling.

"Oh, of course. And the two boys don't make it easy for him," Angela chuckled lightly. "But I just wish he'd give them more of a chance. I do think that he expects you to take care of them completely now that you're here …" she said gently, but with a cautionary note in her tone. "You may need to assert your boundaries as a governess."

Biddie nodded; she had noticed that Arch had said she was there to look after the children. To some extent, this was true. But primarily, her role as a governess was to teach them manners and give them the knowledge they need as children.

She was happy to do a few things outside of that, like helping to keep them entertained or watching over them, but Angela's words did ignite a small amount of concern in her mind.

"I'm sure we will figure it all out," she replied simply.

"I don't doubt that! You seem plenty capable," Angela replied.

Biddie smiled to herself. It was nice to see that she had already made a strong impression, even though she'd only been here for half a day. She only hoped that she would be able to live up to it.

***

15th May 1885

She'd fallen asleep early her first night — the day of traveling and meeting everybody had worn her out. She slept peacefully, and awoke to the sunlight shining through her bedroom window, beating down on her. Sitting up from her bed, Biddie yawned and looked around.

Dust was dancing in the air, caught in beams of sunlight, and the fresh Southern spring air filled her room. She inhaled deeply, twisting so that her feet touched the cold wooden floor of her bedroom, and wiggled her toes.

With one large stretch, she stood up from her bed and, grabbing her spectacles from on top of the wardrobe, plodded over to the window. Looking out across the ranch, Biddie smiled to herself.

"Good morning, Texas," she said softly.

She returned to the wardrobe and pulled out a light purple dress. Quickly dressing, she glanced in the looking glass and pinned her hair back into two small coils at the nape of her neck. Rummaging through her bag, she collected some basic books to go through with the boys that morning and headed downstairs.

She walked through the hallway, conscious to ensure that she did not wake anybody as she moved through to the stairs and down towards the lounge. Leaving her books in the lounge, she walked through the house and into the kitchen, grabbing herself a glass of peach lemonade that had been made — she assumed by Angela — the day before. She drank it quickly and placed the glass on the side.

As she went to head out and back to her books to wait for the boys, Arch walked into the room. He wore gray linen trousers and a shirt that had not yet been tucked into them. His hair was neatly tousled and his eyes, whilst sleepy, were as blue as ever. She had to stop herself from smiling at the sight of him — it was a welcome change from waking up to her meemaw's snoring.

"Oh, good morning," Biddie greeted him. Arch looked up and smiled at her.

"Good morning indeed," he replied, a small look of shock passing over his face at the sight of her. He quickly tucked his shirt into his trousers. His voice was deeper than it had been the day before, his half-awake state providing an almost gravelly tone to it. "What's for breakfast?" he asked, looking around the kitchen as if he was searching for plates of freshly-cooked food.

"Oh, uh, well," Biddie's eyebrows furrowed. Suddenly she wasn't paying attention to the depth of his voice or the blue of his eyes. "I wasn't aware that I was making breakfast," she replied. She was a governess, not a maid. Arch had not hired her to cook for them all.

"Oh. Right. Well, could you?" He asked, heading over to the jug of peach lemonade.

"I am supposed to be teaching the boys this morning …" She started but stopped in her tracks. It was her first full day — she should really try to impress her new employer. He was clearly not fully awake yet; maybe he was just a little out of sorts. "Well … Yes, alright, I suppose I could make breakfast." She turned away from him, searching through the pantry to gather the ingredients to make omelets.

"Thank you," he said simply, yawning and taking a seat at the dining table. She replied with a brief hum and continued making the household their omelets. Before long, Angela and Pauline came into the room, and the two of them took a seat around the dining table. Shortly after, David and Fred came darting into the room.

"Good morning, Bridget," Angela greeted from across the room. "Did you sleep well?"

"Good morning, Angela, morning boys," Biddie called from her place in the kitchen. "I did, thank you," she replied. Angela smiled over at her warmly and placed Pauline in her seat.

"Thank you for preparing breakfast for us," Angela said after a moment. "It smells lovely — where did you learn to cook?"

Biddie smiled slightly to herself — it was nice that Angela was making an effort. It was more than she could say for Arch so far that day. She had thought that she'd managed to read him pretty well on their short journey from the station, but his assumption that she'd cook, along with Angela's warning, made Biddie worry a little.

"My grandmother," Biddie replied. "She's a fantastic cook, and taught me all that I know."

"Grandmothers are wonderful like that," Angela replied. Biddie looked over and nodded quietly.

Once the omelets were cooked, Biddie plated them up and passed them out at the dining table. She handed each person a plate and sat down next to Angela and Pauline.

"So what do you have planned for your first day?" Arch asked as he dug into his omelet.

"I was hoping to go over some basic etiquette with the boys," Biddie said, smiling over at the two lads. "And then we would do some reading lessons." She took a bite of her own omelet. "Then once that's done, I was hoping to spend some time in the sun planning the next few weeks worth of lessons for both Pauline and the boys," she said.

Arch nodded gently and hummed.

"And you, Angela?" he asked.

"Well, I figured I could make myself useful and maybe make some dinner and supper for us all."

"Ah brilliant, Biddie can help you." Arch grinned, finishing up his omelet.

Angela shot Biddie a look, and she pulled her lips tight across her face. She'd do as Arch asked today — but if this continued she was going to have to say something.

***

Biddie sat across from Fred and David, holding *The Princess and The Goblin* in her hands as the midday sun began to pass through the window of the lounge. She had decided to read a chapter of the book to the two boys, and then pass the book around — that way she could best gauge their current reading abilities. As she read, the two boys sat quietly and listened.

Every now and then, Fred would get distracted and would start nudging his brother in an attempt to start a fight or to get him in trouble. David scowled at his brother each time, and Fred resignedly went back to listening. Once Biddie had made her way through a chapter, she passed the book down to David.

The young boy took the book and began to read. He seemed to be doing alright, but Biddie noticed that his voice wobbled as he spoke — he had so little confidence in his own reading skill, it seemed. Nevertheless, he made it most of the way through the chapter without the need for her interjection. She gazed down at him proudly.

"Wonderful job, David," Biddie said as she took the book from David's hands. "You have clearly had a great reading teacher in the past."

David nodded and looked at Biddie sadly. "Our mama used to show us how to read," he said quietly.

Biddie's breath hitched in her throat — this was probably the first time the boys had read or been read to since their parents passed. Angela and Arch had definitely been too busy handling the situation to teach them. She smiled down at David with sympathy.

"Your mama was clearly a very smart lady, then," she said gently. "Are you ready for your turn, Fred?"

Fred nodded, his usual attitude gone and replaced with a small, solemn expression.

"You know what, boys? How about we take a small break," Biddie suggested. She didn't want to overwork them, especially so early in their work together. "We'll carry on in a little while — you can play for a bit."

The two boys nodded, and David stood up from the floor.

"Let's play tag, Freddie," he spoke quickly.

Fred nodded and stood up. "We'll come back and read soon Miss," he said politely, then ran out of the room, David sprinting after him.

Biddie listened to them giggle and smiled slightly to herself. She pulled herself out of her chair and walked out of the lounge and to the front door. She opened the front door and stepped outside, quietly closing the door and heading towards the porch steps. She took in a deep breath, taking in the warm midday air.

The sun was just about at its peak, and she placed herself down on the porch steps as she watched over the space laid out beneath it. There were dragonflies zooming around the ranch, and she could hear the mooing and whinnying of the barn animals ahead of her.

From where she sat, the ranch workers were visible but she was unable to make out any of their faces, which unsettled her slightly. She made a mental note to go and introduce herself to them all eventually.

As she sat, enjoying her break and listening to the boys chasing each other around the house, laughing and squealing, she heard the door behind her creak open.

Arch stepped out and walked over to her. He'd added braces and a tie to his outfit, and she couldn't help but look him up and down. Even though his request for breakfast had frustrated her a little, she could not deny that his company was pleasant. He had a comforting presence, and she enjoyed looking at him more than she liked to admit.

"Hello," he said softly.

"Hello," she replied.

"The boys seem to be running awry," he said, one strawberry-blonde eyebrow raising on his forehead.

"I let them take a break to get their energy out. Children work better when they're not bubbling under the surface," she replied matter-of-factly.

"Hm, well could I ask you to do some chores whilst you wait?"

Biddie paused. She went to roll her eyes but restrained herself — this man was her employer. And he was *clearly* new at running a household.

"Well I won't be free for long — so it depends on what you'd like me to do," she replied diplomatically.

Arch nodded and ran a hand through his blonde, tousled hair.

"Well the playroom kind of needs tidying, and I was wondering if you could maybe start the laundry? I haven't done my own laundry in a while, and I'm not really su–"

Before Arch could finish, the two boys darted out of the front door, skidding to a stop just before the porch stairs.

"Miss Edwards!" Fred yelled, and Biddie flinched at the loud noise and then chuckled.

"Yes, Fred?" She replied, happy to have escaped the conversation with Arch. She was going to have to talk to him about her role. She had been hired as a governess. *Not* as a cleaner or a nanny.

"David cheated at tag, and I don't want to play anymore," he said, squinting his eyes at his brother. Biddie held back a small giggle, and she peered up at Arch who looked suitably confused.

"Ah, I see," she nodded. "Well then, how about we go back into the lounge and continue reading? Nobody can cheat at reading." She grinned and raised her eyebrows, praying that they'd take the bait and she could briskly run away from her conversation with Arch. She watched for a moment as the two boys carefully considered her proposal.

"You're sure David can't cheat at books?" Fred asked hesitantly.

"I don't cheat!" David whined.

"I'm sure, and David definitely didn't cheat when he read earlier," she said softly. Fred nodded slowly as he processed what she was saying.

"Hmm ... then let's read. Can I win at reading?" He asked.

"There isn't really a winner at reading," Biddie said as she stood up. "Sorry, Arch, please excuse me," she said as she offered the two boys her hands and the three of them wandered back into the house, leaving Arch alone on the porch.

"But if there *was* a winner, it'd be me, right?" Fred asked as the front door shut behind them.

Biddie giggled in response and led them into the lounge. She picked up the book and handed it to Fred, and as he began to read, found herself lost in worries about how much more Arch expected of her than she was willing to give.

He paid her well for a governess, but not enough to cover all of the extra duties he seemed to expect of her. She hated conflict, and really did not want to upset him, but there was going to have to be a conversation about her place in the household.

***

Angela and Biddie tucked the two boys into their beds as the sun set through the window. The boys had well and truly worn themselves out and were practically asleep before their heads even hit their pillows. Angela grinned as she straightened up and turned to Biddie.

"They're sweet when they're sleepin'," Angela said quietly.

"They're sweet when they're awake sometimes, too," Biddie replied.

The two women walked out of the room and pulled the door shut gently. Listening for a moment to make sure they hadn't awoken the boys, they stood still. Once they were sure that David and Fred were both sound asleep, they wandered around the mezzanine and downstairs to the kitchen.

"So how was your first day?" Angela asked.

"It was good. It's just–" Biddie shook her head. "I think I need to have a conversation with Arch. You were right," she sighed, talking quietly to ensure that Arch didn't hear.

"I thought that might be the case. You seem tuckered out," she said sympathetically. "I did tell Arch he needed more than one woman," she shook her head.

"I'd happily do the things he's asking, you see, but he only pays me a certain amount. And I feel that doing all of that for such little pay isn't right," Biddie explained. Angela nodded.

"Oh I agree, sweetheart. I think talking to him's the best course of action," Angela replied. "I'm gonna take myself off to bed now; little Pauline's been a handful today. I'll catch you in the mornin'." She smiled and waved, and Biddie waved back. Angela had warned her about Arch not knowing what he needed, but it seemed like she was hesitant to talk outright about it. Biddie was going to have to just be brave. She was going to have to go and speak to Arch.

Using the boiled water left from heating the children's milk earlier that evening, Biddie made herself and Arch a coffee each. *A peace offering,* she thought to herself as she took both cups and headed upstairs toward Arch's office. Knocking on the door, she stood just outside and waited anxiously.

"Come in," Arch called, and she pushed the door open, stepping inside. The office was much more lavish than the rest of the house. The walls were painted, there was a carpet much thicker than elsewhere, and the lamps were more ornate than the ones in the main hallway.

"Good evening," she greeted, walking over to Arch's desk and placing his cup down on the wood. "I brought you a coffee."

"So I can see." Arch smiled up at her. "Thank you," he took the cup in his hands and took a sip. "Is there anything I can help with?"

Quite a bit, Biddie thought to herself. She pushed at her spectacles unnecessarily.

"I was wondering if we could discuss my responsibilities," she said, speaking a touch too quickly to sound confident.

Hm?" Arch asked, peering over at her from above his cup of coffee.

"I think that you might have overestimated the responsibilities of a governess," she said simply. Biddie's heart raced in her chest and she fought the urge to stare down at her feet as she spoke. "You are asking me to clean, to cook ... And well, I am paid merely to teach the children." She kept her eyes up off of the ground, but refused to look Arch in the eye whilst she spoke.

"So you won't do it?" He asked, a small amount of frustration in his voice. His brows furrowed and he placed the cup down on his desk. She watched as his face contorted, his charm fading as the frustration took hold.

"I would be happy to do it if it was a part of my role," she replied. "But I am not paid the wages of a maid nor a nanny, I am paid the wages of a governess."

Arch's eyes widened and he sat back in his chair. He looked at Biddie for a moment, his jaw slack and one eyebrow furrowed inquisitively.

"So what are you saying?" He asked.

"Either I am simply a governess, nothing more, or you increase my wage to account for the additional responsibilities. And, the way I see it, once Angela moves back home, we're going to be between a rock and a hard place if there isn't somebody picking up the slack." She looked him in the eyes this time, to prove that she was entirely serious about what she was saying.

Arch's eyebrows raised and he blinked slowly, processing what Biddie had said.

"You want a raise? It's your first day."

"And I've already gone above and beyond what my job role entails," she reiterated. "All I am asking is that you consider it."

"Hm," Arch said finally, his face relaxing again. "I'll think about it," he said simply. Biddie nodded, and as his brows unfurrowed, she felt herself relax, her guard lowering as she looked into his eyes.

Stop it, she scolded herself.

"Thank you," she said quickly before turning to leave. As she walked to the door, she could feel Arch's eyes still on her. She turned around at the doorway to look back at him, and he very quickly averted his gaze. "Goodnight, Arch," she said gently. "I look forward to hearing from you in the morning."

Chapter Seven

The Sutton Ranch, Paddington, Texas

15th May 1885

Arch looked at his face in the mirror and lifted the razor to his cheek. Carefully, he steadied his hand and used the razor to trim away at the stray hairs above and below his impeccably groomed beard. He watched his own hand move in the mirror as if it were controlled by someone else, and lost himself in thought.

He'd spent much of the night before thinking about Biddie's suggestion, and thinking about how taken aback he was by her confidence to be so forthcoming with such matters so early in her employment. He'd had female employees before, but they'd never done something like that.

Many of his male employees wouldn't even consider such things. He felt an odd excitement rush through him when he thought about how confident and straightforward Biddie had been in her proposal, and it concerned him.

The more he thought about the suggestion itself, he realized that Biddie was certainly within her rights to bring it up. He had asked her to do substantially more in her first day alone than a governess would usually do — he just hadn't been thinking.

He was so used to having a secretary and a maid that it had become second nature. Biddie had also been right to point out that once Angela moved home, the house would quickly fall to shambles 'less he hired a maid or paid Biddie the extra wage. Angela had been doing much of the cooking and cleaning whilst caring for Pauline, and Arch had, to some extent, come to rely on it.

Still deep in thought, Arch placed the razor down on the small dresser in his room. Dipping his hand into the bowl of water beside it, he gently patted his skin, washing away any excess hairs and freshening himself up.

He turned away from the dresser and pulled open his wardrobe, standing in the center of the room as the early morning sun beamed down on him. He pulled out a pair of trousers, a union suit, and a large white shirt and began to dress. Once ready, he headed out of his room and down the stairs.

He was still stuck about Biddie's request; on one hand, it made sense. She could do more, the house would function better. But on the other hand, the excitement that he felt at her confidence, the way she made him feel just by being in the room simply due to her looks alone — it made him uneasy. Biddie was a beautiful, likable woman, and he was unsure whether it was wise to keep her around, let alone pay her more.

The last thing he needed was to be pining over a governess.

Arch sighed to himself and shook his head — he was going to have to discuss this all with someone. He was just going in circles, and it was getting harder and harder to figure out what the right thing to do was.

He wasn't used to having to make decisions that so clearly affected other people — usually, it was just himself that he had to consider, but now there were the children and Biddie. He reached the kitchen and looked around for the usual jug of lemonade perched on the side. He strode over and poured himself a glass, and then leaned on the counter.

Before he could fall back into his circular train of thought, Angela walked into the room. He looked over and smiled, and she grinned back. Her light blue dress looked almost white in the bright spring light, and Arch smiled to himself — she looked like some kind of guardian angel.

"Mornin'." Arch waved.

"Good mornin'," she said with a small nod.

"Did you sleep well?" He asked. He poured her a glass of lemonade and held it out to her as she approached from the other side of the room.

"Well enough," she said softly, taking the glass. "Thank you."

"I'm glad to hear. You're welcome," he said, taking a sip from his drink.

"How about yourself?" She asked, standing a small distance away with her glass held tightly between two hands.

"I didn't get much sleep, actually," he answered. "Thinking too much."

"Ah, yes, Rudy often gets the same," Angela smiled sympathetically and nodded.

"Mm, I find it is happening more and more since coming back to Texas," he remarked. "Perhaps there's something in the air."

"Perhaps," Angela mused. "What were you thinking about if you don't mind my asking?"

Arch placed his glass down on the counter behind him and folded his arms across his chest.

"I was actually hoping to discuss it with you, so no, I don't mind your asking at all," he said simply. "Last night, Biddie visited my office," he began to explain.

"Oh?" Angela asked, moving slightly closer. Arch had clearly piqued her interest.

"She wanted to discuss her responsibilities moving forward," Arch continued. "She'd noticed that I was asking a lot of her and that many of the things I was asking were not typical responsibilities of a governess …" As Arch spoke, he watched Angela's face for a response in the hopes that it would give him an idea as to how to feel about Biddie's suggestions. But she seemed to remain unmoved. One eyebrow was furrowed in concentration, and she nodded slowly along with his story. "She thinks that it is unfair of me to ask these things of her, things like cooking and cleaning, on top of her governess role, without additional pay."

"I see," Angela said quietly.

"We spoke about it and she was very straightforward, very to the point. She is happy to do the extra work, but not for the same pay," he said.

"That is not unreasonable," she replied.

"No, it is not," Arch agreed. "I'll admit I was a little taken aback by it all at first, but I've since thought on it and come to that same conclusion."

"Right," Angela said, knitting her brows together. "And so why did you want to talk about it with me?"

"Well," Arch began to explain. "I am a little bit stuck on whether to give her the raise she is asking for."

"But you just agreed that it's reasonable?" Angel asked, her head tilting.

"Yes, but I am worried that having Biddie around the house is going to cause issues," he said, his voice quieter than before.

"Whatever do you mean?" Angela asked. "Biddie is a lovely girl."

"She is, and that's the problem," Arch replied, looking down at his feet gingerly. "She's so confident and so kind — she's incredibly likable, and well," Arch looked up at Angela for a moment. "She's beautiful, too."

Angela chuckled gently. "Ah, I understand," she nodded. "May I speak frankly?"

Arch paused for a moment — it was rare that someone asked to speak frankly and then said anything nice. But, he'd asked for her opinion, and it was better than just going around and around in his own mind. He nodded.

"You're clearly struggling with the children — Pauline seems to frighten you, and I see the way you tense up when the boys act out. Between your work, the ranch, and growing accustomed to family life, you're barely going to have time to cook and clean. You'll have to hire a maid eventually, and likely a nanny, too. If this young woman is offering to do all of that for you — you ought to take her up on the offer. It's only going to come once," she paused. "Plus, Biddie is already handling the boys incredibly well, and she's a good cook — she helped plenty with dinner yesterday. I'm sure she's capable when it comes to chores, and realistically, you can afford to pay her," Angela said, looking at Arch. She seemed to be nervously awaiting his response.

He took a moment, processing what Angela had said — she wasn't wrong. He was busy. And he was finding it hard to father the children. Biddie seemed to be a natural at it, and she was likely going to cost less than paying for three separate women to come and help.

He'd just have to make sure he kept his distance. He was a grown man; surely he could keep himself from falling for her, regardless of how wonderful she was, and how her smile lit up a room …

Stop it, he scolded himself

"Mm," he said aloud after a moment, and Angela visibly relaxed at his response. "Maybe you're right," he sighed and pinched the bridge of his nose. "This entire situation has been incredibly tiresome. Thank you so much for helping out. I feel like I've known you forever, even if we only met a couple of weeks ago," he smiled warmly at Angela. "Your help has been invaluable."

Angela blushed. "You're more than welcome, love. I'd do anything for these kids, and I'd have done anything for your brother and sister-in-law. No reason why that courtesy would not extend to you," she said softly. "Anyway, I best go and wake the little ones — I'll see you around, Arch," she placed her now-empty glass on the counter and turned to leave.

"I'll see you later," he called as she began to walk out of the room.

Once she was gone, he let out a small sigh. *You can do this,* he reassured himself. He picked his glass back up and finished his drink, and then wandered out of the kitchen and toward Biddie's room. He checked his watch to make sure it was an acceptable time, and seeing that it was five past seven, he knocked confidently on the door.

He heard footsteps and a yawn, and then the door swung open, revealing Biddie with her hair not quite finished. She wore a dark brown dress with a higher neckline than the day before and a small choker decorating her neck. Her hair, in its incomplete state, was half pinned up on the back of her head, and half was undone, falling down her back like a black waterfall, cascading across her shoulders.

Something was different, and it took him a moment to realize that she had taken off her spectacles to do her hair. Her usually bright green eyes were slightly misty with sleep, and Arch felt himself smile, a warm feeling spreading across his chest.

"Oh, hello Arch," she said warmly. "Sorry about the state of my hair, I was in the process of putting it up."

"Morning, don't worry," he replied. "I've reached a decision," he said simply.

"Oh! Right, yes," she nodded and rubbed her eyes.

"I will up your wages to three dollars fifty per week in exchange for you also fulfilling cleaning and cooking chores, but I will need you to really focus on teaching the boys. No more breaks for tag. And I'd like you to start teaching Pauline, too. They're all behind, and I don't want their behavior to worsen," he tried to speak sternly, but could feel that he was failing to do so.

Biddie said nothing for a few seconds and then nodded.

"That sounds perfect," she said simply. "Thank you for agreeing; I'll get started on breakfast shortly, and follow it up with the laundry and then their lessons." She gazed up at Arch. "And I really appreciate the opportunity."

Arch's heart warmed at Biddie's gratitude. He was glad he'd spoken to Angela and reached this decision; Biddie was good with the children, and she was clearly a smart woman. She was going to be a great benefit to the house.

He just had to not fall in love with her.

Chapter Eight

The Sutton Ranch, Paddington, Texas

17th May 1885

Whilst the children were getting ready for their afternoon lessons, Biddie sat at the small table in her bedroom. She'd set out her letter-writing kit and was carefully penning a letter to Evangeline back in St. John.

She was excited to share updates with her grandmother and had been waiting for a moment when she had a few spare minutes to herself to write out what she wanted to say. Once she'd set it all up, Biddie tried to make a mental list of everything she needed to tell her grandmother, and then began to delicately pen the letter.

Dearest grandmother,

I write to you from my own room in a large, elegant house. The ranch that the Suttons own (Archibald Sutton is my employer, in case you have forgotten) is vast and beautiful. They grow corn and wheat, and there are a plethora of animals too.

My room is sweet; it is smaller than that which I had at home with you, but it has in it everything I could possibly require. Besides, I do not spend much time in it, as I am now not only a governess, but I am to care for the house and the children, too.

My employer realized that he required much more support than a mere governess could provide, and so, after discussing it, we agreed that I would get a higher wage and in exchange would do as many of the chores as I can and care for the little ones. I do not mind this, as the little ones are very pleasant most of the time — although the eldest, Fred, does not take well to schooling.

The people in Texas are lovely. I have so far met my employer, a handsome man who is incredibly gentle and warm. He seems to really want the best for the children. I think he's just uncertain on what that entails. Then there's the neighbor, Angela, she's sweet. You'd like her. The children are adorable, of course. Three little wonders. I think I'll be happy here.

Biddie went on to recount her last few days to her grandmother, and to tell her of the sadness she felt for the children and for Arch after they had to suffer such a loss. She spoke of the first reading lesson she had with the boys, and how they mentioned that their mother was their previous teacher. Biddie poured her heart out into the letter, telling her grandmother every minute detail that she could possibly recall, and then finally, ended it with:

I do hope you find this letter interesting, and by no means think that my excitement about my new life means I do not miss you terribly. You are in my thoughts each and every day. I look forward to when we can next see one another, and I pray that you are safe and happy and that your pies are just as tasty when they are cooked for one.

Your beloved granddaughter,

Bridget x

As she signed the letter, Biddie's eyes began to sting with tears. She sniffed them away and carefully ran her fingers under her eyes. She blinked a few times to clear her eyes of the mistiness that tears bring, and then folded her letter just so and placed it in an envelope. She sealed the envelope and wrote out Evangeline Edwards and her grandmother's address carefully on the front.

With a small smile, she placed the sealed envelope on the table and stood up to leave the room. She walked out of her room and into the hallway, peering into the lounge to see if the boys were in there. When she saw that the room was empty, she sighed and waited for a few moments. Still, they did not arrive.

"Fred! David!" she called, rolling her eyes to herself.

She was met with silence.

"David! Fred!" she tried once more.

Rather than silence, this time, she was met with one set of footsteps. David came plodding out of his bedroom and down the stairs, stopping right in front of her.

"Yes, miss?" he asked.

"It's lesson time," she reminded him. "Where is your brother?"

"Gone, miss," David said with a shrug, taking himself into the lounge.

"What? What do you mean gone?" Biddie asked, getting increasingly frustrated.

"He didn't want to read. So he left," David said as if he were simply talking about the weather and not his brother running away.

"Left to go?" Biddie asked, panic starting to bubble away inside her.

"Outside," David sighed. "Can we read now?" He picked up the book that they were working through from the table. "If he doesn't want to read, let's just do it without him," David said, holding the book out to Biddie. Biddie shook her head and let out a long exhale.

"You wait here, I'll be back in a moment," she said quickly to David as she whisked out of the room and toward the front door.

She barreled out of the house and down the porch steps, frantically searching for any sign of Fred. Her heart was thudding in her chest anxiously as she looked around — she could not lose one of the children within less than a week of starting.

She'd surely lose her job, and what if Fred got lost, or injured? Jogging down toward the fields, she spotted him lying down on the grass just before the crop fields. A wave of relief flooded over her, followed quickly by a flush of anger that he'd quite literally run away from her.

"Fred, I need you to come into the house. It's time for your reading lesson," she spoke sternly but maintained her composure as best she could.

"I don't want to read," Fred said from his spot on the floor.

"I am the adult in this situation, and I am your teacher. Therefore, you do what I say. Now, I would like you to come inside with me, right this second," she remained stern and straightened her back as she spoke.

"I don't want to read," Fred repeated.

"Fred, it is only one lesson. You will only have to read one small passage," she sighed. "Come now, inside."

"No," Fred replied, sitting up. "I'm not doing it."

"Fred," she warned.

"No," he repeated.

"Fine," Biddie said, a splash of heat making its way into her tone. She turned on her heel and stormed back into the house. Her mind reeled with frustration. *Why would he not just come indoors? The lessons are not that fun, but they're only short ... I'm doing my best,* Biddie thought to herself as she stomped up the porch steps. She walked into the house and took a deep breath whilst she tried to figure out what the best course of action was. *Arch,* she decided. Biddie walked up the stairs to his office quickly and knocked once before opening the door.

"I need your help," she said simply. "Fred will not listen to me, and he ran away from the lesson."

Arch looked up from his desk with a perplexed expression, his eyebrows knitted across his forehead and his eyes wide.

"Sorry, hello, what?" He asked.

"It was time for the children's reading lesson, and David came downstairs fine. But Fred literally ran out of the house and hid out in the ranch to avoid lessons. He's still there. He won't come back in," she sighed. "I tried, I promise."

"I believe you, Biddie, don't worry," Arch sighed and ran a hand through his hair as he stood up from behind his desk. "I'll have a word with him."

He walked out from behind his desk and slipped past Biddie at the door. She watched as he walked downstairs, and then followed him quickly as he walked out of the house. They reached the porch, and Biddie pointed toward where Fred was laying in the field. Arch sighed again and nodded.

"I'll be back in one second," he said simply, and then wandered off toward Fred. Biddie watched, grateful that Arch did not blame her for Fred's behavior. She was glad that he was so willing to help, and hummed happily as she watched him approach the young boy.

Arch knelt down next to Fred, and Biddie could see the two exchanging words. It started off relatively peacefully, and she could see from Arch's facial expressions that he was essentially pleading with the young boy. But, as time passed, Biddie watched as Arch's fist clenched by his side. He'd been begging and pleading with Fred for a solid ten or fifteen minutes, and she could see his patience wearing thin.

What had been a peaceful, concerned facial expression quickly changed to frustration, and as Fred continued to wind up his uncle, Biddie could see that frustration grow to anger. She felt a lump rise in her throat - this wasn't going well. All she wanted was Fred to come in to read. She'd hoped that he'd listen to his family — but it seemed, if anything, that he was listening even less to Arch.

One thing led to another, and Biddie watched as Arch snapped. He leant forward, and his anger erupted out of him in a fierce yell.

"You get back in that house right now, and you go to your room. Don't make me have to show you what happens when little brats misbehave!" Arch yelled.

Fred froze and scrambled up to his feet. He sprinted away from his uncle and into the house, not even stopping to look at Biddie on the porch. She watched him run past, then turned her attention back to Arch, who had sunk down into his knees, his head hanging in front of him. It was like somebody had deflated him. He wiped his cheek with his hand and then slowly pulled himself up from the ground.

"What …" Biddie said to herself.

She watched as Arch slowly walked back to the house, ignoring her and heading straight up to his office. His face looked as if he'd seen a ghost; it was bright white, and his eyes were filled with a sadness she'd not encountered for many, many years. Her heart still felt as if it were sitting right at the base of her throat, and she couldn't grasp what had just happened — Arch had seemed like such a gentle man. She quickly turned and followed him inside.

"What was that?" she asked once they reached his office.

"I spoke to him for you," Arch replied, his voice tight and curt.

"No, you yelled at him," she said slowly.

"I told him off, he came indoors. What's the matter?" Arch sighed, his eyebrows knitted together in an emotion that Biddie couldn't quite place. It was somewhere between anger, sadness, frustration and guilt, an unusual cocktail of them all. She felt a mixture of emotions herself; shocked that a man as kind-hearted as Arch had seemed could release such anger, confusion as to Arch's own reaction, and frustration that he yelled at Fred. There was something else, too. As she looked into Arch's eyes, searching for an answer, she felt sympathy for him. His eyes glistened with fresh tears, and she had seen him wipe moisture from his cheek. The boys were wearing him thin, she could see that much. But that didn't excuse his yelling.

"He came indoors, but he's not coming to lesson now, is he?" she said exasperatedly.

"Well no, I sent him to his room for the night. He's to stay there and think about how he disrespected you."

And you're disrespecting me by not listening to what I'm saying, Biddie thought to herself.

"But that's not ... He's not going to learn up there," she said. "It's fine, I'll catch him up at dinner." She shook her head with a sigh and turned to leave.

"Oh, no, I told him to stay up there," Arch said. His voice sounded cold, but his face still wore a forlorn and frustrated expression. Biddie couldn't believe what she was hearing — he'd sent a young boy who had just lost his mother up to his room by yelling at him, and was now refusing to let him eat? The frustration she felt bubbled away within her, and she left the room briskly without saying another word.

Walking down to the kitchen, Biddie paced for a moment, trying to calm down before returning to David, who no doubt was wondering where on Earth she might've gone. She wanted to defy Arch's punishment of Fred somehow, but she knew she wouldn't be able to sneak a dinner up to him, nor outrightly bring him to the dinner table.

Wiping a smudge off one of the lenses of her spectacles, she started to look around the kitchen and suddenly got an idea. Quickly, she began to gather food like bread, fruit, cheese, and jerky into a bowl. She piled it up until the bowl was full, and then quietly tread out of the kitchen and up to the boys' room.

As she got closer to the room, she heard a sniffling noise. By the time she reached the door, she could hear that Fred was crying. She decided not to knock, for fear that it'd alert Arch to her plan, and instead slowly creaked the door open.

"Fred?" She whispered.

"Go away!" Fred hissed through his tears.

"I bought you some food," she said gently. She stepped into the room and closed the door behind her. Placing the bowl on the floor, she stepped over to Fred and wrapped an arm around his shoulders. "What's the matter?" she asked.

"It's nothing, I'm fine," he said, shrugging her arm away. She furrowed her brows and tried to look at his eyes, but he refused to look up from the floor.

"I'm here for you, Fred. If you need to talk about anything …" she spoke softly.

"I don't," he said rudely. Biddie watched as he almost winced at his own words. "Sorry, I don't mean to be rude," he said weakly. "I'll be alright. Thank you for the food."

"It's alright," she said, walking back over to the door. "I'll see you later, okay, Fred?"

He nodded, sniffling, watching her go. As she was about to shut the door, he rushed over to her.

"I am sorry for not going to the lesson, Miss," he said quietly.

"I know you are," she replied, a small smile on her face. He nodded again and shut the door. She sighed gently and walked quietly away from the door and back to David. Running over what just happened in her head, she was still in a state of disbelief.

It appears I have more than three people to teach manners to, then, she thought to herself as she returned to David's side.

Chapter Nine

Downtown Paddington, Texas

18th May 1885

Biddie and Angela sat side by side in a small buggy that belonged to the ranch. One of the ranch workers had agreed to drive them into town and collect them a few hours later so that Arch could stay to care for the children.

They needed to collect some essentials for the home such as soap, whisky, and bread, and Angela had said that she wanted to take Biddie around town to show her where things were. Biddie had happily agreed, reveling in the opportunity to get some time away from the ranch and to get some time one on one with Angela.

She had a few questions and concerns about the Sutton family, questions and concerns she hoped that Angela would answer. As the two of them traveled, though, they sat in silence. Biddie once again found herself watching the scenery as they passed through Texas, looking across other ranches and small residential areas as they approached the city center.

"Is it much different to where you're from?" Angela asked, watching Biddie as she gazed out at her surroundings.

"Where I'm from is a tiny town with a handful of shops; I think the ranch is likely larger than the town itself," Biddie replied, turning her head to face Angela, who chuckled gently.

"Ah, right. I get why you watch the scenery, now," she replied. "I've never really paid the view much attention." Angela shrugged. "It's nice to see someone appreciating it, though."

"It's just nice to be somewhere new," Biddie replied. She had spent so long in St John that being anywhere else would be an improvement in her eyes, but Texas did have a certain feeling; it made Biddie feel warm, and like she belonged. It was something she had never felt before.

Angela nodded, but before either of them could say anything more, the buggy slowed to a stop alongside a raised sidewalk.

"We're here, ladies," Henry James, one of the ranch workers, declared as the horses whinnied in agreement. "I'll be back in three hours, alright?" he said, stepping down from his seat on the buggy and walking over to where the two ladies sat.

"That's perfect! thank you, Henry," Angela replied sweetly. Biddie wondered what exactly they would be doing for three hours, but was happy to be exploring her new home nonetheless.

He opened the door and offered his hand to help them out. Biddie stood up and gently took the man's hand, stepping down and out of the buggy. She felt her eyes sting and squeezed them shut, protecting herself from the bright sun that the roof of the buggy had previously been shielding her from.

She stepped away as her eyes watered, dampening her spectacles, so she removed them and dried the lenses on her skirt. It wasn't perfect, but it would have to do. Listening as Angela stepped down, Biddie turned to face her and smiled.

"Where to first?" Biddie asked, looking around at the small streets around them. There were a few residential streets, and then Main Street, on which Biddie could just make out a bakery, grocers, butchers, and what seemed to be a hardware store. There were a few other stores on the street, but she couldn't see exactly what they were.

"Well we need to pick up some things from the bakery and general store, and I believe the haberdashery, too, so I think we should go to the haberdashery first, and then the other stores," Angela replied. "That way we don't have to carry heavy things like the meat around other stores." She glanced at Biddie's smudged lenses. "They may have a cloth you can use to clean your spectacles, too."

Biddie simply nodded in agreement, a little self-conscious, and the two of them headed toward Main Street. Taking a deep breath, Biddie continued to look around her, taking in her new home through the streaks on her lenses as they meandered down the street toward the haberdashery, which sat at one end of it.

The shop was wide, with one large window dominating the front of the building. Inside, Biddie could see rolls and rolls of fabrics, and baskets piled high with balls of cotton and wool. *Meemaw would love this*, she thought to herself.

"I just need to grab a few things; I won't be long. I'll ask about a cloth, too," Angela said, turning to look at Biddie.

"Oh that's alright, I'll come in — I love these sorts of stores; they remind me of my grandmother," she replied.

The two of them walked into the store, and the man standing behind the counter nodded at them politely. The walls were stacked high with shelves and rolls of fabric, and behind the counter there were all sorts of knitting and sewing needles, thimbles, thread and buttons. Biddie couldn't quite believe the extent of it all. She watched as Angela confidently strode from the door over to the shop counter and began to read off a list of the items she needed.

The small, tanned man behind the wooden desk nodded with each item that she named, and then whisked around once she was done to begin compiling it all. He pulled down sheets of fabric, a few spools of thread, a handful of thimbles, two large knitting needles and a selection of sewing patterns. He piled them all up in a small paper bag and handed it to Angela.

"A dollar and five cents, ma'am," the man stated, holding the top of the bag as if to stop Angela from running away with it.

Biddie was worried that Angela might have forgotten about her spectacles, but then she asked, "Do you by chance have a cloth suitable for cleaning glass? My friend here has need."

Biddie felt her skin grow hot as the proprietor eyed her, seeming to zero straight in on her spectacles and their dirty lenses. He made a low sound deep in his throat, as though he were thinking, then turned and grabbed a ragged swatch of plain medium-weight linen.

"Will this work?" he asked.

Biddie nodded. "As long as it's clean; I'm not too particular."

Angela smiled, turning back to the shopkeeper. "How much will that add to the bill?"

He paused for a moment, as though undecided, then tipped his head to the side. "No charge. It's an odd bit, fit for nothing but the rag bin in any case. I'm glad you can put it to good use," he said to Biddie, then looked expectantly at Angela.

She nodded and reached into her small bag, pulling out the necessary coins. She placed them delicately on the table and then looked at the man with a satisfied smile. He took the coins and let go of the bag, making a small grunt in thanks.

Angela turned away from the counter and walked back toward the door and to Biddie. She walked past Biddie and out of the building, and Biddie hurriedly wiped the cloth across her spectacles and quickly followed. Once again, the two women found themselves standing on Main Street.

"Better?" Angela peered at Biddie.

"Much," Biddie replied, holding her spectacles up to the light, then placing them back on her face. She tucked the linen into her apron with a satisfied sigh.

"So is this your first time in town?" Angela asked, leading the way to their next stop.

"It is, yes. Well, apart from the day I arrived at the station. I saw the other end of Main Street that afternoon," Biddie replied.

"Oh, of course," Angela nodded as the two of them walked slowly along the sidewalk.

"It's a nice town," Biddie added. "It's certainly bigger than what I'm used to — St John truly was a tiny place," she chuckled. "It's all a lot to get used to — but I'm getting there." She looked around again, taking in the small storefronts and the wide main road. There were more people around than she was used to: couples, families and friends walking up and down, dipping in and out of stores and chattering away to themselves. But the best bit, undeniably, was that they weren't all avoiding her. Nor were they staring at her. She was just a normal woman, a working woman, doing her household duties with a friend.

"I can imagine it is. New town, new house, new job, new boss …" Angela replied. "How are you finding it all?"

Biddie paused for a moment; she had always been told by her grandmother that sometimes when people ask how you are, or other such questions, they don't always want the truth. She looked Angela up and down from the corner of her eye, and thought about the fact that Angela had been there each day so far to help her. She'd stayed with them to make the transition easier. Biddie already considered her a friend. *I'll be honest,* she decided.

"In all honesty, I'm a little bit concerned," she began. Angela turned her head and gave Biddie an encouraging look. "I'm thoroughly enjoying teaching the boys, and getting to know you has been lovely," she paused to give Angela a sweet smile. "But I do have some concerns about the way that Arch seems to treat the children ..." She shook her head. "It seems ... oh, I don't know," she sighed and then paused for a moment.

"Like he's way out of his depth?" Angela asked.

"Precisely," Biddie answered, grateful that Angela seemed to understand what she meant. "But more than that, he seems to go from one extreme to the other. Some days, I feel like he loves the children endlessly and just wants the best for them. And then others, it's as if they've personally wronged him, and he seems to be unable to even look them in the eyes." She furrowed her brow. "I don't understand, but most of all, I worry about the effect it'll have on those poor children. I don't think he means to act this way, though. From what I can gather, he's a nice man ..."

Angela nodded as she listened to Biddie, and then hummed gently before speaking.

"I think he's also adapting," she said simply. "But I do agree that he doesn't treat those children consistently — or particularly well." She let out a small sigh.

"I'm glad I'm not alone in my frustration with him," Biddie replied, shaking her head again.

"Well, I wouldn't say I'm frustrated," Angela replied, shooting Biddie a sympathetic look. "You've got to understand, Bridget, that he's gone through a lot. The children are acting out because they miss their parents — especially the two young boys. But he is doing the exact same thing. He just lost his brother and sister-in-law. He is filled with sorrow, with grief, and likely with guilt." She shook her head and frowned. "It's a horrible situation to have two young people die in such a way."

Biddie thought for a second about what Angela was saying — for a moment, the way she described the deaths confused Biddie, but she brushed it off. She had not considered that Arch was acting out just like the children were, but now that it had been bought up, it made a lot of sense.

She knew he was struggling to adapt to parenthood, and she'd dismissed his frustrations as simply maladjustment. In reality, though, he had lost his brother and was feeling all of the emotions that the children were, and probably more besides, and his life had been completely upturned — anyone would feel lost. He just didn't know how to process it.

"I hadn't thought about it like that," Biddie admitted as they reached the next store.

"Perhaps try to be a bit more gentle with him — I think he just needs someone to show him that everything is going to be alright," Angela replied, pushing open the door of the butcher's.

"And you think that person is me?" Biddie asked, following her in. Her face contorted as she was met with the smell of drying meat and the stagnant aroma that all butchers' shops had.

"He seems to trust you." Angela nodded, browsing the selection of meat. "And trust goes a long way."

"Hm," Biddie replied. *He trusts me?* she thought to herself. A small flutter passed through her chest. Perhaps Angela had been paying more attention to Biddie's interactions with Arch than she had. She felt a small pang of guilt for not being there for him more, and for blaming him for his behavior, but quickly tried to push it away. She had only been there for a few days, after all.

Whilst Angela considered the meat and discussed with the butcher which was the best value for money cut to feed a large family, Biddie let her mind wander. She tried to process everything that Angela had just said.

She *did* need to be more gentle with Arch, but she also needed to try and encourage him to talk about his feelings rather than to take them out on the children, she decided. He was clearly struggling to adapt, and her working around the house would definitely help that, or at least she hoped it would. He needed support in the same way the children did — how had she not thought about it like that?

Biddie's mind continued to wander as Angela chatted with the butcher, and she couldn't help but think about what Angela had said about Thomas and Sylvie. She said it was horrible for them to die *in such a way,* but as far as Biddie was aware, the two of them had died of stomach ailments.

Was there something more? Were the kids at risk of being sick? Was she? Or was it something sinister? She wondered whether there was something secret going on that she, and maybe even Arch, didn't know. She hoped not. She was unsure that Arch would be able to cope with much more stress. As it was, the poor man was struggling.

Once Angela had collected and paid for the meat, she handed the bag to Biddie, and the two of them left the butchers. Continuing down Main Street, the two of them walked in silence for a few moments.

"What did you mean, when you said that Thomas and Sylvie died 'in such a way'?" Biddie eventually asked. It was probably just a case of odd phrasing, but something told her that she should at least ask. She deserved to know what was going on with the family, especially if it was anything untoward.

Angela's face dropped. A frown took the place of her usually jolly expression, and she looked around them, seeming slightly panicked.

"Never you mind that — and lower your voice," Angela replied. Biddie's heart began to quicken in her chest. It seemed that Angela's choice of words had not been a poorly phrased accident, but something else.

"Angela, please," Biddie said quietly. "I need to know. If I'm to care for the boys, for Pauline … and for Arch, then I need to know what's happened," she pleaded. "You made it sound like there was something sinister at play."

Angela sighed and stopped in her tracks, turning to look at Biddie. Biddie stopped and looked at her friend with wide eyes, confused as to why they had stopped in the middle of the street, since a moment ago Angela seemed to not want to attract any attention.

"There is more to their passing than a bad stomach flu, but I cannot say more. If you want to know, you should speak to Arch. It is not my place, and I should not have said anything at all, let alone in public. We will *not* speak anymore on the matter," she said, her usually friendly smile and warm eyes filled with a stern fierceness that shook Biddie to her core. Something wasn't right.

"I– okay." Biddie nodded. "Sorry," she said, looking down at her feet.

"Don't be daft," Angela said, a smile quickly returning to her face. "It's just not my conversation to have," she said simply, turning to face forward. "Now, let's go get the bread."

Biddie looked up and followed Angela's lead, walking ahead alongside her. She walked in silence; suddenly she had very little interest in the town around her, regardless of how new and exciting it had been mere moments ago. Instead, all she could think about is what Angela had said.

What had happened to Thomas and Sylvie Sutton?

Chapter Ten

The Sutton Ranch, Paddington, Texas

18th May 1885

Arch held Pauline against his chest, bouncing her gently whilst she napped, just as he had seen Angela do so often. He hummed gently to keep her asleep, and looked across the front yard. He had slowly begun to improve his relationship with Pauline. Since she was young, it was much easier to build something with her than with the boys.

He was steadily learning her quirks, what made her sad, what made her giggle. He was hoping that soon he and Biddie could work on getting the little tot to talk and walk again. For now, though, he was satisfied with her sleeping peacefully in his arms while the two younger boys were playing knucklebones on the porch.

Arch stood leaning against the barrier, watching them closely. Things felt alright, for once. He felt like he had finally started to figure out how to handle the three of them. A small smile appeared on his face and he looked down at Pauline for a moment. She was very sweet when she wasn't screaming — almost angelic. He stroked a piece of her hair back from her face gingerly with his index finger and she stirred slightly against his chest.

"No, no no no," he whispered. "Ssh, sssh now …"

Pauline began to calm back down, and Arch relaxed, letting out a long breath. The two boys looked up at him, and Arch could have sworn that Fred had stared daggers at him. He tried to shake off the frustration that it caused, and continued bouncing Pauline gently. Stepping away from the boys for a moment, he looked out across the yard again.

"I'll learn to love it," he told himself quietly. He took a moment, looking over the fields of crops that he now had sole responsibility for, and breathed in shakily. He was still very much struggling to come to terms with all that had happened, and Angela's theories only made it harder.

As he tried to regain his composure, he heard a clattering behind him, followed by a rapid succession of footsteps on wood and then on ground. He darted around to see what was going on, only to see that the boys had disappeared. He scanned the surroundings frantically, desperate to try and find them, but before he could even fathom what his next step should be, Pauline squirmed in his arms.

His heart quickened in his chest, and almost instantaneously, Pauline began to scream and sob.

"Oh wonderful," Arch hissed through gritted teeth. He started to bounce her, patting her back gently, and quickly jogged down the steps of the porch. Looking around, he tried to listen for the boys, but could hear nothing that indicated where they could possibly have gone. His chest tightened — he'd lost them.

His brother had trusted him with their care, and in the one day he had to care for them alone, he'd lost them. In his arms, Pauline's crying worsened as she picked up on his anxiety. She started kicking and wriggling, desperate to be free of his grasp. She was hard enough to hold as it was, but with her writhing around, Arch could feel himself struggling to keep her in his hands.

He adjusted his hold and tightened his grip, and then began to jog around the house, shushing the toddler and scouring his surroundings for any signs of the two boys. After a lap of the house, he stopped still. He took a deep breath in, trying to relax the taught muscles in his chest — but to no avail. He looked across the fields, and then looked across to the right side of the house. Behind the barn there was a small patch of forest; he had used it to hide from his father as a child. *That's got to be it,* he thought to himself.

Quietly, he rushed over to the barn and pushed the door open, just to be sure that they weren't inside. He was met with a few curious whinnies and a boisterous oink, but no children. Nodding to himself, he held Pauline tightly and continued around the barn. As he approached the treeline, he began to hear giggles, and his chest slowly began to relax. Before he went any further, he looked down at Pauline — who was still sobbing about something or other — and smiled gently.

"I best handle you first," he said simply. He maneuvered his hands around the young girl, placing them under her arms, and mimicked what he had seen Angela do with her a few times when she was tired or upset about nothing in particular. He lifted Pauline into the sky above his head, and her crying began to slow. Her eyes widened, filled with a wonder that could only be felt by children.

Her screams turned into giggles, and eventually, she wasn't crying at all. After about five minutes, Arch was raising her in the air and then dipping her down toward the ground, and she was squealing and giggling with such excitement that he had almost forgotten about the boys. Once he was certain that her tantrum was well and truly over, he placed her down on the ground.

"I know you don't want to walk, but I'm going to need you to," he said, trying his best to be gentle. He held his hand out to Pauline, and she hesitantly took it. Slowly, the two of them walked into the forest. The trees towered higher than the barn or the house, and had definitely been here longer than either. In the mud, Arch could see footsteps where the boys had rushed in, and began to follow them as quickly as he could with Pauline walking beside him.

He could still hear their laughter, but he could not for the life of him see anything other than their footprints. His chest began to tighten again, and he could feel the sweat beading on his forehead and his palms. Hastily, he stalked through the woods with little Pauline at his side, and peered around nervously, his heart thumping away in his chest.

He began to worry that the laughter he had heard was a trick of the wind, and that he had indeed lost the children. The panic in his mind made him speed up, forgetting that at the end of his arm was a two year old who struggled to walk on flat ground, let alone in a forest.

After a few minutes of rushing, he heard a thud followed by a scream, and suddenly his hand was empty. He turned to see Pauline in a puddle, crying her eyes out. Her foot was caught on an unruly root behind them, and her dress was soaked in mud.

"Oh darn it," Arch muttered under his breath. He stepped over to her and pulled her up from the forest floor, getting her back to standing. Gently, he wiped the tears from her face, and dusted some of the dry mud off of her dress. "It's alright, it's just a bit of mud," he whispered. "Did you hurt yourself?"

Pauline sniffled and played with the hem of her dress, looking down at her muddy feet. She pointed to her ankle weakly.

"Ouchie," she said quietly.

"Okay, let me look," he replied. He looked around again, trying to see if the boys were near. When he couldn't see them, he held Pauline's small ankle in his hand. It didn't feel broken, and there was no bruising — she'd likely just twisted it. Which meant he was going to have to hold her again. "It'll be okay; let me carry you," he said with a small smile. She nodded, and he stood up from the ground, pulling her up against his chest again.

As soon as he had a secure hold on her, he continued into the woods. Only a few moments had passed when he heard a rustling in one of the smaller trees to the right of the path. His head turned, and he saw Biddie and Angela walking toward him from a small passageway between two of the trees. Both of them looked very confused, and, when they spotted a very muddy Pauline, slightly concerned. *Oh, no*, he thought. The last thing he wanted was the women to see that he'd messed up.

"What is going on? We heard crying," Angela asked almost immediately.

Arch went to reply, but was distracted by a rustle behind him. He turned on the spot, and noticed a pair of legs hanging from one of the branches in a small tree on the left of the pathway.

"There you are," he grumbled. He turned toward the women and handed Pauline over to Angela, and then walked back to the tree. Standing by the trunk, he looked up, and upon realizing how high up the two lads were, his heart began to race again; they were a mere misstep away from falling to their deaths. Did they not know that? Climbing trees is all well and good, but they were not dressed for it, and the forest was covered in a coating of spring dew that made the bark a slippery nightmare.

"You boys get down from there, right now!" he yelled.

"Why should we?" Fred yelled back, climbing another branch higher whilst David remained seated on one of the lower branches. The tree shook, dropping little beads of dew onto Arch as he watched Fred climb.

"Because, Fred Sutton, I am your uncle and I am in charge. Get down here now before you break your necks!" His voice slowly got angrier the more Fred pushed. He could see the hesitation on David's face, unsure whether to follow his brother or to obey Arch's demands. "David, come on, hop down," he encouraged.

"David you stay there," Fred called down, and David's eyes darted between the two opposing forces frantically.

"David, come on," Arch tried again, his voice a mixture of frustration and desperation. "Just climb down, before you get hurt."

Arch could hear Angela and Biddie chatting behind him, entertaining Pauline. The fact that the boys were humiliating him in such a way in front of people, especially Biddie, made his blood boil. She'd already seen him lose his temper, and he didn't want her opinion of him to be jaded further. He desperately wanted her to like him, and to respect him. The boys were really testing his patience; he could handle them being brats, but this was endangering themselves, and making him look ridiculous.

"Last chance, boys. Down. Now. Or no supper for the rest of the week," he said finally. David looked up at his brother, and swallowed harshly. With a small, curt nod down to Arch, he began to slowly clamber down from the large red cedar. On the last branch, his foot slipped, and Arch dashed his arms out to catch him, holding his breath in a wild panic. Just before he reached the floor, Arch caught the young boy and pushed him up straight. "This is what I was talking about," he said, his breath ragged. "Are you alright?"

David was shaking slightly, but looked up at Arch with wide, thankful eyes, and nodded.

"Now go and stand with your sister," Arch said simply, returning his attention to the child still up the tree. "Fred, if he had slipped and hurt himself ... do you know whose fault that'd be?" he shouted up.

"Yours, for letting us run away," Fred replied, rolling his eyes.

"Not yours for encouraging him? For making him climb the tree?" Arch hissed. "Get down, now. Or you won't be eating at all for the rest of the week." His voice had turned malicious now, and he could feel it. Despite his best efforts, he could no longer keep his composure. A part of himself was screaming at him to stop — the women were watching. He needed to manage his frustrations, otherwise both Angela and Biddie would think badly of him. He worked so hard to portray himself as a nice, hard working man, and he could feel himself about to break the whole image. This boy had pushed him too far. He had endangered himself, his brother, and spoken back one too many times.

"Whatever," Fred huffed. "This is boring now anyway," he said, rolling his eyes. He started to climb down effortlessly, landing almost elegantly in front of Arch. "See, not dangerous," he said with a shrug before turning to walk away.

A rage rushed over Arch, and before he could even establish what he was doing, he grabbed ahold of both of Fred's shoulders and vigorously shook him back and forth.

"Do you not understand, boy? You could've gotten yourself killed. Your brother almost injured himself. Do you want to lose a brother? Really?" He yelled.

Fred froze, his eyes red with tears as Arch shook him.

"Answer me!" Arch yelled again.

"No, I— no," Fred replied, his lip quivering. Arch watched as the young boy's face contorted into fear, and he quickly let go, stepping back. All at once, he was both horrified and terrified. His actions had sprung himself back to his own childhood, and he remembered exactly what it was like to be in Fred's position.

He darted his eyes down at his hands, holding them in front of him, and then back up at Fred. With tears in his eyes, Fred ran off toward his siblings and the women, and when Arch looked over at them, the children all looked at him with fear in their eyes. His gaze shifted to Angela, and a lump rose in his throat.

She looked furious and disgusted. His heart truly broke, though, when he looked at Biddie. Her eyes were wide, so much so that he could see their emerald color from across the clearing, and she stared at him in terror and in shock.

What have I done? Arch panicked. *I'm no better than my own father ...*

Chapter Eleven

The Sutton Ranch, Paddington, Texas

18th May 1885

Arch watched as the children began to step away. Their lips quivered, and Fred's eyes were bloodshot, his small nose pink with sniffles. His eyebrows had raised so far up his forehead that his eyes seemed to almost protrude from his face, and any color his skin had once held had washed away. Arch's heart ached; an hour earlier he'd felt that things had finally been going his way, and now he had ruined it all.

He looked from the children to Biddie, whose eyes were wide and full of righteous indignation. She even seemed to be shaking. Looking across to Angela, he saw the same. The two of them exchanged words, and Arch sank back into the tree, leaning on the dewy bark, and pinched the bridge of his nose.

He knew better than anyone that encounters like this don't just leave you, no matter how young you are when they happen. He had just single handedly changed Fred's life for the worse, forever; and David's, for that matter. All because he just could not keep his composure.

They were just children. He was no better when he was young. How could he have lost his temper like that? With a deep sigh, he looked back over to the young boys, and watched as Angela led them away. She held their hands as the four of them walked back out of the woods the way that Angela and Biddie had entered.

Arch let out a shaky breath and tried to stand back upright, away from the tree, but his legs had lost all strength and he wobbled for a moment before thudding back into the bark. He winced on impact, and looked across the clearing at Biddie, who still shook with frustration.

"Biddie, I–" he went to speak, but could not find the words to explain away his actions. He just wanted her to understand. But there was no way that she could.

"No, Archibald," Biddie replied, closing the space between them with fierce, purposeful steps. "I cannot *believe* you just did that."

Neither can I, Arch thought to himself. He looked into Biddie's eyes for a moment, hoping that she'd somehow see his remorse, but she seemed to only grow more frustrated at his silence. He looked down at his feet. The mixture of guilt, anger, and desperation for Biddie to understand swirled around in his head, making him feel sick.

"I didn't mean to," he said simply. He knew there was little use in trying to explain that he had lost his temper - she had seen the evidence of that.

"You are not fit to be a parent if you cannot learn to keep your composure, even when they are misbehaving," Biddie said, her voice stern. "Those boys have just lost their parents, for goodness' sake." She shook her head. "I thought you were better than this."

Her last comment made Archie's chest ache. She *had* thought highly of him. He'd ruined it. She'd never think of him the same way. A new wave of frustration, this time at himself, built within him.

"I'm, I-I," he sighed, looking down at the ground again.

"This isn't about you!" Biddie raised her voice, and Arch flinched slightly. She seemed not to have noticed. The frustration within him continued to grow, but he was no longer able to tell who or what it was directed towards. It felt like it was at everything, and everyone. He was angry that he couldn't protect the boys. Angrier still that they'd run away and Fred had spoken to him like that. He was angry that he'd ruined Biddie's impression of him. Yet, he was also angry that he cared about that. On top of it all, he could feel himself getting frustrated that she was yelling at him. He did not like being yelled at, let alone by a woman, and let alone by a woman that he employed. It all bubbled away inside him, and despite his best efforts, could feel his composure slipping away once more.

"I'm fed up with all of this — with the boys and their stupid behavior, the way that you and Angela let them get away with all of it because 'they lost their parents'." He shook his head. "It's ridiculous! Are we just going to let them grow up to be hooligans? When do we draw the line?" Arch's voice was too loud, but he had convinced himself that he was right. He was the man of the house. Just because she was beautiful, and made his heart skip a beat each time she looked at him, did not mean he was going to stand by and let her talk to him like that!

"They need *gentle* guidance, Arch," Biddie said, looking at him in disbelief. Her stern tone began to soften into a pleading one, but her face remained the same — frustrated and shocked at his behavior and his words. "Please, I'm just trying to help."

"No, they need teaching. By a teacher. Which is *supposed* to be your job. That's how you're supposed to help. But clearly you're not doing enough; otherwise they'd be behaving." He raised an eyebrow. He'd completely lost control. Words were falling out of his mouth before he had a chance to stop them, and he felt his chest tighten as he spoke. "We cannot keep just letting them get away with things like this. They'll grow up to be criminals!"

"It's only been four days, Arch — I can't completely change their behavior in less than a week!" She looked up at him, her eyes meeting his. They were wide and pleading, and in any other situation his resolve would have melted. But in his angry daze, it just infuriated him more. How dare she plead with him when she was yelling at him mere moments before?

The pitch of Biddie's voice raised and her eyes shone as she continued. "It's just a phase — they've gone through a lot. Give them time, and they'll improve. I'll work with them on it, but four days simply is not long enough."

"Then perhaps I should reconsider your position. This negative attitude and inability to provide results isn't good enough." He felt his tone turn from just angry to vicious, but was unable to stop himself. He'd always had an issue with lashing out when he was upset or scared; it came from his childhood. As a boss, he'd never had to learn how to change it — he'd never really been scared. In Texas, though, things were different.

"Arch, come on. You're being unrealistic." She shook her head, and he watched as her wide eyes began to fill with tears — though whether they were of frustration or sadness, he wasn't sure. "Their behavior will improve, but not if you're going to lay hands on them." Her eyebrows remained knotted. She sniffed and wiped one rogue tear from her cheek.

"They're my responsibility; I will do what I must," he said simply. He had no intention of laying hands on them again, but he needed to get away from Biddie. He knew he was just going to continue to upset her, and even in his fit of anger, a part of him was desperate to prevent that. He pushed himself off of the tree. His legs felt much sturdier now, and he stood up straight, a mere few inches from Biddie's face.

Biddie stepped back and stared at him for a moment. Her frustration seemed to worsen.

"Arch, you will *not* place your hands on them again," Biddie said sternly. "They are just boys. Don't you remember when you were a boy? I'm sure you climbed trees, ran away, misbehaved …"

Arch shivered. He did not want to think back to when he was a boy. He'd left this town, this house, this ranch for that exact reason. Ever since he'd returned, he'd done everything within his power to fight off the thoughts of his childhood. They still came, mostly at night, and they filled him with anger and a deep sadness that he spent every day trying to ignore.

"You forget your place," Arch said back. He wanted this conversation to end; she had no right to tell him off like this. He knew what he'd done wasn't right, and he had felt remorse. But now, all he felt was frustration, indignation and disbelief. "I think I will reconsider your position. You're starting to seem more and more like a poor fit."

Biddie froze. Suddenly, her eyes began to stream. Where before one rogue tear had dripped, her face was now covered in flowing droplets, and the wire rims of her eyeglasses were swimming in the puddles that her cheeks had become.

"What do you mean?" she asked.

"I mean that if you're going to act this way to your boss, I'd rather hire another governess. I'd like you to have your belongings packed by morning," he said simply. If for no other reason, at this point, he just never wanted her to see him like this again. He'd ruined any chance of a friendship or anything else with her, and he was sure she'd hate him after this. He couldn't bear to live with her if she hated him. Besides, he could find another governess easily. One that wasn't such a distraction. "You're fired."

"Don't be ridiculous," Biddie replied, stepping closer to him.

"I am entirely serious. You seem to have a poor grasp on what is appropriate to say to your employer, you show little ability to control the children, and you have already asked me for a raise without any evidence of success on your part," Arch said, his voice strained. In reality, he knew that, given time, she'd be an amazing governess. But this was all too complicated now, and he just wanted her gone. He wanted to be alone, and to mourn his brother. He wanted someone who would raise the kids and stay out of his way. He was still wracked with guilt about what happened with Fred, and now he was also angry at Biddie and could feel himself slipping into the sadness that always came when his childhood was mentioned. All of the emotions flooded his brain, and he simply could not think straight. "You will be gone by midday tomorrow, and I will provide you payment for the four days you were here at the rate we first agreed."

Biddie shook her head. "You cannot just fire me for telling you not to harass a child," she said, wiping the tears from her face. He looked away from her.

"I can fire you for whatever reason I deem suitable," Arch replied. He could feel his emotions fizzing within him just like he had on the day that he'd moved to Texas. Nervous, angry and sorrowful energy flooded through his body. All he wanted right now was to disappear into his office.

"I can't believe you!" She shook her head, sniffling loudly. She looked over her shoulder at the house and then back to him. "Those children deserve so much more than you," she said simply, before turning on her heel and storming away back to the house. As soon as she was out of sight, Arch let out a long sigh and leaned back on the tree. He let his body slip down the trunk until he was sat on the dirt ground, and buried his face in his hands.

"I know they do," he said softly, to nobody but himself. His chest felt tight, like his heart had waited for Biddie to leave to beat. His entire body still tingled with emotion, and his head felt foggy, like an entire sky of clouds had just rolled in. He had never liked himself much, but at that moment, he hated himself more than ever. He had felt himself lose his composure twice, and twice he had not managed to stop himself from lashing out at people who he outright knew did not deserve his viciousness.

He was no better than his father.

Chapter Twelve

The Sutton Ranch, Paddington, Texas

18th May 1885

Biddie stormed away from Arch and from the forest. Her heart thumped in her chest and her body trembled with a mixture of frustration, despair and disbelief; had he really just fired her? All because she'd told him not to harm the children?

She shook her head and chewed her lower lip — this was supposed to be her big break, her step to freedom. A day before she'd thought she'd made the best decision of her life; a kind, handsome boss, a lovely neighbor, sweet children … Now it was all gone. She'd have to return to her grandmother, to St. John.

About halfway between the woods and the house, Biddie stopped by the barn, pulling out the linen cloth she'd gotten in town and drying off her spectacles. The tightly-woven fabric turned translucent when wet, and she could already see smudges of dirt appearing on the drab-colored background, even without the aid of the lenses.

She wanted to go and check on the boys, but before she even entered the house she had to make sure she had her own composure; she needed a moment to think and to recount everything that had just happened. She took a shaky breath and walked over to the barn wall.

Leaning against the cool wood, she closed her eyes and exhaled once more, leaning her head back so that her dark curls rested next to her body on the barn wall. Slowly, the tremors began to subside, and in their place she felt a kind of twisting dread in her stomach. Opening her eyes, she looked up at the afternoon sky, and her shoulders slumped.

She'd already fallen in love with this ranch, and with Texas. Each morning since she had arrived she had looked out across the fields and smiled to herself. She'd taken incredible joy at the beauty of the ranch, the warmth of the Texas sun, and the friendliness of those who she had found herself living with.

For that to all be ripped away in the blink of an eye made her heart ache, especially when it was over something she felt so strongly about; Arch should not have placed his hands on Fred. She knew that she was right about that, and she knew that Arch clearly needed help to work on maintaining his composure with the children.

For some reason, though, her reminding him of that had escalated into her dismissal. The man that she had argued with in the forest was not Arch. She refused to accept that the smooth-talking, gentle man she'd met at the train station could treat her with such disregard.

For him to fire her so swiftly … *Well, it just reinforces the point*, Biddie thought to herself. He was a man without control over his own emotions, and that was not going to work if he wished to parent those boys. Nor would it work if he intended to run a happy household.

Biddie sighed. *But what I think clearly doesn't matter,* she thought to herself. She pulled herself up off of the barn wall and rubbed her eyes harshly before placing her spectacles back on her face and pushing them smartly up the bridge of her nose.

She glanced back toward the woods, and then rolled her eyes. She considered going back and arguing her case some more. Maybe she could get Arch to see that she had not intended to upset him, but that she simply wanted to ensure the safety of the boys.

They would not learn to improve their behavior if they were being manhandled, after all. But after a moment's thought, she established that, realistically, there was nothing she could do now to fix this, and trying would likely just make things worse.

Back to Kansas it was, then. Back to her grandmother. Back to being glared at not-so-subtly in the streets. She blew out one last shaky breath and began her walk back to the house. As she walked up the porch steps, her mind began to reel. She tried to block out the thoughts, but to no avail. Her body may have stopped shaking but her mind was clearly having a harder time moving on.

Between the look on Arch's face when held onto the boy and the fear in both Fred and Dave's eyes, it was something that was certainly going to stay with her. She felt a bizarre mixture of emotions, and whilst she tried to ignore them, she could not deny their presence — sadness, shock, and even guilt wreaked havoc within her mind.

Breathe, she told herself. And she did. The emotions remained, but she felt at least a touch more stable, and pushed the large front door open with a creak. She stepped into the house and spotted Angela in the lounge with Pauline.

The two of them were sitting on the floor, and Angela watched as the young girl played absentmindedly with a set of wooden alphabet blocks. *At least she seems not to have noticed,* Biddie sighed gently with a small amount of relief. She wandered from the doorway over to the lounge and stood just inside the room.

"Hello," she said softly, so as not to alarm Angela, who seemed not to have heard her enter. Angela looked up and smiled faintly at Biddie, but her usual radiance was replaced with a grim discomfort, and Biddie smiled back sympathetically.

"Hello," Angela replied. "How did it go?"

Biddie chewed her lower lip again and simply shook her head. She didn't want to discuss hers and Arch's argument, nor the fact that she was to leave first thing in the morning. Angela seemed to discern this from Biddie's movement, and her eyes softened emotionally.

"I see," she replied. "The boys won't speak to me," she said, trying to move the conversation on. "They're up in their room."

Biddie nodded, it made sense that the boys would be isolating themselves. They were likely awfully upset, scared, and confused, and children usually rush to their parents in such a situation. Fred and David didn't have that option.

"Bless them," she said. "I presume this little one is doing just fine?" She grinned down at Pauline, who seemed oblivious to everything going on. She was an odd, quiet child, but in this case, that seemed to have benefited her.

"She doesn't seem to be reacting, no," Angela smiled at Pauline as she bashed two small wooden blocks together and giggled. "I'm glad for that."

"Me too," Biddie said softly. "I'm going to go see the boys; perhaps they'll talk to me." She waved at Angela and received a wary look in return, then stepped back out of the lounge. She walked up the wooden staircase and over toward the boys' room, stopping just outside the door.

She could hear the two children inside sniffling and crying, and her heart ached for them. Pushing away her own frustration and anger at Arch, she inhaled shakily and knocked once firmly on the door. There was a scurry, and then silence. *They're trying to hide*, she realized after a few moments.

"Fred? David? It's Biddie," she said, making sure that her voice was as soft and as gentle as possible, desperate not to upset or scare either of them. "Can I come in?"

There was another scurry, followed by a few sniffles, a muted conversation, and then what sounded like the lock undoing.

"You can come in, but only you," David said.

"It's just me, don't worry," Biddie reassured, placing her hand on the handle and slowly pushing it open. Inside the room, both boys were sitting on the floor, next to one another. Fred had his knees bent up by his face, and his head was buried between them. His body trembled, and he was sniffling with each shaky breath he took. Dave sat cross-legged next to him, also trembling. Biddie stepped into the room and closed the door. She stepped over toward the boys and dropped down onto her knees.

"Hey," she said, her voice still sweet and gentle. She tried to smile at David, but was met with an uncomfortable stare as his quivering lips struggled to make the curve. Instead, he nodded in acknowledgement and then darted his eyes away from Biddie. She watched with sad eyes, and then out a long sigh. "Want to talk about it?" she asked.

David looked at his brother, and then back to Biddie.

"He won't say much." David frowned.

"Do you want to talk?" Biddie asked him.

"I'm just ..." David sniffed loudly. His lip quivered more, and his eyes began to fill with tears. Fred looked up from his legs and over at his brother, and the two of them locked eyes. Within seconds, they were both sobbing.

"Oh boys," Biddie said, shuffling across the floor on her knees. She placed a hand on each boy's shoulder, rubbing across the tops of their arms with her thumbs. "There, there." She could feel her frustration at Arch building again. "It's alright, it's alright, let it out."

"I didn't — I didn't mean t-to make him so angry," Fred said through several ragged breaths. "We w-were just climbing," he sniffled, clearly trying to get his breath back. "It was j-just fun." He managed to take a normal breath, but almost seconds later, a sob shook its way through his body.

"Why does he hate us?" David asked, tears streaming down his face. "It isn't our fault he had to come here."

Biddie nodded and smiled at the boys sympathetically, racking her brain for the right thing to say. She knew that Arch didn't hate the children. He was not a bad man, not really. He was just lost. Stuck. Grieving both his brother and sister in law, but also his old life.

"He doesn't hate you," she said after a moment. She pulled her arms away from the two of them and placed her hands in her lap. The boys looked at her, their tears starting to subside once again. "He's just ..." she thought for a moment longer. "He's sad."

"Why's he sad? His parents didn't die!" Fred's brows furrowed. He wiped the tears from his face and looked at Biddie with an expression that sat somewhere between confusion and anger.

"Yeah!" David nodded, looking at Biddie for a response.

"Well, no, but your father was his brother," she reminded them. "He lost his brother. You wouldn't want to lose one another, would you? That'd make you sad, right?" she asked.

The two of them took a second, looking at Biddie, and then at each other, before nodding slowly.

"Very sad," Fred said quietly. "But if he's sad, why doesn't he talk to us about it? We're sad too."

"He's scared to, I think," Biddie answered. "This is all new to him."

Fred looked down at the floor and then up at Biddie. He nodded simply.

"It's new to us, too," David said quietly. "We really miss our mom, and our dad," he sniffled and looked up at Biddie. "I don't understand why they had to go and be with God so soon. We still needed them …" His lip began to quiver again and Biddie's chest tightened.

She knew what it was like to not understand why your parents had just gone. She remembered how often she used to ask her Meemaw when her mother was going to come back, and she could feel tears stinging in her eyes.

"I know you do," she said gently. "You must miss them both so, so much."

The two boys nodded and she smiled at them with sympathy.

"It's easy to be sad when we lose someone we love, but sometimes, we need to remember to be happy and to honor their memory." It was much easier said than done; she knew that better than anybody, but she'd endeavored, every day of her life, to live for those that she'd lost. And she hoped that this would help the boys do the same. Their parents may be gone, but they still had so much of their lives ahead of them.

"Do you know what? I reckon they'd be awful proud of you both, yeah? Looking after each other, looking after Pauline.

You're so brave. Their big brave boys." Biddie spoke with a confident smile on her face, hoping to instill some happiness in the two boys.

"You really think so?" Fred asked. "But Uncle Arch is always so angry at us."

"He's not angry at *you*," Biddie sighed gently. "He's just … angry. I know he's proud to be your uncle, just like your parents were proud to be your mom and dad, okay?"

The two boys looked at each other for a moment, and then nodded. Fred stood up from his spot on the floor and walked hesitantly toward Biddie. In a motion that was too quick for Biddie to even process, he wrapped his arms around her shoulders and squeezed.

"Thank you, Miss," he said quietly into her shoulder. She returned his embrace, her chest finally relaxing as she hugged him close.

"You're welcome," she said back simply. Fred let go and David smiled at her sweetly. "Now, you boys try and cool off up here, and I'll come and get you for supper, alright?"

"Yes Miss," David replied, and Fred took a seat on the edge of the bed. Biddie nodded and rose to her feet. She gave the two young boys one final smile, then turned to leave the room.

This family needs me, she thought to herself as she went to open the boys' bedroom door. *I can't let him fire me, those boys need someone who understands.*

Chapter Thirteen

The Sutton Ranch, Paddington, Texas

18th May 1885

With a new found sense of determination, Biddie pulled the bedroom door open and stepped outside, only to find Arch leaning against the banister merely a few feet away. She stopped dead in her tracks and quickly shut the boys' bedroom door behind her.

Arch stared at her in silence, his face forlorn and drooping. If she'd thought he looked different when angry, he looked like an entirely different person when sad. The blue of his eyes was overpowered with red, and his usually well-styled golden hair was haphazardly pointing in about ten different directions at once.

She stared back at him, the frustration still bubbling away within her. Her heart raced in her chest and she could feel her palms getting clammy.

"Biddie," he said softly, his voice weak and almost hoarse. Standing up straight from the banister he stepped closer, leaving only a foot or so between the two of them. Up close, she could make out each individual freckle on his pale skin, and could see the sharp, straight lines of his clearly meticulously groomed hay-colored beard.

"Hello, Mr. Sutton," she said curtly.

"I ... well." Arch looked down at her, his eyes gazing into hers for a moment before darting away uncomfortably. He shifted his weight from one foot to another, and wrung his hand in front of him. "I-I o-owe you an apology," he said slowly, his voice quiet as if he were scared someone might hear him admit fault.

The stutter took Biddie by surprise, and her heart quickened again in her chest. She watched his face, unsure whether or not he was being genuine. "I-I-I," he started, then sighed and let his head drop, his frustration evident. She watched as he took a large breath, and then tried again. "I should n-not ha-have spoken t-to you like that, b-back there."

Is he really apologizing? Biddie thought to herself. The stutter made him sound sincere, and almost guilty or afraid. This was the type of man she thought he was — kind, understanding ... A part of her felt sympathy for him, whilst the other, more cynical part of her wondered whether it was an act.

"I should think not," she replied. His eyes widened and his brows furrowed, making his face look even sadder than before. *Maybe he does mean it,* Biddie considered. "You do owe me an apology, yes," she added, trying to reduce the coldness of her voice.

"I-I-I'm really, t-t-truly sorry," Arch said again, his voice still quiet. "I'm n-no good at m-m-managing my emotions." He chewed his lip for a moment and furrowed his brow in vexation. "But th-th-th-that's no excuse."

No, it isn't, Biddie thought.

"I can see that much." Biddie smiled up at him half-jokingly. He seemed to be genuine in his apology, and she would be a hypocrite if she forgave the two young boys' poor behavior on the grounds of grief and not his. "I appreciate the apology," she continued.

"T-th-thank you," Arch said, his shoulders dropping a good inch or so in relief. "I-I-I-I also want-wanted to say that." He exhaled sharply through his nose, gradually getting more upset with himself. "That I acted harshly, a-a-a-nd I should not have dismissed you." He looked her in the eyes again, and where her heart had once been racing, it suddenly felt as if it was slowing right down. "You're a great governess, Biddie," he added. "And I do not think this house would function without you," he said finally.

Biddie continued to look into his eyes, and suddenly noticed quite how close the two of them were. Her frustration at him began to subside; she thought about what she had just said to the boys. Arch was mourning, and was a man who had clearly never had to handle many emotions at once.

He was trying; his apology showed that much. She couldn't hold one lapse of judgment against him, so long as he made every effort to correct the effects of it — and it seemed as if that was his intention. Standing there, in the hallway, his soft voice and shy stutter showed him to be the gentle, kind man she had thought him to be, and a small wave of relief crashed over her. Lost in her thoughts, she only thought to respond when she noticed Arch's eyes move away from her own.

"I'd be happy to stay, thank you, Arch," she said softly, her voice as quiet as his.

"I'm glad," he replied. It seemed as if her forgiveness had relaxed him. His usual, smooth, velvety voice had almost returned. The stutter had dissipated, leaving in its place a small blush across Arch's cheeks. "I really think I need you," he said. "I mean, we, the house, we need you," he quickly continued. His eyes locked onto hers again, and his blush deepened.

I need this too, Biddie couldn't help but think.

"Then it's a good thing I'm sticking around," she replied.

"I think so too," he said. As he spoke, his eyes seemed to take in her whole face, scanning down from her eyes to her nose, and then onto her lips — where they stopped. Biddie's breath hitched in her throat. From where she was standing, she could hear Arch's breath quicken. She could almost feel his breath on her lips and her neck, and imagined it fogging up the lenses of her spectacles. His eyes remained locked on her lips, and she couldn't help but chew her lower lip nervously.

Is he about to kiss me? She found herself wondering. As soon as she'd thought it, her heart began to race, and she wondered what it would feel like to be kissed by a man as handsome as Arch Sutton. The thought made a lump appear in her throat, and she swallowed nervously. She wasn't sure she'd even know what to do if he did kiss her. But before she could think too long, Arch snapped his head up and stepped back slightly.

"Are the boys alright?" he asked quickly, running a hand through his messy hair.

Biddie felt a blush spread across her cheeks, and she coughed to clear her throat. Not even ten minutes ago, she'd been furious with this man, and now she was flustered by him simply gazing at her mouth — how utterly ridiculous!

"They're ... handling it. They were both scared, and sad," she replied, trying to move her mind off of what had just happened and onto the situation at hand. "They thought you hated them," she added.

"Oh no," his eyebrows tightened across his forehead. "I could never hate them."

"I know, I told them that," she smiled gently.

"Thank you, again." He nodded and took a deep breath. "I really am sorry."

"I know, and I accept your apology. But it isn't just me that you should apologize to, it's Fred and David." She raised an eyebrow at him, and he sighed in response.

"I just ..." He let out a small sigh of exasperation and looked down. "I don't know what to say."

"How about we talk to them about it in the morning?" She asked. "Give everyone time to cool down, and then we can tell them why they shouldn't run off like that. Maybe if you explain why you got so upset, they'll understand."

"Will you help me to explain? I'm awful with the children ..." He looked down at his feet.

You're not wrong there, Biddie said to herself.

"I'll help." She nodded. "We'll sort this out."

Chapter Fourteen

The Sutton Ranch, Paddington, Texas

18th May 1885

Arch looked at Biddie nervously as she tried to encourage him. He knew she meant well, and that she had spoken to the boys and so likely knew how they were feeling, but the idea of sitting down and talking to the two of them over breakfast about what had just happened filled him with dread.

His stomach turned and he felt a lump in his throat, but he knew that realistically, it had to be done. Biddie had agreed to help him, and without talking about it, they'd never be able to move past it. He knew that. He'd never spoken about his childhood to anybody, and here he was, a grown man still unable to handle his own emotions, and completely without control of his own anger.

"I'm just worried," he eventually said. Biddie smiled at him understandingly and nodded, and he watched the curls tucked around her head bounce as she moved.

"I know," she replied. Her voice was silky soft, and she looked at him with gentle, truly sympathetic eyes. He could not remember a time he'd felt so listened to.

"I don't, well, I don't know how to discipline children. I know what I did was wrong, but I don't know what the right way to do it *is*." He sighed gently and leaned on the banister. It was hard being so open and honest, but he'd already shown Biddie the worst parts of himself — even if he didn't mean to — so there was no going back now.

"It doesn't always come naturally to people, but that's okay," she said, moving to stand next to him. He could smell her delicate, floral perfume, and a small smile appeared on his face. He quickly cleared his throat and straightened his lips.

"It's more than that. I think that it comes from my own childhood," he said after a moment.

"What do you mean?" Biddie asked, turning to look at him. He quickly glanced at her face and took some relief in her quizzically furrowed brows and slightly tilted head. He'd always feared that if he brought his childhood up to anybody, especially as an explanation for his own behavior, they'd think he was lying.

But at that moment, Biddie seemed genuinely concerned and curious as to what it was that he was talking about. He looked away from her again, staring instead at the wall beside the boys' bedroom door.

It's okay, you can talk about it, he said to himself. He took a long, deep breath in and held it. *There's no harm in admitting that you're out of your depth.*

"Well ..." he let out the breath. "I didn't exactly have the best childhood, and I don't really have any examples of *good* discipline," he said quietly. He turned his head to look at Biddie, and her head remained tilted. Her eyes were wide, processing what it was that he was insinuating. "I only have what I grew up with, and I don't ever want to use those methods on Pauline, Fred, or David. Not ever."

"You mean ..." she began. He nodded, chewing his lip.

"Myself and Thomas were disciplined with a belt. Or sometimes a switch. Father would hit us as many times as we were years old for small acts of misbehavior. For larger things, well, he'd just beat us until he felt we'd suffered enough, I suppose." Arch looked into Biddie's eyes as he spoke, and was shocked to see them widen further.

She began to tear up, and he felt an overwhelming urge to stop what he was saying and to comfort her but was unsure as to whether his efforts would be appreciated. So he stayed where he was and watched as she sniffed her tears away.

"That's horrible," she sniffled. "I'm sorry you had to go through that …"

"Don't be. You didn't do it to me," he said, half-jokingly. "But I suppose it is likely to blame for my approach to parenting … So, in fact, I'm sorry, for not seeking out your or Angela's help. I didn't have any idea it would be this hard." He looked down from her face again and at their feet.

"I understand. I think many people underestimate how difficult parenting really is," she replied, her voice somehow gentler than it had been previously. "But now that I know, we can work on this together. I grew up in a much nicer environment, so I have a bit more experience with gentle discipline."

Arch looked up and nodded hesitantly. If his bad childhood had led to his poor choices, perhaps Biddie was exactly what he needed to balance him out. Together, the two of them could really help the three children.

"Were your parents soft, then?" he asked.

"To be entirely honest, I don't remember," Biddie answered, and a subtle, sad smile appeared on her face. Arch's brows furrowed.

"What do you mean?" He asked, watching her carefully.

"My parents and my siblings all passed when I was very young, not unlike the boys and Pauline." She folded her hands in front of her, and Arch watched as she wrung them and rubbed them whilst she spoke. "They fell ill, all of them. I was only a babe, and somehow I escaped the disease. So my mother, in her last days, gave me to my grandmother. She saved me." Biddie's eyes glistened with a sorrowful nostalgia. "So I grew up with my grandmother. She was — well, is — a kind-hearted woman."

"I see. I'm awfully sorry that you lost all of them," he said, and, despite his best efforts, couldn't help but extend a hand to clasp her arm comfortingly. He ran his thumb over the fabric of her dress and gave her a light squeeze before withdrawing his arm again. Biddie smiled at him appreciatively.

"Don't be, you didn't do it to me," she replied, repeating his own words back to him. "It's okay, I had a good childhood with Meemaw. She was strict, but not in a harsh way. We had rules, and plenty of boundaries, but they were always explained to me. And, when I inevitably broke them, my punishments were always logical. They were consequential." She nodded as she spoke, as if agreeing with herself.

Arch felt a pang of jealousy in his gut — he wished he'd been treated with the same kindness as a child. Perhaps then he wouldn't be the bitter man he was. After all, Biddie was sweet and kind. Maybe he'd be the same.

Maybe he'd even be married. Would he have stayed in Texas? Kept in touch with his brother? Been there for the children? The what-ifs were neverending. He shook his head to brush the thought away. All he could do now was make sure that he didn't make the Sutton children like him. They deserved better than that, and he owed his brother more than that.

"What do you mean by 'consequential?'" he asked.

"Essentially, my punishments directly related to whatever it was I did wrong. If I got in a fight with a neighborhood child, I would have to go to their house and apologize to them and their parents. I'd then have to ask what I could do to make it up to them. It was *so* embarrassing! I only ever did it once, because I never wanted to have to clean another family's stove and grovel to them again …" She shook her head and laughed lightly. "You learn just as quickly if you have to make up for your mistakes than if you're beat for them, maybe more. The difference is, it makes you think about it logically. You aren't running on fear." She looked at Arch, and he felt as if she had, in mere moments, completely understood the baggage he had been carrying alone for all of these years.

It seemed like she knew exactly what his father's actions had done to him, but she wasn't judging him for it; she wanted to help. He was suddenly very, very grateful that she had forgiven him and agreed to stay. He had been completely right when he said that he needed her.

Chapter Fifteen

The Sutton Ranch, Paddington, Texas

19th May 1885

Arch sat up in bed as the sun beamed through his bedroom window. Light filled the small room, and he watched as dust danced around him. Downstairs, he could hear pots clanging in the kitchen as one of the ladies worked hard on an undoubtedly wonderful breakfast for the six of them.

He rubbed his eyes, removing the remnants of sleep that sat around them, and swung his legs out of the bed. Placing his feet on the cold floor, he stretched and yawned. He'd had the best night's sleep since he'd arrived in Texas — likely due to the emotional rollercoaster that had been the day before.

He still felt a pit of guilt in his stomach about the way he had acted in front of the boys, but Biddie's support and her understanding ear had made him feel more confident about parenting them going forward. It was just the matter of apologizing to them that stood in his way. The idea of it filled him with nerves that tingled and made his chest tighten. Knowing that Biddie would be there helped, and whenever the nerves grew to be too much, he focused on that.

With that in mind, he pushed himself off of the bed and plodded over to the wardrobe. He pulled on a pair of fine suit trousers, a button-up, and braces, and then headed to the looking glass. As he combed his hair into place, he found himself thinking about the day before.

He couldn't help but think back to how close he and Biddie had been when they spoke outside of the boys' room. He had been able to see how truly deep and ethereal her emerald green eyes were behind the veil of her eyeglasses, and had smelled her light, floral perfume. Thinking about it, he could still smell it.

Light dashes of lavender, a smell he recognized from drinking tea for head pain as a young boy, mixed with something else. He chuckled lightly to himself and tried to focus back on his appearance in the mirror — now was not the time to lose himself in the idea of an employee.

Once dressed and ready, he left his bedroom and trotted down the staircase to the kitchen. Walking into the room, he spotted Biddie by the stove, whistling as she worked her magic on what smelled like eggs, and Angela standing near the table. Seated around the far end of the table were the children.

As he stepped into the room, David and Fred instantly looked down at the table and tensed, and Angela scowled at him ever-so-slightly. The look made him gulp, and he hoped to God it wasn't audible.

"Good morning," he said, falsifying a bravado that he definitely did not feel. Biddie turned around and gave him an encouraging smile, and a little anxiety faded away. "Angela, first of all, I'm sorry for my behavior yesterday. It will *not* happen again," he shot her an apologetic look, and her scowl softened.

"I appreciate the apology," she said, her voice curt.

"I'm glad. Now, I don't suppose you'd mind watching Pauline in the living room for a little while? I just need to talk with the boys." He smiled at Fred and David, but neither of them so much as looked up from the table. Angela looked from the boys to Arch, and then over her shoulder at Biddie. A small nod from Biddie gave her the confirmation she sought, and she nodded at Arch.

"I can certainly do that," she answered. Arch relaxed a little, his shoulders dropping down as tension he wasn't aware he was holding eased a bit.

"Thank you," he said softly as Angela picked Pauline up from her chair and placed her down on the floor.

"It's alright. Oh, and Arch?" she said, taking Pauline's hand and leading her out of the room. "She seems to be alright walking now."

Arch beamed down at his little niece. She'd been walking before her parents passed; Thomas had told him in a letter when she took her first steps. It felt bizarre to Arch that they'd stunt her development by allowing her to be carried all the time.

His effort to make her walk yesterday seemed to have had some kind of positive effect, and the small turn her ankle had taken did not seem to have caused any lasting harm. His heart warmed; at least his parenting wasn't *all* bad. Angela and Pauline wandered slowly out of the kitchen and across the hallway.

"Did you see that?" Arch asked, looking over to Biddie excitedly.

"I did," she smiled back. "She just needed a reminder," she nodded at him and then returned to the eggs.

"Clearly so," he replied. "How long will breakfast be?"

"I'm just finishing up," she replied, and with a small nod, he swiftly turned to the table. He walked over and pulled a seat out opposite Fred. A few moments later, Biddie appeared. She placed a plate down in front of each of them and sat down next to Arch.

The two boys looked up at her, picked up their forks quickly, and started to eat without looking up again. Arch looked over to Biddie, and she gazed back at him warmly. Their eyes met, and a small shiver traveled down Arch's spine. She gave him an encouraging nod, and he took a deep breath, then cleared his throat.

"Fred, David," he said softly. The boys froze, placing their silverware back down on the table and looking up at Arch through their eyelashes. "It's alright, you're not in trouble," he said, trying to encourage them. Slowly, the two of them looked up properly, and Arch tried to smile at them reassuringly.

"Your uncle would like to talk to you both about yesterday," Biddie said sweetly. "Wouldn't you, Arch?"

"Mmhm," he answered. He could feel sweat beading on his forehead and tapped his foot nervously beneath the table. "I ... well, I—" He sighed and started again. "I want to apologize," he said simply. The boys' eyes widened, and they looked from Arch to Biddie and back again. "I should not have laid hands on you, Fred, nor should I have yelled or spoken the way I did. I was harsh and unfair, and it will not happen like that again — I promise you." He spoke quickly, and while he tried his best to keep eye contact with one of the boys at any given moment, he caught himself simply staring at the table as he spoke. "I panicked. I have not been myself since losing my brother — your father — and the idea that I may have lost his two wonderful boys, or that under my watch you might have injured yourselves ... It scared me. It really scared me."

David and Fred seemed to consider his words for a moment, and Arch watched, waiting for a reply. When one didn't come, his chest tightened, and he continued.

"You boys are my responsibility now, but I've never looked after anyone but myself before. I just want to do right by you, and by your father, and when you both ran off, I thought that was it. I thought you were gone." He shook his head, and tears began to sting his eyes. "I cannot lose you too," he said quietly. "You both, and your sister, are the only family I have left — and so I swear to you, I will not act in such a way again." He smiled at them, desperate to show he was talking from the heart. To his surprise, David nodded and smiled back. A small, shy smile, but a smile nonetheless. Fred, however, remained stoic.

"It's alright, Uncle," David said after a moment of silence. "We knew running away like that was wrong. It's just, well." He furrowed his brows. "We miss our parents, and it's hard having someone new try to tell us what to do …"

Fred glared at his brother and shook his head. As Arch nodded appreciatively at David, the older boy rose to his feet and ran out of the room, rushing upstairs and slamming the door to his bedroom fiercely. Arch watched as Fred went, and slumped in his chair. Turning to look at Biddie, his eyebrows knotted across his head.

"What did I do wrong?" he asked quietly.

"I … I don't know," Biddie replied. "Maybe just give him time."

"He's never been told off before, and definitely not like that …" David piped up, picking at the eggs left on his brother's plate. "We won't run away again, Uncle Arch. I'm sorry that we scared you," he took a large final bite of egg, and then stood up from the table. "Thank you for breakfast, Miss," he said sweetly, and smiled at Biddie. She smiled back at him.

"That's alright. Go and check on your brother, David," she replied.

"And thank you for listening to what I had to say," Arch added. "You're a lot like your father — very smart for your age," he said finally. David grinned in return and walked away from the table and out of the room. As soon as he left the kitchen, Arch let his head drop and sighed.

"You did wonderfully," Biddie said quietly.

"Tell that to the nine-year-old who just ran away from me," Arch replied. He lifted his head and looked over to Biddie. She locked eyes with him and nodded, her eyes gentle and understanding.

"I know, but David forgave you. Fred will too, in time," she said.

"I just wish it was easy." Arch shook his head. None of this had been easy. He knew losing his brother would be a hard thing to handle, but never did he think that he'd also have to look after three children and consider the circumstances of his brother's death, too. He was constantly thinking, be it about work, his brother, or the boys (or sometimes Biddie.) It was exhausting.

"It'll get there; it's a big adjustment to make," Biddie replied.

"It's more than an adjustment." He shook his head. "There's more going on than just a change of pace."

"What do you mean?" She asked. "Your business?"

"Ah, well yes, there's that. But no," he pinched the bridge of his nose. "Before they died, Thomas and Sylvie were being harassed by Mr. Wellington. They — and now I — have the water rights for the area, you see. It would seem that Mr. Wellington wanted to buy the ranch, or the water rights, at least. But Thomas declined. Now I'm countin' the days 'til he comes to pester me for it."

"Have you met Mr. Wellington?" Biddie asked. Her brows were tied tightly across her forehead and she looked almost concerned. Arch wondered whether he should've kept quiet. He hadn't even mentioned Angela's theory, and Biddie seemed to be dangerously curious.

"Not yet, no," he answered. "He's not important, though. I'll just decline." He smiled, hoping to move the conversation on.

"But if he harassed your brother and his wife so much, who's to say he won't make your life unnecessarily difficult, too?" she asked. "Shouldn't you seek him out before he seeks you?"

"Oh no, it's really fine. I'll handle it, he's not worth worrying about," he replied. *He is, in fact, worth worrying about,* he thought to himself. *And I've been worrying every day.*

"Oh, alright … If you're sure?" Biddie replied. Her brows were tightly furrowed, and her eyes were squinted slightly behind their lenses as if she were equal parts suspicious and concerned about what Arch was saying. *It's nice that she cares*, Arch thought.

"I'm very sure. For now, I want to focus on the boys. On Fred. I need to make them feel safe, and I need to work on my parenting skills." He nodded. "And you need to get them to read without running away," Arch forced a cheeky smile onto his face. He didn't want Biddie to worry about anything; she deserved some peace, especially after how he'd treated her yesterday. Besides, he was sure he could handle a bitter rich man.

Chapter Sixteen

The Sutton Ranch, Paddington, Texas

19th May 1885

Biddie knelt in the garden, collecting some fresh flowers for the house. The afternoon sun beat down on her back, warming her to her core. She was always appreciative of the southern sun, especially in the spring. It took away any remnants of the winter and gave everything a brand-new brightness.

As it shone down on the flowers by her knees, they almost seemed to shimmer. The petals of the flowers had a sort of iridescent transparency to them that made her smile. She plucked a small selection of lavender, daisies, and geraniums and held them in a bunch.

Standing up from the ground and wiggling her nose a bit to settle her spectacles, she looked over the fields and watched for a moment as the ranch hands worked. Yet again, she felt intense joy. This was her life now. Beautiful fields of crops, a garden full of flowers.

With a happy sigh, she began to walk back into the house. Today was the last day that Angela was staying with them, so she was looking after all three children for a few hours whilst Biddie got the house together. Angela's husband, the sheriff, would be home soon, and would come to collect her.

Then it would just be Biddie and Arch running the household together. She was nervous, but also excited. Part of her could not wait for some time alone with Arch. Most of all, though, she was sad to see Angela go. The two of them had become friends in the brief time that they'd lived together, and Biddie had never really *had* friends. At the same time, she was excited to meet the sheriff and to let her new life properly start — especially now that Arch had been honest with her.

They could start working together to make life easier for the children, and maybe they could build a real friendship. She desperately wanted to get to know him more, especially after hearing about his childhood. He seemed like such a complex, sweet man.

She just wished that Fred would listen to Arch's apology; she knew that it would make everything so much easier. She knew he'd come around eventually; it would just take some time.

She quickly walked up the steps to the porch and wandered through the house into the kitchen. Grabbing an old whisky bottle that had been rinsed out, she popped the flowers into it. *It will make a nice table decoration,* she thought. She had suggested that when the sheriff came to collect Angela, they all have a meal together. She'd like to know the neighbors, and so would Arch, and it'd be a fitting way to thank Angela for all of her hard work and care with the children since Arch had arrived.

Plus, the way that Angela spoke about her husband made Biddie feel warm and fuzzy; their love seemed so pure, and she was desperate to see them together. Arch had quickly agreed to the idea, and Angela had bashfully accepted the invitation.

So that morning, Angela had watched the children while Biddie ran around, setting up everything for supper and making sure the house was in order for her to begin her full duties the following morning. She had hung laundry out to dry and made a dough using some wild yeast that she and Angela had purchased in town. Then she had moved on to the garden, picking flowers and vegetables, and planned a meal; she was going to make a vegetable soup and serve it with bread. That was easy enough to prepare without any extra help and could be left to simmer while she got on with the rest of it. She popped her flowers onto the counter and then added all of her vegetables into the pot atop the stove.

"Meemaw would be proud," she said to herself, before wandering out of the kitchen and into the lounge where Angela sat with the children.

"Not long now." She beamed at Angela as she walked into the room. "Have you missed him?"

Angela looked up from watching Pauline build a tower out of her alphabet blocks and smiled. She nodded gently.

"I've missed him awfully; always do when he's away. As lovely as it's been being here with you both — well, for the most part — I am looking forward to my own bed, and to spending time with my lovely husband." She let out a small wistful sigh. "He's not normally gone this long; usually it's only the neighboring towns that need him. This time it was a little further out."

"I can only imagine; it must feel like part of your heart has left you," Biddie said. She missed her grandmother, but she just could not imagine what it must feel like to miss someone you loved like Angela loved her husband. She looked around the room. Everything was tidily packed away, unlike when she had first gotten here, and the boys sat in the corner with a set of dominos, a few feet away from Angela and Pauline in the center of the room.

"It does, actually, yes. That's a good way of describing it," Angela replied.

"I look forward to meeting your husband," Biddie said. "Arch said he seemed like a nice man." She walked over to where the two boys sat in the corner of the room playing dominos. "And that these two get on well with him?" The boys both looked up at Biddie.

"Ah, yes, he's a sweetheart. The boys love him. And likewise," Angela answered. "We were often invited around for dinner, you see, so we got to see them grow up. Sylvie and Thomas were real great hosts." She sighed softly. "It'll be nice having a big dinner here again." Her voice was quiet, and Biddie smiled at her in an attempt to provide some comfort.

"I'm glad to bring that tradition back," Biddie said after a few moments. She wanted nothing more than to have a real, solid family and community around her, and by the sounds of it, Angela wanted the same. Angela looked up at her with warm eyes, and then returned her attention to Pauline.

"Boys, do you want to go and get ready for guests and supper?" Biddie said, kneeling down next to them. David smiled and nodded at her, and Fred simply shrugged. "Please," she added, desperate to get something other than an apathetic response from the older boy, but to no avail. The two of them stood up, and Fred led the way out of the room.

"We'll be down soon," David called over his shoulder as he and his brother disappeared upstairs to clean themselves up. Biddie watched them go, a small sigh escaping her lips. Angela seemed to notice and looked over at where Biddie remained kneeling.

"He'll get over it, I promise," Angela said quietly. "I think he's waiting for it to happen again. Like he doesn't believe Arch," she added. "But it won't, and he'll eventually move on."

Biddie looked at Angela as she spoke, a small amount of relief coming from somebody else saying precisely what she had been telling Arch. It also reassured her that Angela also knew it was not going to happen again. She had worried for a while that her judgment was clouded when it came to Arch.

After all, she still found it hard to see him as anything other than the handsome, charming man that had met her at the station.

"I hope you're right," she replied, pushing herself up off of the floor. It looked as if Angela was about to reply, but before any words left her mouth, there was a loud knock on the front door. Biddie watched as Angela's face lit up suddenly. Her eyes widened, and a huge, beautiful smile broke out across her face. She looked at the little toddler in front of her and then to Biddie.

"Do you mind?" She gestured at Pauline.

Biddie shook her head. "Not at all, go, go!" Biddie beamed at her, and within seconds, Angela was on her feet and out of the room.

I want that. Biddie caught herself thinking. *A love like that.* She walked over to Pauline and knelt down again. *I wonder what it must be like to know that you're loved like that ... To have someone care and listen, no matter what. To know that even after time apart, he's there waiting for you.* She let her mind wander for a moment, imagining herself in Angela's shoes, running to the door excitedly to meet the love of her life. Only, when Biddie opened the door in her head, Arch was standing behind it.

She shook her head. *Don't be daft,* she thought to herself, quickly turning her attention to Pauline.

"Hey little one," she said, her voice naturally rising to a higher pitch than usual. "Shall we go and say hello?" she asked. Pauline looked up from her blocks and giggled at Biddie's face. She put the block in her hand down with surprising vigor and then nodded at Biddie. A small smile crept onto Biddie's face. She knew that Pauline *could* speak, but for now, a nod would suffice. It was a start. It was more communication than the young girl had given her when she first moved in. She stood up and offered her hand to the tot, who took it quickly. Together, the two of them walked into the hallway.

Standing in the doorway was Rudy Parker, Angela's husband, a large, muscular man with dark hair and a smattering of stubble across his cheeks. His eyebrows were angular and bushy, and he wore a Stetson on his head.

His shirt had the sheriff's badge pinned onto it and was tucked into dark blue denim trousers that covered the tops of his tattered brown leather boots. Angela stood in front of him, and the two of them were holding each other's hands as if they were about to start dancing. At the sound of Biddie's and Pauline's footsteps, they looked over toward the lounge door.

"Is that little Pauline? All big and walking! Wow!" Rudy grinned down at Pauline. She instantly started giggling and let go of Biddie's hand, running as best she could over to the sheriff. "And you must be Bridget," he added as Pauline gripped his leg in what looked like an almost painfully tight hug. He chuckled and ruffled her hair.

"I am indeed — but please, call me Biddie," Biddie replied. "I've never seen Pauline so excited!" She stepped closer and watched as the sheriff let his wife's hands go and bundled Pauline up, holding her against his chest in a proper hug. She squealed and giggled, and Angela laughed.

"I was here a lot before they ... well, you know." He smiled grimly. "She warmed to me very young."

"So I can see!" Biddie laughed. "It's a pleasure to finally meet you; I've heard so many wonderful things from the boys, Angela, and even Arch." She smiled, and Rudy grinned appreciatively in response.

"Ah, so I have something to live up to, then." He laughed again and popped Pauline back on the ground. "Actually, come to think of it — where are the boys? And their uncle?"

"Oh, they're upstairs. I can call them down if you like?" Biddie replied, gesturing behind her at the staircase.

"That'd be nice." Angela nodded. "Then we can all go and enjoy one another's company." she beamed at her husband with a zeal that Biddie had never seen her display before. She'd thought Angela was a warm person generally, but with Rudy, it was something else. A whole new level of warmth radiated from the two of them. A pang of jealousy took a hold of Biddie, and she tried her best to ignore it. She nodded in reply to Angela and then turned to face the stairs.

"Fred! David! Arch!" she called, trying to keep her tone soft and sweet. "Rudy's here!" She listened for a moment, and then there were two very quick sets of footsteps out of the boys' room and downstairs. As they reached the bottom of the stairs, the two boys grinned at Rudy, who grinned back.

"Hello, fellas," he said cheerfully.

"Rudy!" they shouted together, rushing over to him. He bent down and gave them a hug, then straightened back up again.

"Have you been behavin'?" he asked, raising an eyebrow at them.

"They've been fine," Angela answered quickly.

A second or so later, Biddie heard Arch's door shut and she turned to see him walk down the stairs quickly. He'd put on the same suit he'd worn the day that they met, and Biddie felt a blush spread over her cheeks. He looked wonderful, smart and sleek, and his bright blue eyes shone.

She felt an overwhelming urge to get close to him and brushed it away, as she had tried to with all of her similar thoughts.

"Hi, Sheriff," he said simply.

"Afternoon, Mr. Sutton," Rudy grinned at Arch. The three children stood by Angela and Rudy's feet and looked from Rudy to Arch.

"Please, call me Arch," he smiled, stepping forward to shake Rudy's hand.

"Then call me Rudy," Rudy replied, taking Arch's hand and shaking it firmly.

"Sounds like a deal, Rudy," Arch replied, and Biddie watched as the two men let each other's hands go.

"Shall we go and sit?" Angela asked, and the children nodded. Rudy smiled at her and Arch looked over to Biddie.

"Is that alright with you?" Arch asked. Biddie felt a small shiver down her back as her eyes met Arch's, and she nodded.

"Supper won't be long; let's go and sit," she said softly.

One by one, the lot of them piled into the kitchen and took their seats. Angela and Rudy sat beside one another on the far end of the table, opposite David and Arch. Fred sat at the head of the table between his brother and Rudy, leaving the other end open for Biddie and the highchair for Pauline.

As they waited for Biddie's soup to thicken, they chatted. Rudy told stories of his adventures out to neighboring towns, and the children — especially the boys — listened with great intrigue. He told one story of a time that he was ambushed, and as he spoke, the boys sat on the edge of their seats. Biddie watched as he kept them hooked.

"So there I was, no partner, no gun. Alone in the dark ..." Rudy almost whispered. Angela rolled her eyes; clearly this was not the first time he had told this tale. "I walked down Main Street, and then–" he stopped, leaning forward. The two boys' eyes widened, and they leaned forward too.

Biddie grinned and watched them, and then in the corner of her eye, as Rudy waited to build up tension, she spotted Arch's hands moving toward David's waist. Curiously, she watched him, and just before Rudy continued his story, Arch grabbed David and began to tickle him. The boy squealed, and in turn, Fred squealed, and soon the whole table was laughing as Arch and David tried to simultaneously tickle and fight one another from their seats.

Biddie watched them and smiled. Seeing Arch interact with the children made her heart warm. The longer she watched, the more she felt unable to look away. She caught herself no longer thinking about Arch and David playing but instead about how Arch's arms moved under his shirt, and how his jawline perfectly complemented his angular, tidy beard.

His hair flopped around as he wriggled, and she realized quite how good-looking Arch really was. The thought made her blush, but she just couldn't look away. *Come on, Bridget, get it together!* She thought to herself, but all too late.

Arch looked over to her.

Their eyes locked.

He'd caught her staring.

She quickly looked away and cleared her throat.

"Come now, let Rudy finish his story," she said hastily, chewing her lip and looking anywhere in the room except at Arch.

"Yeah, I want to know what happened!" Fred rolled his eyes at all the commotion.

"Okay, okay," Arch held up his hands in surrender, and Rudy chuckled. He continued his story, and Biddie quickly excused herself to go and check the soup. She stood by the pot and took a deep breath. *You cannot stare at your employer like that*, she scolded herself. She took a few more breaths, stirred the almost-done soup, and then returned to her seat. As she sat down, Rudy was talking about something new.

"So yes, it's next week, and the whole town will be there. You should all really come along. It would be a great chance to get to meet the townsfolk," he said, looking at Arch. Arch nodded along and then turned to Biddie. She quickly darted her eyes away but listened as he spoke.

"Rudy was just saying that there's going to be a fête in town in a few days. Music, apple bobbing — the lot," he explained.

"It would be great for Arch to show his face, what with him owning one of the biggest ranches," Rudy smiled at Biddie. She nodded and smiled back.

"That sounds like a wonderful idea," she agreed.

"And perhaps we'll see you there, too, Biddie?" Rudy asked.

"Time will tell, I suppose!" She laughed gently. The idea of a community fête filled her with childlike excitement, but she certainly didn't want to reveal that to her new friend and the Sheriff. She hoped that she'd be able to go, but figured it would depend on how much needed to be done in the house on the day. If she went, she'd actually get to be a part of something. A part of a family, a community.

Chapter Seventeen

The Sutton Ranch, Paddington, Texas

19th May 1885

Biddie stood on the porch, watching as David and Fred ran around in the garden, wearing off their energy before their reading lesson. She'd realized early on that letting them blow off steam was the best way to ensure that they would pay attention in her lessons, and so before each one, they went and played whatever it was that kept their interest for half an hour.

It wasn't necessarily perfect, but it worked. Meanwhile, Pauline was in the lounge napping in her cot. That way she got some uninterrupted rest, Biddie got half an hour of fresh air in amongst her chores and teaching, and the boys got to run around like loons for a short while. She leaned against the wooden railing that lined the porch, enjoying the warmth of the sun on her face and clearing her mind.

From behind her, Biddie heard the front door creak open. She craned her neck to look and spotted Arch standing in the doorway. He wore deep blue jeans and a button-up, and it took every ounce of effort in her to keep from staring.

Ever since she'd looked at him during dinner, her eyes continuously betrayed her, staring at him whenever the opportunity arose; it was awfully inconvenient. Brushing away the thoughts of him, and of *them*, was becoming increasingly difficult.

"Good morning," Arch greeted her, his voice smooth and warm like honey.

"Isn't it just?" she replied, turning to face him. "How are you?"

"I'm well, very well." He nodded, a warm smile spreading across his face. "How about you?"

"Me too," she replied cheerfully. "I'm just letting the boys wear themselves out," she chuckled, gesturing behind her at the two young lads running in circles.

"Ah, I see — a smart move," he nodded.

"I thought so," she replied. "What can I help you with this morning? Surely you're far too busy to just come out here on a whim?" she added, half-jokingly. Arch was always tucked away in his office. She had very little idea about what it was he did in there, but he seemed to be an incredibly busy man.

"Well, yes, actually," Arch blushed at her comment and laughed. "I was wondering if I could ask a question?"

"Technically, you just did," Biddie grinned, and Arch furrowed his brows in confusion for a moment. Staying silent, she waited for him to understand. A second later, he rolled his eyes and chuckled.

"I suppose I did," he nodded. "I'd like to ask another if that's okay?" he said. "In addition to those two," he added before she could pull the same trick again.

Biddie laughed quietly and glanced over her shoulder to check on the boys — thankfully, they were still chasing each other.

"Mhm, go ahead," she answered.

"This fête," he began. Biddie's heart skipped a beat. "Would you like to join me and the children? You're new to this place. I've at least grown up here — it seems only fitting that you get to know the community." He looked into Biddie's eyes as he spoke, and she found herself lost in them. The depths of the blue that sparkled in the sun were just too enticing, so much so that she had to be reminded to answer his question. "Biddie?"

"Oh! Yes, I would love that. Yes, please." She nodded, looking away from his eyes and focusing instead on his chin. She could not get distracted by his chin. Probably.

"Lovely, I'm glad." He nodded swiftly. "We'll arrange it all later, but I was thinking we could all go in the buggy together? There should be enough room." He leaned against the doorframe as he spoke, and Biddie nodded excitedly — she was just happy to be invited.

"That sounds wonderful! When is it?" she asked.

"In a couple of days. So we have plenty of time," he smiled and straightened back up. "I'll see you later to talk about specifics?"

"Of course," Biddie replied, the large smile still plastered on her face. "I should get back to the boys." She looked over her shoulder at them again.

"Oh yes, and I should get back to work." He nodded again and then turned on his heel. "I hope the lesson goes well, Biddie," he said quickly, smiling at her charmingly before quietly closing the door and disappearing off inside the house. Biddie felt another shiver along her spine as she heard her own name and shook her head. *Oh, stop it!* she told herself.

Turning her head back to the boys, she noticed that Fred had stopped running and was glaring at the doorway where Arch had just been standing. She frowned down at him and he looked away, back to his brother who had occupied himself by digging a hole in the ground with a small stick.

Biddie let out a soft sigh and looked from the boys to the door and back again. She knew that Fred was going to take some time to forgive Arch, but having to handle his attitude in the meantime was exhausting. Especially when David had so readily accepted the apology and moved on.

She just wished Fred would hurry up, but for now, she'd have to just tolerate it and hope that he became more reasonable in the coming days. With that in mind, she cleared her throat.

"Boys, inside now," she called delicately.

The two boys stopped their digging and looked up at the porch where Biddie stood. David shot her a smile and Fred visibly sighed, but both of them dropped their sticks and walked up the small wooden steps to the porch. Biddie smiled at them gently and stepped over to the front door, pulling it open for them both and ushering them inside with a small wave.

They quickly piled into the house and Fred led the way to the living room in silence. There, Pauline lay still asleep in her small cot, snoring quietly and rolling back and forth every now and then as she dreamed about something or other. Biddie gestured toward a plush green armchair in the corner and David wandered towards it, taking a seat on the floor in front of it.

Fred begrudgingly followed, huffing. Biddie rolled her eyes to herself and strolled over, taking the book they were reading together from the small table to the side of the armchair. Sitting carefully in the seat, she opened the book.

"Do you remember where we were?" Biddie asked Fred.

"Curdie had just heard the goblins' plans!" David answered for him.

"Ah, yes, very good David," Biddie answered. She'd hoped to get Fred to show some interest in the lessons, but it seemed that it was not the day to push him too hard.

"So I'll read a page, and then you, David, and then Fred. Does that sound good?" she asked, finding their page and getting comfortable in the armchair. David nodded, an eager smile on his face, and Fred huffed again. With a forced smile, Biddie nodded at the two of them. She was happy to see that David was so interested in their reading lessons, but it really frustrated her to see Fred quite so apathetic. He'd been a pain before, but at least he showed some kind of personality. Now he just seemed glazed over, as if he were barely even in the room with the others.

She decided she'd try to speak to him after their lesson, alone. She'd not had a whole lot of time with just him, and she figured that it was the only thing that she hadn't really tried yet. It couldn't hurt. Maybe if she opened up to him, he'd open up to her. After all, she knew what it was like to lose one's parents.

She began to read from the book, adding in different voices for the characters of Princess Irene, Lootie, and Curdie and making sure that her face was as expressive as possible. It helped to keep their attention, and made an otherwise mundane reading lesson much more interesting for all involved.

She read aloud the goblins' plans for the mines in a low, gravelly voice, and David squealed. Biddie grinned and continued to read until she'd finished the double-page spread. When done, she handed the book down to David who continued where she had left off. To her surprise, he struggled significantly less than he had done in their previous lesson, and even tried to add his own voices for each character.

She couldn't help but giggle at his *very* high-pitched and feminine voice each time Princess Irene spoke, and he took her giggle as encouragement, doing it more and more. He finished his two pages and continued to read, clearly enjoying his own performance and the story. Biddie allowed it, letting him finish another double page before stopping him in his tracks.

"Okay, okay, c'mon now." She grinned down at him. "It's Fred's turn." She gestured toward Fred with her head and David sighed and nodded, handing Fred the book reluctantly.

"Now, Fred, off you go." Biddie smiled at him, but he ignored her kind expression and sighed. She took in a long breath, trying desperately to keep her composure in the face of such disrespect.

Fred began to read. Slowly at first, stumbling on a few words as he went, and then faster and more naturally. Biddie watched as he lost himself in the story, reading fast and paying little attention to the excited face of his little brother or the proud grin that had taken up residence on her own face.

After a double page was done, he continued, only stopping when the chapter ended a few pages later.

"Well done, boys," Biddie said warmly, taking the book from Fred. "You both did so well! We'll continue next week." She placed the book on the table, and the two of them went to stand up. They knew their routine; after reading they were to collect the laundry from outside, and then there'd be an arithmetic lesson before supper. "Just a moment; before you go." Biddie stood up. "I'd just like to speak with Fred about his reading. Would you mind starting on the laundry on your own, David?" She smiled at the younger boy and he furrowed his brow slightly, but nodded.

"Yes, Miss," he answered. Fred looked from David to Biddie, his eyes wide. He almost looked frightened, Biddie noticed.

"Fabulous," she replied. "Off you go — Fred will be out in a moment."

David nodded and left the room, heading out of the front door. Fred watched his brother go and then turned to Biddie, his eyebrows knotted together suspiciously.

"Fred, sit down," she said warmly. He shook his head, crossing his arms firmly across his chest.

"No," he answered.

"Alright, fine, you can stand," Biddie shook her head in disbelief and lowered herself back into her chair. "I just wanted to ask how you were."

"I'm fine. Can I go?" He rolled his eyes.

"No, Fred," Biddie replied. *Why are you making this so hard?* She asked subconsciously. "Sit down, please, I want to tell you a story." She smiled at him pleadingly and he sighed. With another eye roll, he sat back down on the floor. "Thank you."

"What story?" he asked. "We've finished reading."

"Not a fictional story, Fred," Biddie said as softly as she could. "I wanted to tell you a story from my life. I ... well, I think it might help."

"I don't *need* help." Fred shook his head.

"Just listen, please?" she begged. Fred flung his head back and huffed again, and Biddie exhaled sharply through her nose. "I want to tell you about when I was a really little girl, no older than Pauline." She gestured over at Pauline, who remained fast asleep in her cot. "You see, I can tell that you're not alright. We know, us adults. It's easy to tell when someone isn't okay, and when it's someone you care about, it's even easier," she started. "And I've been there. I know how you're feeling."

"You don't know anything!" He raised his voice, and Biddie flinched slightly. "My parents are dead. You don't know anything," he said again, quieter this time.

"My parents are dead too," Biddie said simply. "They died when I was very, very young. So did my brothers and sisters."

Fred's eyes widened and he looked up at Biddie. His eyes were red, and she could see that they were slowly filling with tears.

"When I was a baby, a really bad sickness took over the neighboring village. Somehow, my parents got it. Soon, my brothers and sisters did too. They were all ill. And not the kind of ill that you get better from," she said sadly. "When my mother realized that I was not getting ill, and that she did not have long left to live, she called for my grandmother. And, to save me, my grandmother came to the house. My mother saved my life. She passed me out of the window to my grandmother who risked her life just by being there.

"Days later, they all died, and I was left to live with my grandmother. I had no clue who this woman was — I was very young. But she raised me anyway. And she made me who I am today." Biddie felt the sting of tears in her eyes. She really missed her grandmother. "But I survived it, and I wouldn't have changed my grandmother for the world. But one of the things that helped me through it all, when I got older, was talking about it …" Looking down at Fred, she saw that his eyes were even redder, and as the two of them locked eyes, he broke into a sob.

"I just," he cried. "I just don't know him." His torso shook with sobs, and tears raced down his face. Biddie slipped from the chair onto her knees in front of him and wiped his tears away gently with the pad of her thumb.

"I know, I know," she said softly.

"I miss them so much. I miss my father's jokes, and my mom's cooking. And her singing." He shook his head, tears falling from his face onto his shirt. "Do you miss your parents?"

"Every day," Biddie said quietly. "But, do you know what?"

"What?"

"I'm also grateful, every day, that I had someone as wonderful as my grandmother to raise me. She didn't have to. There was no obligation. I could have had to go to an orphanage. But my family looked after me — just like your family is looking after you," she raised her eyebrows, looking at him with eyes full of sympathy and he stopped crying for a moment, his lip quivering as he looked at her.

"I never thought about it like that," he admitted quietly. "It's just that, I don't know him, we don't know him ... He doesn't feel like family. He feels like a stranger," he sniffled. "An angry stranger."

Biddie nodded, listening to everything he said. She had quickly learned that Arch had not had anything to do with the children prior to Thomas' death, and she knew that it made the whole situation harder for everyone involved.

"He might feel like a stranger," she said, taking Fred's hand in hers. "But he *is* your uncle. And your mother and father trusted him enough to ask him to come here." She cocked her head to the side. "That's got to count for something."

Fred sniffed again and wiped his nose on the back of his hand. He nodded hesitantly.

"I guess," he said quietly.

"And he won't be angry, not anymore. I promise you that," she added. "You just need to give him another chance. He wants to do right by you. For your father. The least you can do is let him try, right? If not for him, for your parents?" She watched his face for any hints of a response, but he remained relatively stoic, his quivering lip the only sign of any feeling.

"Do you really think he's trying?" Fred replied after a moment of thought.

"I know he is." Biddie nodded. Fred sniffed one last time and wiped his face. He took a deep breath and looked Biddie in the eyes. With a sad look in his eyes, he nodded once.

"Then I'll give him a chance."

Chapter Eighteen

The Sutton Ranch, Paddington, Texas

20th May 1885

The light flickered through the windows of Arch's office, filling it with a brightness that made Arch smile. If he had missed one thing about Texas, it was the weather. It wasn't as nice in Georgia. He leaned over some paperwork on his desk and continued to read it, following the words with the nib of a pen as he read.

He'd been reading so much paperwork since he'd got here that it felt like he'd forgotten what accounting actually entailed. But, it would all be worth it in the end — he'd start up a Texas branch of Sutton Accounting, and his second-in-line back in Georgia, Harold, would continue to run that branch.

Together, they'd be able to make double the profit. Or so he hoped. Before he could reach the end of his document, there was a quiet knock on the door.

"Yes?" He called, marking his place on the document with his finger and looking over at the closed door. The door swung open, revealing David.

"There's a man at the door, Uncle Arch," he said simply. "Said he needs to talk to you."

Arch frowned — who in Texas would know he was here? And why would they want to talk to him? He nodded thankfully at David.

"Lovely, thank you, David." He smiled quickly. "You can go back to your chores."

David nodded and waved, then turned and ran back downstairs. Arch chuckled gently. Since getting to know the boys a little — or at least David — he'd realized quite how goofy they were. It made him happy. They were much like their father at the same age. Standing up from his desk, Arch ran a hand through his hair and straightened his braces, then swiftly exited his office, trotting down the stairs.

Standing in the doorway was an older man. Taller than himself, the man wore all black and seemed to not have any luggage, briefcase, or even a pistol on him. He had gray hair that was slicked back and incredibly angular eyebrows that dominated much of his face. Arch's eyebrows tightened across his forehead.

Why do I recognize you? Arch thought to himself.

He straightened his posture as he reached the door and offered his hand out to the stranger, hyperaware that this odd man had just appeared on his property with no warning. His other hand clenched in his pocket.

"Hello, I'm Mr. Sutton," Arch introduced himself.

"I'm aware." The man took his hand and shook it. His skin was clammy and cold, despite the warm summer heat. It was unsettling and put Arch further on edge than he already was. "I'm here with a proposal."

A proposal? Arch thought.

"And what might that be?" Arch asked. Everything about the man standing before him made his skin crawl for some reason. He could not help but want him gone as soon as possible.

"My employer, he's interested in your ranch," the man started. Arch's chest tightened. Suddenly, he thought back to what Angela had said when he first arrived. He tensed his fist even more, trying his best to keep calm. "It's a mighty fine plot of land, and he believes it would be perfect for his cattle to graze on, you see. He's a generous man; you'd be well rewarded." The man smirked as he spoke, and his voice made the hair on Arch's arms stand on end.

"Ah, I see," Arch nodded. "Well, unfortunately, this ranch, Sutton ranch, is not for sale," he said simply. "You'll have to tell your employer to look somewhere else."

The man's eyebrows furrowed and he scowled at Arch. Stepping forward, his voice quietened.

"Now, come on, let's be reasonable," he almost hissed. "I'm sure it is a deal you'll want to consider before declining, no?"

Arch remained in his position, his shoulders back and head held high. He looked the stranger in the eyes.

"No. I will not be considering it," he replied confidently. "Now if you could see yourself off of *my* land, it'd be greatly appreciated."

"Oh dear, Mr. Sutton. It's a real shame that you feel that way." The man raised one angular eyebrow and the corner of his mouth followed suit. "I really think you ought to consider it. We wouldn't want anyone to ... regret anything, now."

"Listen, I am *not* selling. Tell your employer I said no, and leave my property right now," Arch replied. His heart thumped in his chest and he could feel his palms sweating. It was becoming hard to keep his composure.

"Aren't you interested in how much my employer would be willing to pay?" The man asked. Just as Arch went to reply, he spotted someone walking along the pathway to the house through his peripheral vision. Darting his eyes away from the stranger's face, he looked over to the person approaching and realized it was Rudy. A small smile appeared on his face and he stayed quiet. The stranger frowned at him and raised his eyebrow again.

"Hello?" the stranger asked, his voice full of frustration. Arch simply nodded in response. Before the man could say anything further, the sound of footsteps coming up behind him made him jump, and he turned his head to see who it was. The sheriff, as he approached the door, looked from the stranger to Arch and back again, and cocked his head to the side.

"Mornin', Arch," Rudy said cheerfully, stopping next to the stranger. "Monty," he said sternly to the stranger.

"Sheriff," Monty replied grimly.

"Morning Rudy," Arch nodded his head respectfully. "I was just asking *Monty* here to kindly remove himself from my property." He glared at Monty. The Sheriff caught the look and sighed, turning to Monty.

"Turning up unwanted again, are we, Monty? I'd have thought Mr. Wellington's employees would have much better manners," he tutted. "Let's go, come on." Rudy placed a hand on Monty's bicep and pulled him away from the door. Monty resignedly turned with the Sheriff's push, sighing exasperatedly. Rudy continued to lead the peculiar man down the stairs of the porch, then stopped and looked back over his shoulder.

"Won't be one minute," he called up to Arch. Arch chuckled lightly and nodded, watching as Rudy led Monty away and off of the ranch. He stepped out of the front door, shutting it behind him, and took a seat on the porch steps.

As he waited for Rudy to return, he thought about what the sheriff had said about Monty — that he worked for Mr. Wellington, the same man who had been trying to get Thomas and Sylvie to sell the ranch for years. He had known it would only be a matter of time until they came to try again. Poachers. This family had lost enough, did they really think he'd sell the ranch too? Especially to someone as unnerving as Monty? There was something about him that just made every fiber of Arch's being angry and suspicious, but he couldn't quite put his finger on what it was. Whatever it was, he knew it was enough to make him never want that man near him, the children, or Biddie. Monty was not welcome on his ranch.

Not too long later, Rudy jogged back toward the property. He slowed to a halt at the bottom of the stairs and took a second to catch his breath.

"He didn't cause no harm, right?" Rudy asked. Unlike when Monty had been here, Rudy's face looked alarmed and concerned. His eyes bore into Arch's, searching for an answer.

"No, no, not at all. Just asked if I'd sell, then got a little bit eerie when I said no." Arch shook his head. "Angela mentioned people were after the ranch - it's no big deal." He looked up at Rudy reassuringly.

"Yeah, they're after more than the ranch," Rudy sighed, taking a seat next to Arch.

"Oh, right, yeah. The water rights, right?" Arch asked. Angela had mentioned that Thomas and Sylvie owned them and that Mr. Wellington wanted them. Arch's chest tightened. She'd also said the man she saw leaving the ranch was probably connected to it all. The old, tall man. Dressed in black. A lump rose in Arch's throat, and he swallowed harshly. Rudy had seemed to think Angela's ideas were fantasy. It was best that he kept his panic to himself.

"That's the one." Rudy nodded. "You see, your brother owned the water rights. Just like you now do." he took a cigar from his pocket and lit it, then took a long drag on it. "But he was nice, he was a right good man, Thomas. He let everyone who needed the water use it. No quarrels, no issues." Rudy let out the smoke from his cigar. "So when people started showing interest in the rights, he declined. *Especially* Wellington. Nobody in this city trusts that man, least of all your brother." he shook his head and scowled at the air. "There was no chance that Wellington would let anyone use the water. Not without payin'. So Thomas refused. And he continued to refuse. He and Sylvie, well, they were the only ones who stood in that sick man's way." He looked at Arch. "And now that falls to you."

"Well, I can assure you, this ranch is mine and my family's. It will not be falling into the hands of some money-hungry bottom-feeder." He shook his head. "They'll have to do more than send some creep to get what they want."

Chapter Nineteen

Downtown Paddington, Texas

21st May 1885

From where they parked the buggy, Biddie could hear laughter, cheers, and squeals of excitement. Behind the sound of voices overlapping one another, she could just make out music. There was the unmistakable sound of a fiddle, a banjo, and, if she was hearing correctly, even an accordion.

There were some other instruments that her ears could not quite make out from so far away, but the sound of them all playing together filled her with an unruly energy. All she wanted was to rush over there and dance, unwind, and enjoy herself.

The midday sun was high in the sky, and it warmed her face as she walked alongside Arch, Rudy, and Angela. Angela held Pauline's hand as they walked from their buggy to the village fête.

Biddie watched as Fred and David played some kind of game just ahead of them, running around and occasionally stopping, staring at one another, then running again. She didn't recognize the game, but they seemed to be enjoying it.

The seven of them walked briskly along a dirt track through a wooded area not dissimilar to that on the ranch, and Biddie took relief in the moment of coolness provided by the tall cedar trees. She looked across at her companions and smiled to herself.

This was precisely the sort of thing she had moved to Texas for; she was heading out to a community event with her friends, to have fun. She'd had fun in St. John with her grandmother, but this was different. It was something that she'd craved for as long as she could remember.

Her smile widened. *I've found it,* she thought to herself. She couldn't quite put her finger on it, but something about that collection of people, something about Texas ... It all just made her feel at home.

Before long, the group re-emerged into the sunlight; Biddie could hear all the noises of the fête much clearer, and she could now see where the noises were coming from. They had stepped out onto a large field full of people. The usually green grass was trampled and trodden on, making it flat and an almost yellowish color.

Upon it were upturned barrels forming makeshift tables surrounded by people, tens of stalls made out of wood, tall flag poles with colorful bunting hanging between them, and a bar with the band next to it over in the far corner. There were other barrels dotted around too, that seemed to be used for apple bobbing or something similar, and a shooting range opposite the bar.

Biddie could see a few food stalls, and then other craft tables set up by local sellers. The adults were hovering around barrels and watching their friends dance, glasses of iced tea in their hands, and the children ran around like little hurricanes, trying desperately not to run into anyone.

Beside the bar there was a large wooden platform with numerous barrels on, all of which were surrounded by sawdust and had large scoops placed in them.

Biddie's jaw dropped. She'd never seen anything like it. They continued to walk closer to the fête, and as they approached, Biddie got hit by a wave of smells: apple pies, cinnamon, coffee, stew, soup, bread; every food that she could think of all blurred into one exciting aroma that filled the field. The smells were coming from every direction, and she had to stop for a moment to take it all in.

"Are you alright, Biddie?" Arch asked, turning his head to look at her and stopping a few steps ahead of her. Biddie looked at him and nodded, her mouth slowly closing and reforming into a grin. She looked around at the fête, and then at Angela and Rudy.

She let her eyes travel over to the boys, who were entirely oblivious to the fact that the group had stopped, and then finally, to Arch. He'd put on his Sunday best for the fête, and was dressed in a well-tailored suit, complete with a waistcoat that hugged his lean body. His hair had been slicked back, and in the sun, she could see all of his freckles.

"Oh, uh, yes." She nodded, realizing she had not yet replied. "I've just never been to a fête before. It's a lot to take in." She smiled at him and then looked past him at the fête. "I'm so glad you invited me," she said softly.

"Me too," he replied, a small smile on his face. "Let's go and explore."

Biddie blushed and nodded once more, and they continued walking toward the fête. The boys stopped their running and walked alongside her. Before long, Biddie found herself standing within the main ring of the fête, next to one of the stalls run by a local woman.

Looking around, Biddie spotted couples embracing one another, dancing along happily to the music, which she could now tell also featured a washboard. She watched them for a moment, the ladies' dresses swinging around as they skipped and dashed happily alongside the well-dressed men, and jealousy filled her mind.

She wanted to dance. She wanted to be held like the women were being held, and to clear her mind as her feet followed the beat of the music. She let out a small wistful sigh and turned her attention to the vendor beside them, where all of the others were focused. Looking down at the small wooden table, she noted a selection of homemade soaps decorated with small ribbons and dried flowers.

There were soaps with lavender, daffodils, rose petals, and other flowers that Biddie couldn't quite place. They were all beautiful, and the smell of them was so incredible that she couldn't help but grin like a child.

"These look divine," she said gently.

"Thank you, miss," the woman standing behind the table replied, beaming from ear to ear. She was around the same age as Biddie, and her smile filled Biddie's heart with joy.

"Would you like one?" Arch asked, moving to stand beside Biddie. "I'm sure I can spare a few pennies." He looked over at Biddie, and she felt a shiver travel down her spine. She nodded excitedly and he smiled in response. He turned back to the lady and she looked at him expectantly. "How much?" he asked.

"One bar is five cents," she answered cheerfully. Quickly, Arch reached into his pocket and pulled out the necessary change. He placed it on the table and then scanned the bars of soap with his eyes.

After a few seconds, he picked up a round bar with two lavender flowers pressed into the top. He handed it to Biddie gently, his eyes meeting hers. Her stomach filled with butterflies as he handed her the small gift, his fingers gently grazing her own.

"Thank you," she said quietly. She was very aware that a blush was spreading across her cheeks and that Angela, Rudy, and the children were all nearby. Quickly clearing her throat, she darted her eyes away and toward the young woman on the other side of the table. "And thank you," she added. The woman nodded politely in return, and Biddie turned away from the table.

With butterflies still running rampant within her stomach, she led the group away from the soap stall and into the rest of the fête. They walked past stalls selling food, various types of iced tea, and even a few selling jewelry. Biddie took it all in as they walked, Angela holding Pauline's hand as she waddled carefully alongside them all, the boys playing tag and running along beside the adults. She looked over to Arch and noticed him watching the two boys, a happy, peaceful expression on his face. She sighed contentedly and stopped for a moment.

"So, what should we do?" she asked, the others stopping shortly after her.

"We want to go play!" David said, grinning. "They have apple bobbing!"

Biddie and Angela chuckled in response. It came as no surprise to anybody that the two young boys wanted to run off and have their own fun. Looking over at Arch, Biddie caught him rolling his eyes jokingly and then watched as he reached into his pocket.

She furrowed her brow as he fumbled for a moment. He pulled a few coins out from his pocket and held them out in his palm toward the children.

"Off you go, then," he said simply, his tone light and happy. "Don't go causing any issues now, alright? Or I'll have to send Rudy after you!" He winked and David's grin somehow got wider. Fred snatched the money and scowled at Arch. Biddie's heart sank.

Please don't snap, she thought to herself. Fred was still not over what had happened the other day, and he was making it very hard for Arch. Biddie reckoned he was testing him — trying to make sure that he wouldn't snap again. Whatever the boy was doing, it was getting tiresome.

Biddie eyed Arch for a moment. His hand remained outstretched. His brow furrowed. He leaned forward, his body tense, and Biddie braced herself. But rather than yell, or reach for Fred, she watched as he took a long, deep breath. He dropped down onto his knees gently in front of the boys and looked Fred in the eyes.

"I work hard to make the money for us as a family, Fred," he said gently. "So when I offer some to you, it would be nice if you could say thank you." He raised an eyebrow. Biddie let out a small breath that she hadn't been aware she was holding. *He did it,* she thought to herself. *He's trying to teach them to be better, not punish them. He's finally showing them that he cares.*

Fred watched Arch suspiciously for a moment and then nodded curtly.

"Thank you," the young boy said quickly, then turned and ran away, toward the apple barrels. David followed shortly after. Arch let out a small sigh and craned his head to look up at Biddie. She gave him a warm smile and a nod and tried desperately to ignore the heat that filled her as their eyes met again. Arch pulled himself up from the ground and turned back toward Biddie, the Parkers, and Pauline.

"Well, that should keep them busy for a while," Arch chuckled. "I'm sure we'll hear all about it later."

"Inevitably," Rudy laughed, nodding. "So what would you both like to do?" He asked, looking from Arch to Biddie. Biddie looked over Arch's shoulder at the couples dancing and smiled wistfully for a moment. What she really wanted to do was to go and dance, to enjoy herself, and to get closer to

Arch. The idea of it made her chest tighten with a mixture of giddiness and nervousness.

She had not planned on even really spending time with her employer when she first moved here, let alone feeling this way about him. But she just couldn't help it. Every time they were near one another she got this tingly feeling all over her body, and when they were apart, it was never long before she found herself thinking about him.

It all started with that moment outside the boys' bedroom. She felt like a schoolgirl!

You need to answer, she reminded herself.

"I don't mind, what about you, Arch?" she asked, turning her attention back to him and smiling. She wanted to dance, but she'd settle for just spending the afternoon with him and the Parkers. Even that was much more fun than anything she'd had the chance to do back in Kansas. Arch furrowed a brow at her and then looked over his shoulder, seemingly following her gaze. A cheeky grin formed on his face and he turned back to Rudy.

"I think I'd like to head over there." He gestured with his head. "I've not danced in a long time. Perhaps you could remind me how, Biddie?" He looked back at her, and their eyes met. She felt herself melting into the shimmering blues of his eyes, and could barely keep herself from giggling at the offer. She glanced over at Angela on her right who was grinning and nodding encouragingly. Locking eyes with Arch once more, Biddie nodded, smiling.

"It'd be my pleasure," she said softly, her voice weak with nerves and excitement.

"Well then, would you two mind keeping an eye on this little one?" Arch pulled his eyes away from Biddie, a small blush spreading across his cheeks, and looked toward Pauline, who was watching everyone with wide, eager eyes.

"Of course not," Angela answered quickly. "We love Pauline," she smiled. "Go on, you two, have fun."

Biddie felt the butterflies in her stomach speed up as heat spread across her cheeks. Arch nodded at Angela before turning to Biddie and offering her his arm. She chewed her lower lip and threaded her arm through his, and together, the two of them walked away from their friends and to the dance floor.

"I'm not the best at dancing," Biddie said as they reached the space where the other couples danced cheerfully to an upbeat folk song played by the band. On the small makeshift stage, the musicians bobbed cheerfully from side to side, smiling and watching the crowd dance to their songs.

The washboard player, Biddie noticed, seemed to be especially enjoying himself. Each movement of his hands seemed to ripple through his body as he danced a fun little jive on his stool. All of them wore dark linen trousers, braces, and white button-up shirts. The fiddle and the banjo player wore ties that matched the braces, and they swung as they danced.

"That's okay, neither am I." He grinned and unthreaded his arm from hers. Stepping back, he bowed courteously and offered her his hand. She took it, and, following his lead, began to dance an almost polka to the music playing behind them. She could feel the warmth of his smooth hand against hers, and it sent a shiver across her body.

As the two of them danced, she watched his often too-serious face turn into one of childlike joy. A great smile split his face, one which made his eyes sparkle and his whole face seem brighter somehow, and all the stress that he had been carrying in his posture seemed to dissipate. She felt her own worries lifting away, too, and couldn't help but grin back at him as they jumped and danced around to the beat of the music.

This is it, she thought to herself. *This is the life I wanted.*

They continued like that for a couple of songs, and then the music began to slow. A polka was no longer appropriate, it seemed, as Biddie watched the other couples embrace one another for a slower dance. It was like the waltz her grandmother had told her of, but a little faster to allow for the instruments at hand.

Her heart began to race as Arch caught on, and he held her hand tighter, pulling her in much closer than she had been before. There was only a foot or so between them, and she could feel his breath on her face as he helped her to position her arm up at an angle between them.

Holding her forearm, he led the dance, and she felt as if she were floating. His strong, protective grip on her arm made her feel all fuzzy inside and being so close to him allowed her to see all of his freckles again. She found herself watching them as if they were the constellations in the sky.

The two of them danced, hand in hand, for the length of the song. Biddie stopped looking at the other couples entirely, and instead let her eyes lock with Arch's. At that moment, she felt, it was just them in the world.

As the song began to end, Arch pulled Biddie closer still. Her heart rose into her throat — their torsos were almost touching at this point. *What is he thinking?* She asked. They were surrounded by people! He leaned forward and Biddie's breath hitched in her throat.

"Biddie, I," he whispered as he gazed down at her, only a few inches from her face. "I have something to confess."

Biddie let out a small sigh as she relaxed. She looked up at him and arched an eyebrow. *What could he possibly want to say right now?* She wondered. She hoped it was nothing related to her work or the boys. She just wanted this moment to stay perfect.

Arch went to open his mouth to speak more, but before a word could leave his mouth, a hand appeared on his shoulder. The hand was large, veiny, and pale, and Biddie's eyes traced up the arm that it was attached to, all the way up to the face. Arch quickly let go of Biddie and turned, still smiling, to the stranger.

The man had a very large, square head, and wore a suit better than anyone around them. His hair was gray and parted meticulously on one side. Above his small, pink lips sat a well-groomed, equally gray mustache.

"Can I help you?" Arch asked politely.

"Are you Archibald Sutton?" the man asked. Biddie frowned. *So much for a perfect moment,* she thought.

"I am, and you are?" Arch replied. His posture straightened, and Biddie watched his smile disappear.

"I'm Henry Wellington the Second," the man replied. "I knew your brother."

Arch's brows furrowed, his fists tensed by his sides, and he stepped back, making more space between them and the man. Suddenly, Biddie thought back to her and Arch's conversation about water rights.

It had been Mr. Wellington who had pestered Thomas and Sylvie. And now he was here to cause Arch trouble, too. But Arch was smart. He'd assured her that he could handle some rich old man. So why was he acting so frustrated?

Chapter Twenty

The Town Fête, Paddington, Texas

21st May 1885

"You didn't *know* my brother, you pestered him," Arch spat. His voice was full of venom, and Biddie couldn't quite figure out why. He'd said Wellington had irritated Thomas, but surely that was not a crime ... Unless he'd missed out some crucial information, there was no reason for him to be so angry.

"I did no such thing." Wellington shook his head, letting out a small chuckle. "I simply persevered with a business ambition." He smirked at Arch and then at Biddie. The expression made the hair on her arms stand on end, but she was unsure why.

His eyes seemed to swallow her whole, traveling down her body and then back up. It made her skin crawl and, from the looks of it, Arch's too. She hadn't been looked at in such an uncomfortable way since leaving Kansas, but somehow, the way that Wellington looked at her was worse.

"Business ambition." Arch rolled his eyes. "Sure."

"Rumors are not to be trusted in such big towns, Mr. Sutton," Wellington said, grinning. His eyes glinted mischievously as he spoke. "I assure you, all I have ever wanted of the Suttons is a business relationship — nothing more. But your brother never seemed to fancy what I had on offer. It's a shame, really ... He could have been a very wealthy man. Those children could have lived a life of pure luxury."

"Well they're gone now, and I assure you, you won't get anything from me," Arch said simply. "Those children are absolutely fine with what they've got. They don't need your money, and neither do I." He turned to glance at Biddie, and she spotted a glimpse of concern in his previously happy and carefree eyes. She began to worry. From what she knew of Arch, he didn't seem like the type of man to grow concerned over trivial matters. Something was off; she could feel it. She just wished he had told her.

"At least let us discuss, no?" Wellington raised an eyebrow. "But beforehand, let me introduce myself to your lovely lady here." He held out his hand to Biddie and bowed his head. She looked to Arch for direction, and he nodded begrudgingly. Carefully, Biddie placed her hand in Wellington's, and he brought her knuckles up to his mouth. He kissed them gently and then let go. "And who might you be?" he asked.

"I'm Miss Edwards. I work for Arch." Biddie said, quickly pulling her hand away from the strange old man. Something about him was unsettling, but she couldn't put her finger on it. He was perfectly polite and courteous but seemed to exude an off-putting aura that put her (and Arch, it seemed) on edge.

"I see." Wellington nodded, frowning ever so slightly at her haste. "Well, Archibald, will you listen to my offer?" He turned his attention back to Arch, a small smirk on his face.

Biddie looked over at Arch. His eyes were locked on Wellington, but where they had gazed at her, they bore into him. It was as if he hoped to destroy the man with a look alone. After a moment of silence, he replied.

"Fine," Arch said curtly.

"How gracious of you, truly," Wellington remarked, his smirk stretching. "I would like to buy Sutton Ranch. All of it. You will be handsomely rewarded; name a figure and I will pay it. Money is no object here, boy," he continued. "My only condition is that you and your employees, the children, and whatever else you store on the land must be gone by the end of the week."

Arch laughed and shook his head, not breaking his stare. He slid his hands into his pockets and ran his tongue along his top teeth.

"No amount of money will make me leave my family's ranch, let alone sell it to a letch like you," he replied, his voice quiet but clearly malicious. Biddie's eyes widened; she'd never heard him talk like that.

She glanced up at the older man and watched as Henry Wellington's own eyes widened in shock, too. His previously suspicious and mischievous look turned foul instantly, and he scowled at Arch.

"Fine, then. But I'm sure the same can't be said for this pretty thing." He darted his eyes across to Biddie, and she frowned, unsure of what he meant. "What price would I need to pay to get you on my arm and not his? I gather it wouldn't be too much." He raised a brow and moved his hand up, toward Biddie's face, as if to cup it.

She stepped back, her jaw open in shock. *How dare he?!* She thought to herself. She was nobody's to buy, and to insinuate such things … Her body filled with rage. Before she could respond, Arch stepped forward, closing the space between himself and Wellington. His body shook with anger, and she could see the tension across his back.

"Don't you *dare* speak to my …" he paused very briefly, "… employee like that!" he yelled. "You are not to come near me, or my family, ever again. Step foot on my ranch and I'll have you carted away to jail … If you're lucky," he hissed.

Without giving Wellington a chance to respond, Arch turned around and grabbed Biddie's hand, pulling her away.

As the two of them half-jogged out of the dancing area, Biddie noticed that Arch's outburst had grabbed the attention of almost everyone at the fête.

Suddenly, her chest tightened and she felt her forehead and palms becoming sweaty. She didn't want to be the gossip of the town. Not again. But he hadn't done it intentionally. He'd tried to defend her.

Her mind was awash with emotions; shame, nervousness, gratitude, and what was left of the rush she'd felt when dancing. They all bubbled away within her. She let Arch lead her away from the crowd, confused and overwhelmed. After a few minutes, he let go of her hand. She followed him toward the apple bobbing barrels, where they found Fred and David sitting with a small collection of apples that they had clearly won.

"Boys, get up," Arch said. His tone was tense but gentle. He was still trying not to lose his composure around them. "We're heading home now."

The boys looked at Arch as if they were about to argue. But Biddie looked at them both, catching their attention. She shook her head swiftly, and the two boys said nothing. Standing up from the ground, they simply nodded, and Arch led them all back to Angela and Rudy. They were over by the entrance to the fête, drinking cider and chatting whilst Pauline watched everyone walk by with a large grin on her face.

"We're leaving. You two can stay if you wish, but I need to get back to work," Arch lied as they reached the two of them. "And we'll take Pauline with us." He leaned down and offered Pauline his hand, which she took excitedly, waddling over toward him. Angela frowned and looked to Biddie for an explanation, but Biddie just shook her head. Rudy caught the exchange and furrowed his brows, but said nothing more on the matter.

"Alright, then, well we'll see you around, folks," Rudy said simply, his brows still furrowed across his forehead. Arch nodded, giving the two of them a tense smile before leading Pauline, the boys, and Biddie away. Biddie took one last glance over her shoulder at the fête.

A sadness washed over her as she walked further and further away from the beautiful dancing ladies, the cheerful music and the wonderful mixture of smells. As much as she knew there'd be other fêtes, and she was in Texas to stay, part of her felt heartbroken that they had to leave. From where she was, she could just see Wellington, still standing in front of the bar. He seemed to have spotted her too, and waved eerily, a grin on his face that she could only describe as slimy.

Chapter Twenty-One

Downtown Paddington, Texas

21st May 1885

Arch led Biddie and the children to the buggy in silence with his hands clenched into balls in his pockets. He had been waiting for Henry Wellington to find him, but he had not expected the man to be so inherently vile. Now that he had seen Wellington himself, Angela's once far-fetched ideas of foul play were becoming less and less unreasonable.

If anyone was going to commit such an atrocity, it would be a man like Wellington. Arch had only met him for a matter of minutes, but that was enough to deeply unsettle him. The way he spoke, the way he dressed, the way he looked at Biddie … Let alone what he had *said* to Biddie.

All of it filled him with loathing. That man needed to stay as far away from him and his family as possible. He wasn't going to risk anything. He *definitely* wasn't going to sell the ranch to him. Not now, not ever.

He let out a sigh. He'd thought moving to Texas was bad enough. Now he had an enemy who may or may not have had a part to play in his brother's passing, and he had Biddie to worry about. He knew she wasn't just going to let this go, but he didn't want to worry her or put her in danger.

He glanced over his shoulder at her as they reached the buggy. She looked concerned but was clearly trying to hide it for the sake of the children. As they reached the buggy, he turned to her and smiled half-heartedly.

"If we pop the children in the back seat, you can sit up front with me," he said quietly. Biddie looked up at him and nodded. Her eyes seemed to scan him for answers, but she wore her own plastered-on smile in an attempt to hide it.

She gently loaded the kids into the back seat of the buggy, hauling them up from the ground and propping them up in their seats. Once they were all in, Arch climbed up into his seat at the front of the buggy and waited for her to join him. A moment later, she slid onto the bench next to him.

He glanced over at her. The fake smile was now gone. In its place was a small, worried frown. He opened his mouth, looking for the words to say to explain his own anger at Wellington, or to explain why he whisked them away in such a manner, but he couldn't find them. He shut his mouth and looked ahead again, pulling the reins and steering the horses away from the fête. He steered the buggy out from the field and onto the gravel road that led back to the ranch, trying desperately to focus on the road ahead.

No matter how hard he tried, though, his mind reeled. All he had wanted was to dance, drink and spend time with his family; it was the first chance he'd had to enjoy himself since moving to Texas. This was not how he had wanted his day to end.

After a little while, the children fell asleep in their seats. Arch could hear their snoring from the front and let out a breath he wasn't aware that he'd been holding. At least they weren't bothered by what had just happened. He glanced over to Biddic again, but this time she caught him. She turned her head to look at him, her brows furrowed.

"What was all of that about?" she asked. "I know that's the man who tried to buy the ranch off of Thomas, but why were you instantly upset with him? And why did he speak to me like that?"

Arch sighed; he had really been hoping that she'd uncharacteristically just let everything go, but had known that was unlikely. He was going to have to either lie or tell her everything. He didn't want to lie, not to Biddie — she'd been there for him so much since moving in — but he also didn't want to scare her. He shook his head and released one of the reins to pinch the bridge of his nose.

"I, well ... Do you really want to know?"

Biddie nodded slowly, eyeing him.

"So everything I told you about Wellington was true, but there might be more to the story," Arch continued. "You see, Angela mentioned that she had some suspicions about my brother's death when I first arrived here." He glanced over at her and then back at the road, hoping to judge her response. She remained unmoved. "She said that she thought she saw someone on Sutton Ranch hours before Thomas' death. Someone mysterious, and a little suspicious."

"She did suggest there was something going on when we were in town the other day," Biddie said quietly. "She told me to ask you, but we've been so busy I had forgotten about it."

Arch nodded. As much as he wished Angela had not said anything, at least it meant that this news would be easier for Biddie to hear. For that, he was grateful.

"Well, the man who was on the ranch, I think, was a guy called Monty. He stopped by the other day to give me an offer on the ranch from 'his employer.' He fit Angela's description perfectly. Rudy helped me to identify him as a worker of Wellington's," he huffed.

"And you think...." Biddie asked, trying to connect the dots.

"It doesn't seem like a far stretch to imagine that a man like Wellington could ask one of his cronies to 'make a sale happen' ..." Arch nodded. "I'm not sure how, but I feel like something isn't right."

"I see," Biddie replied. Arch looked over at her; she didn't appear to be shocked, but she still looked concerned.

"Thomas never said anything about being ill; he was perfectly healthy. To just suddenly die, so young ..." He shook his head. "I think Thomas and Sylvie were murdered for their ranch. And I think Henry Wellington had something — maybe everything — to do with it."

Biddie went silent for a moment. She looked away from Arch and straight ahead, and Arch felt his chest tighten. He desperately wanted her to reply, and quickly. A few moments passed, and she remained silent. He kept looking over to her, trying to prompt a reply, but got nothing.

"If you want to go home to St. John, I'll understand," he said eventually. "You didn't sign up to be involved in any of this. I'll pay you until the end of the month, and you'll get a shining reference, that's for sure. I'll understand completely, Biddie, it's alright," he started to babble, his mouth running away from him in an attempt to fill the silence that she had created.

She turned to look at him and shook her head. Her brows had relaxed, and the frown that had been on her face had broken into a small smile.

"Arch," she said softly. "This is my home now. You, the children, you're like a family to me already." She moved a little closer so that he could hear her. His heart warmed at her words; she was so sweet. He did not deserve someone so kind, but God had brought them together and he was grateful for it.

She made Texas bearable. She made all of it more bearable. Her smile made each one of his days better, and at that moment, it was making him forget about the stress he'd just gone through. For a second, it was just them against the world.

He felt warm, and at peace, and before he could stop himself, he felt his eyes lock onto her lips again. It was becoming hard to ignore it. The way she made him feel was becoming clearer than day.

Oh dear, he thought to himself. *This is awfully inconvenient.*

He scooted along the bench, closing what little space was left between the two of them. It might not be just them in the world, but, there on the buggy, it was.

He moved his eyes up from her lips and into her eyes, flashing behind their veiling lenses. Her gaze locked on his, and a shiver traveled down his spine.

I could do it, he thought. *Maybe she feels the same.* Looking into each other's eyes, it sure felt like the feeling was mutual. He bit his lower lip nervously and counted down in his head. He needed to know whether she felt the same.

You've got this, he told himself. He leaned forward, and she leaned forward too. His heart began to race as her perfume filled his nostrils. He was a mere inch away from her face, and ready to ruin their friendship; but before he could, there was a cough from behind them. Biddie jolted back, away from Arch, and he let out a long sigh.

"Are we there yet?" Fred asked sleepily from behind them. Biddie let out a shaky breath, and Arch cleared his throat.

"Not yet, but nearly," he answered. He glanced over at Biddie, whose face was a rosy pink, with a small shy grin perched on it.

Maybe it is mutual, he thought to himself.

He'd hoped that he'd be able to keep Biddie at arm's length when she first moved here, but she'd been his rock since she'd arrived, and now he couldn't keep from smiling at her presence, and when she wasn't around he was always trying to find reasons to speak to her.

Now he was going to have to try and find a reason to be alone with her, too. He couldn't help but think about how that almost kiss would have felt. He hoped one day soon he'd be lucky enough to find out.

Chapter Twenty-Two

The Parker Ranch, Paddington, Texas

22nd May 1885

The Parker kitchen smelled like fresh bread and cloves. It was smaller than the kitchen at the Sutton Ranch but functional enough. There was a small stove in one corner and rows of shelves lining two of the walls.

Biddie was sitting at the wooden table, admiring the fresh flowers in the glass vase at its center as she leaned delicately on her elbow. From where Biddie was seated, she could feel the warmth of the afternoon sunlight streaming through the kitchen window and she removed her spectacles, closing her eyes for a moment to bask in the light.

Opening them again, she smiled at Angela, who was dashing around the kitchen, preparing items for her supper.

"Can I talk to you about something, Angela?" she asked, settling her spectacles back on her face. She'd been mulling the events of the previous day over in her head all morning, and whilst she intended to keep the close moment with Arch entirely to herself, she desperately needed to discuss the revelations that Arch had revealed to her.

She wasn't going to run away from it as he'd suggested, she knew that for sure, but she wasn't certain how to best react and behave with the information that she'd been given. She hoped Angela would have some insight.

Angela looked up from the kitchen side and nodded as she grabbed the jug of cider that sat on the counter and wandered over to the table.

"Sure thing, doll." She pulled a chair out and sat down opposite Biddie. "What's on your mind?" Angela poured out two glasses of cider.

"So yesterday, when Arch and I left the fête so hastily," Biddie began, taking one of the cups of cider. Angela looked at her intently and nodded. "Well, we left because we'd bumped into a man — a Mr. Wellington," she spoke quietly and slowly, hoping to watch Angela's face for a reaction.

At the mention of Wellington's name, Angela's smile faded. Her usually happy face contorted into a tense expression, but she remained silent. "He was, well, to be frank, vile." Biddie shook her head. Even the thought of that man made her skin crawl. There was just something not right about him.

"I've heard similar reports." Angela nodded somberly and took a large swig of her cider. "What did he want?"

"He wanted to give Arch an offer on the ranch. When Arch said no, he insulted me — he insinuated that *I* was for sale!" Biddie huffed. Angela's eyes widened.

"He did *what?*" she gasped. "Oh goodness, that man is a nightmare." She shook her head. Biddie nodded and sipped her own drink.

"Indeed. Well, naturally, Arch defended my honor, and that's when we left. But even before that, Arch was furious with the man before he'd even said anything other than his name. I didn't really understand why until we were on the way home, and, well I had to ask," she sighed. "He said that you told him there was suspicious behavior on the ranch on the day of Thomas and Sylvie's death... and that he believes it can all be traced back to Wellington."

Angela paused for a moment and looked around. Biddie frowned, unsure what Angela was checking for. She'd acted the same way that day in town, but they were in her home...

Nobody but her husband would be around, surely? After a moment, Angela nodded.

"There was a man on the ranch that day, yes. Someone I didn't recognize. He looked shifty, as if he weren't meant to be there," Angela explained. "Add that onto their symptoms ... and well, it doesn't all add up."

Their symptoms? Biddie thought. *What does she mean?*

"They had stomach flu, what do you mean about their symptoms?" Biddie asked. As far as she was aware, symptoms of stomach flu were fairly straightforward.

"Officially, yes." Angela nodded. "But, well," she said, then paused and took a sip of her drink. "My mother used to be really interested in natural medicine, and herbs; she wanted to open an apothecary when she was a little girl. So when I was younger, she taught me all she knew, in the hopes that I'd be able to use it if ever I got sick." Angela smiled warmly in nostalgia. "So when I heard about Thomas and Sylvie's symptoms ... it didn't sit right."

"You think they ate something bad?" Biddie asked. That would be reasonably easy to do, and it would explain why Thomas had never said anything to Arch about being unwell. But it didn't necessarily mean that they were murdered.

"No, I think they were *fed* something bad. There are bushes of a plant called spurge laurel near here. It's beautiful, but it's also really, really poisonous. You eat one of those berries and you'll die. Stomach discomfort, mouth blisters, an urgent need for the toilet, and then a quickening of the heart, before finally passing away in great amounts of pain — all from one little berry." Angela raised her eyebrows and shook her head. "And those are exactly the symptoms that Thomas and Sylvie had."

Biddie's heart stopped for a moment. If their symptoms lined up so perfectly, it couldn't be a coincidence. Arch was right. *That evil, evil man,* she thought to herself. *Wellington cannot get away with this.* She shook her head and looked at Angela with sympathy. Not only had she lost her neighbor and her friend, but they were murdered by a man who walked free!

"That's awful ... Does Arch know about the berries?" she asked.

"It's horrific," Angela agreed. "What makes it worse, though, is those berries taste awful. They're so bitter, it'd be hard to disguise them in something. I don't know how they didn't suspect something. That's why I haven't told Arch about the poisoning; I wanted to be sure. He knows my theories, and he clearly agrees ... But I don't want to give him information before I know for sure." Angela sighed. She took a big swig from her drink. "I just wish I'd thought of it when they first fell ill. It's curable, the poison. If they'd have come to us sooner... They were sick for a few hours before passing. It was only in the last hour that we found out. I could've done something." She began to tear up and shook her head. "All I'd need is agrimony and hawthorn."

Biddie watched her friend tear up and began to fill with anger. Wellington had robbed three little children of their parents, Angela and Rudy of their friends, and Arch of his brother and sister-in-law, all for the sake of some water rights? It took every ounce of her being to keep from shaking with anger. She reached her arm out across the table and offered Angela her hand.

"I'm so sorry, Angela," she said softly, doing her best to hide how she was feeling. "Those people are evil."

Angela nodded and sniffed, wiping a tear away as it fell from her eye. She placed her hand in Biddie's, and Biddie squeezed it gently. She clasped her other hand over Angela's and looked into her eyes.

"They won't get away with it, I promise," she said.

"They already have," Angela sighed. "Rudy can't prove anything … And I just, I miss them so much, Biddie. Sylvie was like a sister to me." She shook her head and suddenly tears began to stream from her eyes. "I still can't believe they're gone." She desperately tried to battle the tears falling down her cheeks, wiping them away as quickly as possible. Biddie wished she could do more to comfort her friend. Seeing Angela like this was making her heart ache.

"I know," Biddie said, unable to think of anything more useful. "I'm sorry. Really, I am," she continued. Angela cried for a while longer, and the two of them just sat quietly, hands clasped across the table in support.

"Thank you," Angela eventually said, wiping the last tear from her eyes. "I don't think I've really cried about it yet."

"Well, you've had a lot to do." Biddie smiled at her gently. The poor woman had lost her best friend and instantly been dropped into a babysitting role. It couldn't have been easy.

"I suppose so," Angela chuckled lightly. "Was there anything else you wanted to say? Sorry, I didn't mean to interrupt the conversation with my tears!" She blushed gently and Biddie chuckled.

"I just wanted to see what you had to say. To check Arch wasn't being paranoid. To be honest, I just wanted to make sure I wasn't making it all up. Yesterday was a blur," Biddie let go of Angela's hand and smiled awkwardly.

"I understand," Angela nodded, a small smile on her face. "Well, neither you nor Arch are making anything up. There's definitely more at play here. We should all be very careful."

Angela picked her glass up from the table and stood up from her chair. "I won't lose another person," she said defiantly, before taking the glass back over to the counter. "Now, if you wouldn't mind, I have supper to make," she looked over at Biddie with a gentle expression, and Biddie nodded. She needed to get back home to the children anyway. Besides, the talk with Angela had helped more than she could've imagined.

"No, no, of course," Biddie replied, standing up. "Thank you for the cider," she said and carried the cup over to Angela. "I shall see you soon, I imagine."

Angela took the cup graciously and nodded. Placing it down on the counter, she embraced Biddie. Her warmth made Biddie relax a little, and she let out a soft sigh, embracing Angela back.

"I would imagine so," Angela said, releasing Biddie. "Stay safe, love," she said finally before returning to her vegetables.

"And you." Biddie nodded, turning to leave the kitchen and the Parker home.

She stepped out of the kitchen and wandered over to the front door. Gently pulling it open, she walked out and down the small porch steps. The sun still sat relatively high in the sky, and despite it being late afternoon, almost evening, the air was still warm enough that Biddie was glad she had worn only her dress and not a coat.

She looked around once, briefly, before setting off down the path that led straight from the Parker house to the gate at the back of the Sutton ranch. As she walked, she tried not to focus on the conservation that she'd just had. She'd just gotten comfortable here; the last thing she wanted was to live her new life in fear.

After all, if Wellington *had* poisoned Thomas and Sylvie, he wouldn't do the same thing twice. That'd get him caught. As horrid as that man might be, she couldn't imagine him being so blindly ambitious.

To try and get her mind to focus on anything else, she looked around her as she walked. It wasn't a long walk; she just needed to keep herself occupied for a few more moments. Looking around at the scenery that she'd come to love, her eyes scanned the fields of the Parker ranch to her left.

They largely grew corn, so the fields were stacked high with tall plants, and she could just about make out ranch men's heads in the distance. She smiled as she watched the heads bob around in the corn for a moment. She looked over to her right at the large field which bordered Angela and Rudy's property.

It was a huge space, interrupted only by one large hill at the far end. Sometimes she'd spot children or animals enjoying the space, but it seemed to be empty. She let out a small sigh as she neared the gate to Sutton Ranch.

She took one last look around, glancing back at Angela's home. She hoped that she hadn't left her friend alone and sad. As she turned her attention back to the gate, a movement across the field caught her eye, and she froze.

Don't look. She told herself. But she needed to know.

She slowly turned back around and looked across the empty field. Sure enough, standing atop the hill there was a man. He was too far away for her to make him out, but she could tell that he was watching her. He had nobody with him, not even a dog, and was standing in such a way that he was directly facing her.

Her heart began to race.

Suddenly all of the ways that somebody could hurt her rushed into her mind, and she felt her hands and forehead begin to sweat. She rushed through the gate to the ranch and ran down the path that led through the fields.

Occasionally checking behind her, she only stopped running once she reached the porch. Gripping the wood harshly, she bent over, leaning one hand on her knee to catch her breath. She checked behind her once more, and once she was sure the man had remained still, she had mostly calmed down. It was just somebody trying to scare her. She'd handled much worse.

"If they think intimidation will work on us, they've got another think coming," she muttered to herself as she regained her composure.

Chapter Twenty-Three

The Sutton Ranch, Paddington, Texas

22nd May 1885

Arch watched Pauline and the boys play in the lounge. Biddie had asked for an hour or so away, and he'd relished the opportunity to step out of his office for a moment, and to check on how the children were doing after their rush off from the fête the day before.

As he watched the three of them build all sorts of towers and turrets with Pauline's wooden blocks, he smiled to himself. They seemed completely unaware of the panic that he had felt a day earlier. At least he could take some relief in having kept that from agitating them.

He let out a small sigh and picked the newspaper up from his lap to continue his reading, but just as he found an article that piqued his interest, he heard the creak of the front door as it eased open and then shut again. He listened eagerly as Biddie entered the hallway, glad that she was home.

As he listened, he noticed that she seemed a touch out of breath. He watched the doorway, waiting for her to say hello. When, after a few minutes, she hadn't, he began to worry. He stood up from his seat and discarded the paper onto the chair.

Looking over at the children, he noticed that they were looking in the direction of the door, too. He wandered over to the door to the lounge calmly, turning to look at them.

"You all behave now, I'll only be a moment," he said, a smile on his face that did very little to hide his furrowed brows. As he stepped out of the lounge, he looked around, spotting Biddie sitting on the stairs. She *was* a little out of breath, which was unlike her, and paler than usual.

"Biddie," he said carefully. She seemed like she'd been spooked by something, a coyote or cougar perhaps? "Everything alright?" he asked, his brows furrowed. She looked at him, her eyes wide, and nodded uncertainly.

"Uh, yes, I," she blinked rapidly a few times and removed her eyeglasses, pinching the bridge of her nose. "No, not really, actually." She took a deep breath and smiled at him nervously. Looking over his shoulder and into the lounge, she gestured towards the kitchen with her chin. His brows knotted across his forehead, but he nodded and she stepped quietly away from the lounge as she rubbed a dingy scrap of linen across the lenses of her spectacles.

"I was at Angela's," she said in a hushed tone once they were away from the door. He nodded slowly, still confused about what was going on. She'd just gone to visit Angela whilst Rudy was at work. Why was she so on edge?

"Yes, you said that was where you were going." Arch nodded.

"Well, on my way back, I was enjoying the short walk and the scenery, when, well," she held her eyeglasses up to the light, squinting as she frowned at the still-smudged lenses. *Come on, tell me,* he thought to himself frustratedly, though part of him just wanted to stare at the emeralds that were her eyes, freed as they were from their glass cages.

"There was a man watching me," she finally added. "I'm not sure whether he was just watching … I think he may have been following me, but I don't know. He was on the hill. I ran home as soon as I realized."

Arch's breath caught and he froze.

"Did you see who?" he asked after a moment. Biddie shook her head.

"No, but he was tall," she replied. *Monty,* he thought to himself.

"I'm sorry, Arch, I wish I could give you more information," she said sadly. "It's got to be one of Wellington's men, though, right?" she whispered.

Arch let out a small sigh and nodded. They were trying to get under his skin, more than Wellington already had. *That man is relentless,* he thought to himself.

"It must be," he answered. "I'm sorry, Biddie." He'd wanted to keep all of this away from her, or at least keep her safe from it, but now she was being followed home by strange men... He wanted to put a stop to Wellington's torment of his family; he just didn't know where to start.

If Wellington's men were happy to follow innocent women, what's to say that they wouldn't go near the children? He couldn't continue to put his family at risk, but the only other option was to agree to Wellington's terms, which would mean that his brother died for nothing.

"It's alright," Biddie said softly. She gazed up at him nervously and placed her hand on his arm. "You are not to blame for any of this," she reminded him. "They're nasty men. We're stronger than they are, and we will not be perturbed by strange men on hills."

"I'm just worried," Arch said, sighing. "What if they go after the children?" he whispered. Biddie chewed her lower lip and looked over at the lounge.

"We'll just have to do everything we can to keep them safe," she said. He nodded and smiled gently in response. She was right, but the issue was that he didn't know *how* to keep them safe. As long as they were in this house, they stood in Wellington's way. That made them fair game.

"I suppose so," he replied.

"I've handled things worse than strange men and business venturists," Biddie said, half-jokingly. He knew she was trying to cheer him up, but it was having little effect.

"I'll go and watch the children to give you a moment," she said gently before replacing her eyewear and walking quietly into the lounge. He watched her go and let out a long sigh.

He was in over his head.

He already had three children to keep happy and alive and a ranch to run. Now he had to protect both, and the woman that he had come to care so much for. He thought about what Biddie had said, that she had handled worse.

He thought about maybe asking her what she thought they should do to keep the children safe. *Would she even have an idea? I don't ...* He groaned softly in despair and rubbed his eyes. Taking a deep breath, he went to walk back into the lounge, when suddenly, he remembered what Biddie had told him about her mother and grandmother.

She'd been in a position of danger when she was no older than Pauline. And yet, here she was, supporting him. All because her mother had sent her away from her home.

That's it! he thought. *If they're not in the house, or on the ranch, they're not in Wellington's way. They'll be safe.* He thought about it for a moment and nodded to himself. He could send them to Angela's until this all brushed over. They would be close enough to visit, but far enough away that they'd be safe from any cruel or terrifying plot that Wellington had planned. With a small, shaky breath, he walked back to the lounge.

Biddie looked at him as he walked in, one eyebrow raised as if she were asking a silent question. He smiled and nodded, hoping to answer her. Walking over to the children, who were once again engaged in building, Arch knelt down on the floor. Biddie watched quizzically from her seat on the armchair.

"Children, can I have your attention for a moment?" He spoke softly. Ever since the incident with Fred, he was always over-conscious of his tone around the children. At the sound of his voice, they gently left the wooden blocks alone and turned to face him. Pauline smiled a toothy grin at him, and David watched him respectfully. Fred, on the other hand, eyed him suspiciously. *He'll get over it,* Arch told himself. He'd been telling himself that for days.

"Sorry to interrupt your building time." Arch smiled, trying to ignore Fred's look. "But I just need to talk to you about something that's happening."

"Arch–" Biddie said, and he darted his eyes up to look over at her. He smiled reassuringly and shook his head. She raised her hands in apparent surrender.

"I'm going to take all three of you to stay with Angela and Rudy for a little while," Arch began. He kept his eyes on the children — he'd talk to Biddie about it afterward. He was hoping she'd go with them. Then they'd all be safe. The children all looked at one another and then up at Arch, puzzled looks on their faces. "There is a nasty man who wants to take the ranch, and he used to annoy your Papa. He's now decided he wants to annoy me, too. So to keep you from having to see him or meet him, I'd like you to stay with them," he said slowly. "I love all three of you so very much, you see," he said, smiling, and to his surprise, he felt tears begin to sting his eyes. "So I want to keep you as far away from nasty men like him as possible. I'll miss all of you so much, but I know you'll have an amazing time with Angela and Rudy." He sniffed away the tears and watched for a response. David's little eyebrows were knotted tightly across his forehead, and he was the first to speak.

"Is he why we left yesterday?" he asked. Arch nodded sadly. "Then he must really scare you, Uncle Arch ... Where are you going to go?" David asked.

"I'm going to stay here. Defend our home, and get him to leave us alone. Once I know he won't come back, you can all come home again," Arch answered. "But yes, he does scare me a little bit."

"You'd stay to protect our home?" Fred said quietly. Arch's eyes widened — it was the most the boy had spoken to him in days.

"I would do anything for you," Arch replied simply. David smiled at him and stood up. "You're my family, Fred. You, your brother, and your sister mean the world to me," Arch continued.

Just as he finished his sentence, David strode over to him and threw his arms around Arch's middle. Arch's heart warmed and he returned the embrace, wrapping his arms around the young boy. Not a moment later, Pauline waddled over, all but falling into the hug.

Arch began to feel the familiar sting in his eyes again as he squeezed his nephew and niece. He meant what he'd said — he'd do anything for them. They were his only family, his brother's legacy, and, though he had never imagined in a million years that he'd feel this way, he adored all three of them.

A tear fell from his cheek as they hugged, and before he got the chance to wipe it away, Fred joined the embrace. He wrapped one arm around Arch and the other around his younger siblings. All at once, the tears began to stream down Arch's face silently.

The four of them stayed like that for a moment. Arch felt more loved then than he ever had before, and suddenly, moving to Texas, handling Wellington — it was all worth it to keep them happy. To keep them safe. He sniffed, blinking gently to stop the tears, and pulled away from the children. He looked each of them in their eyes with a small smile.

The boys returned the smile, but Pauline's face was contorted into what appeared to be confusion. She raised her little hand and wiped her head. Arch looked at the spot that she'd wiped and chuckled — his tears had landed on her.

"Sorry about that, little monkey," he said gently, and the boys laughed. Pauline looked from the boys to Arch and held out her damp hand. She looked at her hand intently for a moment.

"Wet," she said simply, her brows furrowed.

Arch's heart skipped a beat.

That was the first word she'd said since he'd been there, possibly the first since Thomas and Sylvie's passing. A huge grin spread across his face, and the boys looked from Arch to their sister in shock. Arch looked over at Biddie who shared the same expression, her emerald eyes open wide in surprise.

"Yes, wet," he replied to Pauline. The response seemed to satisfy her, and she relaxed her eyebrows, rubbing her hand on her dress.

"She spoke!" David exclaimed.

"That she did," Arch agreed. "A miracle." He put his hand out and ruffled Pauline's hair, then pushed himself up off the floor. "Now, boys, can you go and pack a bag for your little adventure? And pack one up for Pauline, too?"

The two young boys nodded and stood up. Fred offered Pauline his hand, and she took it happily.

"Thank you, Arch," Fred said, louder than last time. "For looking after us." A warm happiness spread throughout Arch, and he looked Fred in the eyes.

"Always, Fred," he said softly.

With that, the children rushed off upstairs to pack up their bags. Arch looked over to Biddie, who was sitting with tear-stained cheeks on the edge of the armchair.

"That was beautiful, Arch," she said softly. "And a really good idea, too." He walked over to her, a small blush on his cheeks and a smile still on his face.

"Will you go with them?" He asked quietly, looking down at his feet. She inhaled sharply and stood up. He looked up, locking eyes with her. Taking a step toward him, she shook her head.

"I will not abandon you," she said quietly, but defiantly. Her sparkling eyes looked into his and he felt a small shiver down his spine. He wasn't going to win this fight.

"But you're not safe here," he said gently. "I want to keep you safe."

"And somebody needs to keep you safe," she replied. "I will not let you cart us all off to safety and put yourself right in that madman's line of fire." She shook her head, looking into his eyes. He let out a small sigh; she was so stubborn. He knew she wasn't going to back down easily, but he'd never forgive himself if he didn't at least try.

"Biddie, please," he begged. "It won't be for long, and you could continue your lessons with the children."

"If that's what this is about, you don't need to worry about paying me for the days that they are at Angela's. But I'm still staying here. With you." She spoke with an air of confidence that he had never seen in a woman, but it suited her incredibly well.

"It's not about that; I don't mind that they'd miss lessons, I mind that you'd be in harm's way." Arch shook his head loosely, trying not to think of all of the things that Wellington and his men could do to Biddie if they wanted to. He couldn't bear the thought of it. He hated the idea of someone else even being as close as he was to her in a non-threatening way, let alone with malicious intentions.

All he wanted was to keep her safe and happy, away from all of this. "It's not your battle to fight," he added after a moment. He looked into her eyes desperately, hoping that she'd understand that he was pushing for this because he cared about her so deeply.

"If it's your battle, it's mine too," she said softly. She stepped closer, and he became acutely aware that it was the closest they'd been. He could feel the warmth from her body; her torso was mere centimeters from his own, and their hands were almost touching.

He could see little puffs of fog appear on her smudged eyeglass lenses where his shallow breaths hit them, and just as rapidly dissipate. Arch found himself fighting every urge to thread his fingers through hers.

What does she mean? He asked himself.

He'd wondered the day before whether or not her feelings were the same as his, and had found himself at a loss. But surely she wouldn't say that, or insist on staying if she didn't feel *something* for him … His heart quickened within his chest, beating so hard he worried she might hear it.

He tried to find the words to reply, but with the new thoughts of her feelings for him, he was unable to. All he could think about was their closeness, how much he wanted to hold her hand, how beautiful she looked, their almost kiss on the buggy, and, most of all, how much it'd break him to lose her.

Instead of speaking, he simply shook his head and let out another small sigh. His words were failing him; he needed to show her how much he cared. Maybe then she'd do as he asked.

I hope this isn't a mistake, he thought briefly, before threading his fingers through hers and clasping their hands together. As he did so, he continued to gaze into her eyes. His eyebrows knotted softly across his head into a concerned and caring expression, and he held his breath, waiting for a response.

Biddie's eyes widened, and she glanced down at their hands. Her small, pale hand was soft against his larger, slightly darker skin, and their fingers fit together perfectly, as if by design. She bit her lower lip nervously and looked back at him.

"Arch," she whispered. "I know you're asking this of me to protect me, and I know it's because you care for me …" A small blush spread across her cheeks and the tip of her nose. "But I have been the one sent away from those I love for protection before. This time, I want to stand strong. I want to stick with the ones I love." She spoke quickly, and her eyes seemed to flicker between his eyes and his lips, whether nervously or as an enticement, Arch couldn't tell.

He felt his whole body tense; she'd just confessed her feelings.

She loved him.

She was his, just as much as he was hers.

His heart fluttered in his chest and he scrambled, trying to find something to say. She watched him expectantly, but for some reason, the idea of telling her his own feelings filled him with nervousness that overpowered the excitement she brought.

He'd never confessed his feelings to anyone. Feelings were not something he'd ever been taught to be proud of or open about. No matter how hard he tried, he couldn't get himself to say it, to tell her. He felt his eyes travel down from her eyes to her lips just hers had done, and for a moment, they stood there silently.

He could feel her breath on his lips, and every fiber of his being was compelling him to close the space between them. To press his lips on hers. To show her he felt the same.

But before he could, he heard the boys' footsteps coming down the stairs. Biddie's eyes darted to the door, and the two of them quickly stepped apart. Arch's heart continued to race in his chest.

"Alright, then," he said quietly before the boys entered. "You can stay."

She quickly reached and grabbed his hand, giving it a firm squeeze in response before letting go. As she did, the boys entered the room, Pauline sitting on Fred's shoulders.

"We're packed," Fred said as they walked in. He looked between Arch and Biddie, and Arch panicked; they were both still blushing, and he could feel that his breathing was a touch more ragged than it should have been. He prayed the boy didn't notice.

"Well then, let's get you to the Parkers," he replied quickly.

"Rudy's away for the night, so we'll just drop you all off with Angela. Rudy will be back in the morning," Biddie smiled at the children and walked over to them. "Let's get your coats," she said, leading them out of the room.

Arch watched them walk out and let out a long, shaky breath.

You swore you wouldn't fall for her, he said to himself. *So much for that.*

Chapter Twenty-Four

The Sutton Ranch, Paddington, Texas

The Night of 23rd May 1885

Biddie lay in her bed, the sheets pulled tightly around her. The house was eerily quiet now that the children had gone to the Parkers', and she could hear the sound of the wind in the trees outside and the animals in the barn chattering away as the night passed. Usually, she'd be asleep by now.

Looking after the children was a rewarding job, but it was exhausting. She would often get ready for bed in a half-asleep stupor, only to fall into a deep slumber as soon as her head hit the pillow. For some reason, though, her mind was restless. She kept thinking about the events of the day, replaying them over and over.

It started off with the man on the hill. She couldn't get the image of him out of her mind. She kept trying to figure out who he was, and what he wanted. Her heart raced each time. It was the closest to real danger she could ever remember having come.

When she could take no more anxiety, her mind moved on to focus on Arch and the children, and she relaxed. Watching Fred finally open up to his uncle and the moment that the four of them shared ... It warmed her heart and made tears spring to her eyes.

It had been such a sweet scene, and she felt incredibly lucky to have been there for it. Naturally, after that, she found herself dwelling on the moment she had shared with Arch.

Her heart raced yet again, but for vastly different reasons, as she thought about his hand in hers, the way he spoke to her, his voice soft and warm like honey, or velvet. His sky-blue eyes had gazed into hers. They'd begged her to reconsider her decision.

But they'd also shown her how he felt. There'd been real affection and raw emotion in the way he'd looked at her. He might not have said anything, but she knew without a doubt that the two of them had a connection beyond that of an employer and employee. After all, Arch had almost kissed her — twice, now.

The idea of it made her blush, and her stomach twisted nervously. A small giggle escaped her lips. Even in the dire situation that they found themselves in, her and Arch's relationship put a huge grin on her face. She was grateful to have met him, and, despite everything, she was grateful that she'd moved to Texas.

She desperately tried to hold onto those thoughts as she lay in bed, hoping that they'd bring her good dreams. Closing her eyes, she tried to remember how Arch's hand had felt on hers, how he'd looked at her lips as if he were ready to envelop her in his arms and press his lips on hers, how giddy she felt each time he was in the room, each time he looked at her.

Slowly, she felt sleep approaching. Her breathing began to slow, and the thoughts running through her mind grew slower and slower as slumber took hold, pulling her under and providing her peace.

Not long after she'd fallen asleep, Biddie bolted upright in bed. A loud crash echoed through her room, making her heart beat erratically in her chest.

"What on earth?" she said quietly. Reaching over to her bedside table she found a large candle and some matches. She pulled them over to her and struck the match, lighting the candle quickly and shoving her spectacles onto her face. She cast her eyes around the small room once more. On the floor, she spotted something shiny and moved the candle over to it.

"What might you be?" she speculated aloud, reaching out to touch the shiny triangular thing on her floor. She prodded it gently. "Glass?" She frowned and looked up at the window. It was smashed to bits, with only two shards of glass left in the wooden window frame. She gasped and her heart began to beat harder in her chest. Lowering the candle to the ground, she surveyed her bedroom floor. Sure enough, it was covered in glass. Over in one corner, by the door, was a large, gray rock. Biddie reached for it carefully, lifting it onto the bed. She held it up to the candle. For the most part, it was a plain gray rock, clearly picked up from near the woods, judging from the mud on it. But on one side there was a message painted on in haphazard handwriting:

GET OUT OF SUTTON RANCH NOW OR SUFFER THE FATE YOU DESERVE.

Biddie frowned and shot out of bed. Carefully dodging the glass on the floor, she moved to the wall and looked out of the window. Right by the fields, she spotted a man on a horse.

Squinting to see more, she noticed he wore a pistol on one leg, and her chest tightened. He waved at her in the window, and then with a malicious chuckle, turned and began to ride off.

"Oh, no you don't," Biddie growled. She tip-toed over the glass and grabbed her house dress. Pulling it quickly over her nightwear, she grabbed the rock and ran up to Arch's room. With ragged breaths, Biddie knocked hard on the door. In an instant, Arch was up and she could hear him scrambling to the door. He opened it a moment later. His hair was messy, and his usually light blue eyes were dark with sleep but wide with panic.

"What is it?" he asked quickly. She handed him the stone.

"There was a man. He threw this into my room. He's riding off now, through the fields," she said, speaking so fast she wasn't sure that Arch would even be able to understand her. "He waited for me to see him, then waved. They're taunting us. And threatening us."

Arch growled and threw the rock on the floor angrily.

"I'll get him." He reached behind the door and grabbed a coat. Pulling it on, he rushed past Biddie and out of the stairs. "Stay here. Stay safe," he said sternly, shooting her a quick look that Biddie was sure was supposed to be reassuring before sprinting out of the door. Biddie's heart continued to race in her chest, and she jogged down the stairs and out of the front door, watching Arch run after the man on the horse.

You stay safe, she thought.

***

Arch's mind raced as he sprinted along the dirt track that led from the house to the fields. In the dark, he could not see the man he was chasing, but he could hear the drumming of horseshoes just off in the distance. His palms and forehead were sweating profusely with a mixture of exertion, anger, and fear.

As he ran, the cool night wind licked his face, stinging his cheeks and cooling his damp forehead. He could feel his body reaching its limit as he began to approach the barn, and struggled to push himself on. He could just about make out the figure on the horse by the time he'd reached the barn, and he wondered why the rider had slowed down; he couldn't have caught up on his own.

It's got to be a trap, Arch thought, stopping by the barn for a moment to catch his breath.

The rider was by the entrance to the woods and had all but stopped by that point. Biddie was right; they were being taunted. Anger bubbled up inside him, and with one more deep breath, he pushed off of the barn and continued to follow the mysterious rider into the woods.

Passing through the leafy threshold, suddenly the darkness he'd been running through previously felt like daylight. In the forest, there was no glimpse of light. There were no breaks in the tree canopy to let in star or moonlight, and within seconds of entering the forest, he lost sight of the rider.

He stopped for a moment, desperately trying to regain his bearings. He'd grown up in this forest, on this ranch; surely he could figure out where someone might ride off to or — at the very least — where he was. Darting his eyes around in a moment of panic, Arch heard a rustling from behind him and froze.

Please be an owl.

He heard the rustling again, and Arch felt his whole body tense. *I'm not alone,* he thought to himself. There it was again, and it lasted for longer this time. Arch turned on the spot, trying to face whoever it was hiding out in the bushes, but in the dark, he couldn't quite locate the source of the noise. His heart pounded in his chest. He'd walked straight into some sort of trap or ambush, and left Biddie alone in the house.

He was so naive. How did he think he was going to catch a rider on foot? At night? He growled at himself under his breath. The rustling started again, but louder this time, closer. Arch tensed. He could not see who or where the noise was coming from, but he was certainly not going to go down without a fight. He braced himself and exhaled slowly as the noise got louder and louder.

Come on ... He thought to himself.

As if summoned, someone came barreling out of the bushes toward Arch. In the dark, he still couldn't make out who it was, but they ran with force, head low and shoulders tensed. They collided with Arch head-on, making him fall backwards onto the ground with a thud.

He gasped and tried to follow the figure with his eyes. Quickly pushing himself up from the ground, Arch looked around, panicked. To his right, he spotted the figure. Tall and slim, he could not make out a face, but the stature was enough to tell him exactly who it was: Monty.

"What are you doing here, Monty? The Sheriff'll have you put away for stepping foot on my property," Arch called over to him, standing up straight. He could just make out the whites of Monty's teeth as he grinned, and the sight made Arch shiver.

"I don't think your friend Rudy will be able to catch me in time," he replied. "It's only a brief visit," Monty spoke in an almost lyrical way, a slight musical intonation behind his voice taunting Arch even further.

"It's no visit at all. Get off of my property, and tell your boss he'll be paying for the broken window," Arch replied. His heart was still racing in his chest, and he could feel the sweat on his forehead beading despite the cool wind around him. Monty laughed loudly in response, and Arch felt himself getting increasingly frustrated.

"Not a chance," Monty said simply, his voice full of venom. "I'm here to tell you that you need to take the boss' offer. You, uh, might regret it if you don't." As he spoke, he walked closer to Arch. Close enough that Arch could actually make out his face, for the most part.

"Leave, now," Arch hissed. "Last chance."

"Or what?" Monty grinned. "You're not a fighting man."

"For my family I am," Arch replied. He'd never been in a fight, but he was happy to start today. Monty snorted and shook his head, and before Arch could even think, Monty had balled his hand into a fist and driven it into Arch's gut.

Arch let out a loud gasp as he doubled over, all the breath in his lungs suddenly gone. He coughed loudly and grabbed his torso with one hand. Glaring up at Monty, he took a deep breath.

"Ah yes, what a vision of strength," Monty teased.

"I should've known you wouldn't fight fair," Arch replied as his breath returned. He straightened back up.

"A fight with someone as pathetic as you was never going to be fair," Monty replied.

That's enough, Arch thought to himself. He balled his own fist up and swung for Monty, aiming for the face. His knuckles made contact with Monty's jaw, hitting with such force that Monty's head was whipped to the side. He groaned on impact, snapping his head back straight as soon as Arch's hand left his face.

"Oh, so you do have *some* bite, then," Monty replied, the grin still on his face. "Not enough, though. Sorry, Mr. Sutton, you'll have to try harder next time."

Arch furrowed his brows. *Next time?* He thought to himself. They weren't done here — or so he thought. But a mere second after Monty had finished speaking, he punched Arch directly in the temple. Arch felt a thud followed by pain spreading across his head and face. Unsure what was happening, he felt himself fall to the forest floor, unable to react.

"One punch and you're down. Really, you need to work on that," Monty said. Arch could just make out the words as he lay on the cold mud. Looking up, he noticed that the darkness in the woods was spreading, and soon, everything was black as his eyes fluttered closed.

Chapter Twenty-Five

The Sutton Ranch, Paddington, Texas

24th May 1885

Biddie stood nervously on the porch, looking out across the fields. She listened eagerly, trying to determine whether Arch had managed to catch the rider. He'd run off so quickly that she had not had a chance to even think about whether or not it was a good decision.

He'd just left her in the dust, waiting anxiously for him to return safely to her. But more and more time was passing, the sun was beginning to rise, and she was becoming restless.

He should've caught the rider or given up by this point, she thought to herself. The ranch was large, but he'd run off a good three quarters of an hour ago. He'd have reached the end of the ranch within fifteen minutes, so where was he? What was going on?

Biddie began to pace up and down the porch, a wave of concern passing over her and only worsening as more time passed. Every now and then, the wind would rush through the trees, or a bird would caw in the distance, and Biddie would jump, darting her attention in the direction of the noise, but it was never Arch.

She stopped pacing for a moment and wandered down the steps of the porch nervously. He'd been gone for too long now. He'd told her to stay in the house, but her concern was becoming too much to handle. Something felt off. Somewhere, deep within her, she knew something had happened, and she wasn't about to leave Arch out there on his own.

She peered up at the house and then over towards the barn and let out a shaky breath; she'd been in real danger for the first time earlier that day, and now it almost seemed she was seeking it out.

Gingerly, she began to walk away from the house and down the dirt track, keeping her eyes peeled for any movement among the corn or any noises from around her.

She was unsure what she'd do if there was anyone nearby; she had no fighting knowledge or skill, and was sure that she probably had very little strength, but she could at least run if someone approached, she figured.

Biddie continued through the fields, wringing her hands in front of her as she walked hastily. Soon enough, she'd reached the end of the crops. The only places left to look were the barn, the woods, and the fields past Sutton Ranch. She took another shaky breath. She'd check the barn first — she was at least familiar with the building — and then she'd go into the woods, but she'd stick to the path. The woods were hard enough to navigate in full daylight, let alone in the early hours of the morning.

Approaching the barn, Biddie looked around quickly. She reached the large wooden door and rested against it, taking a deep breath before peering around the corner of the building. She could not hear anyone inside, and didn't wish to disturb the animals.

They'd make noise and then people would know she was coming. Once she'd double-checked that the space around the barn was clear, she continued on toward the forest.

She walked carefully, testing her steps before taking them and trying hard to avoid any unruly roots laid by the cedar trees, which formed the blackest night sky above her. As she walked through the trees, she scanned the space on either side of the path, her heart beating quickly in her chest.

The ranch was tolerable at night, but walking alone through the woods in the dark was beginning to make her panic. She continued on anyway, and just as she was beginning to give up hope, she spotted a large man-shaped lump on the floor in a clearing up ahead.

Oh dear god, no.

Suddenly, Biddie threw all caution to the wind and ran over to the lump. Kneeling down, she quickly identified the man as Arch, and tears began to fill her eyes. She placed a hand under his head and moved her ear to his lips to see if he was breathing. A warm breath flooded over her face and she let out a small shaky sigh. Carefully, she placed her hands around Arch's torso, pulling him up into a sitting position.

"Arch?" she asked breathlessly. "Arch, can you hear me?"

For a moment, nothing happened. Biddie felt a tear fall from her eye down her cheek and sniffed to try and stop any more. But before she said anything more, Arch jolted awake in her arms.

"Monty, you ev–" Arch began to growl. He stopped himself in his tracks and looked at Biddie. His brows knotted across his forehead, and he winced. Lifting his hand to his forehead he groaned and blinked slowly. "What happened?" he asked.

"Your guess is as good as mine," Biddie replied. "But it's okay, I've got you. Let's get back to the house," she said softly. He had been outside in the cold and the dark for ages; if they didn't get him home soon he'd catch a chill. He looked at Biddie, his sparkling blue eyes wide and confused, and he nodded gently.

"Home sounds good," he said quietly. With a small smile, Biddie nodded back and stood up. She offered him a hand and he took it carefully, pulling himself up onto wobbly legs. Together, the two of them hobbled out of the woods and back to the house in silence, both jolting and jumping at any noise around them. By the time they reached the house, Arch was beginning to shiver.

"I'm going to go and put some warmer clothes on," he said as they entered the hallway. "I'll be down in a moment." He smiled gently at Biddie and then wandered off upstairs. She watched him go, still a little shaky on his legs, and let out a large sigh. He could've died out there. She was starting to realize quite how serious all of this was, and was very glad that she'd convinced him to let her stay in the house and not at Angela's. She walked through to the dining room and took a seat, trying to relax a little. She'd found him; they were home now, and it was alright. But, no matter how hard she tried, she could not slow the mad dashing of her heart.

"Oh come on now," she said aloud to herself, shaking her head.

She was no use to Arch if she was going to be so emotional. She placed her spectacles on the table and rubbed her eyes with the heel of her hand, trying to relieve some of the stress. By the time she opened her eyes again, she could hear Arch trotting down the stairs. He wandered through the hallway and into the dining room. Almost instinctively, he pulled a chair out opposite Biddie.

"So you have no idea what happened?" Biddie asked, her voice inquisitive but gentle.

"It's starting to come back," Arch said, frowning. He pinched the bridge of his nose and sighed. "Monty."

"He's one of Wellington's men, right?" Biddie asked, setting her eyeglasses carefully on the bridge of her nose. "Was he the one Angela saw?"

Arch nodded, and Biddie's heart dropped. He'd killed Thomas and Sylvie, and he was lurking in the woods waiting to get Arch. Wellington was not holding back.

"Oh dear," she replied. "That doesn't bode well."

"Not at all," Arch agreed, slumping back in his chair with a small sigh. He looked Biddie in the eyes, and she couldn't help but notice that the usual hopeful sparkle that she'd come to love was replaced with a dull slate. They shared a look for a moment, and Biddie could see the anxiety within him. Whatever had just happened with Monty had really thrown him, and all she wanted was to make it all better, but she didn't even know where to start.

"It'll be okay," she said after a few seconds of silence.

"Mmhm," Arch replied.

"I promise," she continued. In reality, she knew as well as he did that there was every chance that it wasn't going to be okay. But she had to try to comfort him at least.

After that, the two of them sat at the dining table for a little while without saying anything. Occasionally, they'd share a look, or something would bump outside and the two of them would jump. It seemed as if neither of them knew what to do or say next, so they opted to just do nothing.

After about twenty minutes of nothing, there was a loud knock on the door. Biddie jumped up out of her seat and stared at the door, and Arch gripped the table. Slowly, he stood up from his chair and stalked over to the door. He signaled at Biddie to remain at the table, and she nodded begrudgingly. Carefully, he opened the front door, standing behind it and craning his neck around it as if to protect himself.

"Oh. It's you," Arch growled.

Oh no, Biddie thought to herself. The only people that would justify such a response would be Wellington or one of his men.

"May I come in?" The person behind the door asked. Biddie would've recognized that voice anywhere. Prickly and cold, it belonged to exactly the man she did not want to see — Henry Wellington. A wave of anger washed over her and she rushed to Arch's side.

"No you may not," Biddie replied. Arch shot her a warning look, but she ignored him. "You're not welcome here."

"Oh, look, it's the pretty little thing," Wellington smirked. "And she's got an attitude. Y'know, Archibald, you should really keep your pets on a shorter leash." He raised an eyebrow.

Biddie's blood boiled. She was *nobody's* pet.

"Don't talk about her like that," Arch said sternly. "She's right, you're not welcome here. Leave, now."

"You don't want to keep telling me to leave," Wellington sighed. "It'll just end badly for you. I'm here to offer to pay you whatever price you name for the ranch. You really ought to consider it. Who knows what might happen if you don't ..." Wellington smiled widely, revealing all of his teeth. Arch's brows tightened across his forehead, and Biddie felt herself begin to tremble with frustration and nervousness.

"You cannot come to my home and threaten me, Wellington. You won't get away with it." Arch shook his head.

"I think you'll find I'll get away with it just fine," Wellington replied. "In fact, I could even tell you my plan, and I don't think you could do a single thing about it."

"Leave," Arch hissed. Biddie felt him tense up beside her. She subtly moved her hand and placed it on the back of his arm in an attempt to comfort him. She knew how he felt; she felt it too. Wellington made her skin crawl, and, after what he'd just done to the house and to Arch, he filled her with rage. Arch's comment seemed to amuse him, and his grin merely widened. He looked from Arch to Biddie, and back again.

"Consider my offer," he whispered, and his eyes returned to Biddie. "If you don't, I *will* have to act. I'll take away the things you love one ... by ... one." Wellington spoke slowly, and the malice in his voice filled Biddie with foreboding. He winked at her, and a shudder rippled across her body. Arch scowled at him and shook his head.

"Goodbye, Mr. Wellington," he said finally, before slamming the door. He turned to Biddie, his eyes full of concern. The blue in them was softer than usual, light and gentle, inviting her to be honest and reassuring her. "Are you alright?"

Biddie nodded nervously; she was lying, but he didn't need to worry about her right now. There were bigger issues at hand than whether or not Wellington's wink had unsettled her.

"Are you?" She asked quietly, and Arch shook his head in response. He bit his lower lip and ran a hand through his tousled sandy hair.

"I need to find the sheriff," he replied. "Will you come with me?" he asked. The idea of leaving the ranch unattended filled her with dread, but she knew that Rudy needed to be made aware of what was going on, and being left alone was scarier.

"Sure," she said, a small, nervous smile on her face. He matched her smile and let out a sigh.

"Alright, then. Let's go and let Rudy know what's going on," he nodded.

He opened the door back up an inch or so and peered outside. Once he'd confirmed that Wellington was long gone, he opened it fully and stepped outside. Cautiously, he led the two of them down toward the barn. As they approached, Biddie spotted that one of the doors was ajar. She thought back to earlier in the night, but couldn't remember whether or not it had been open then.

"You might want to have a word with your men," she said, a small frown on her face. "They really ought to shut the barn doors completely."

"They do ..." Arch replied, squinting at the barn in confusion. Biddie looked at him and then at the barn. *Someone's broken in,* she thought.

"Oh, no," she said, speeding up. Arch matched her pace quickly and the two of them half-jogged the rest of the way to the barn. Arch led, pushing the barn door open carefully. The door creaked open, and Arch stepped inside. A moment later, he reappeared. His face was red with anger, and his hands were trembling.

"They're gone," he said, shaking his head. "All of the animals ... They're all gone. There's only one pony left ..." He kicked the ground and yelled, making Biddie jump back. "Sorry, sorry," Arch said, putting his hand out to apologize. "It's just ... My brother worked so hard to keep this ranch going, and they've just gone and taken all of it ..." He exhaled shakily. "There isn't even a horse we can ride into town.

There is only the pony, and he won't be able to carry us both."

Biddie sighed and shook her head.

"So Wellington was a distraction, then."

"Seems like it." Arch nodded. "I still think Rudy needs to know. Would you be alright if I went into town alone?" He looked into Biddie's eyes, and she nodded weakly.

"I don't like the idea, but I'll manage," she replied. The idea of being at home, alone, when those men were loitering around made her stomach turn, especially knowing what they had done to Thomas and Sylvie. But Arch needed to get Rudy; she knew he was right about that. She couldn't ride a pony into town, she'd just get lost. This was the only way. She was just going to have to stomach it.

Arch smiled at her nervously, his eyes restless and uneasy, and then looked behind him, into the barn.

"I won't be long, I promise," he said gently. "Now go back to the house, and stay there. Do not leave for anyone, got it?"

She smiled softly, his need to protect her made her feel a little bit better. She knew he'd be as quick as possible.

"Got it," she said.

He smiled at her once more, and then dashed into the barn, leaving Biddie to run back to the house. Once inside, she locked the doors, pulled all of the curtains, and sat in the dining room. As Arch rode by, she listened to the sound of the pony's hooves hammer on the ground.

It'll be alright, she tried to tell herself. *Why would you be their target?*

AN UNEXPECTED GOVERNESS TO TAME HIS WILD HEART

Chapter Twenty-Six

The Sutton Ranch, Paddington, Texas

24th May 1885

Biddie sat at the dining room table. She was too nervous to do anything but wait for Arch to return. Even though she knew losing herself in her thoughts was only going to make her more anxious, she couldn't help it.

She kept finding herself thinking about the children, whether or not they were safe, Angela, and what she'd do if Monty or Wellington figured out that they'd stashed the children there. She thought about Arch and wondered if maybe Wellington had followed him into town. He could've been ambushed.

He could be injured by the side of the road and she wouldn't know any better. She even thought about Thomas and Sylvie Sutton. She wondered how they let it get this bad, and thought about how Wellington could have poisoned them. Angela said that the plant tasted awful, so they must have known ...

She sighed and shook her head.

"Stay positive," she said to herself half-heartedly. She thought about maybe getting up and doing some chores — the kitchen needed mopping, the lounge needed dusting — but her nerves kept her planted firmly in her seat. She tried instead to think about something positive, but just as she started thinking about her grandmother and their life together, she heard a creak at the back of the house.

She froze.

The creak appeared to come from one of the back rooms. She listened carefully and heard another. Shooting up from her chair, she walked around to the back of the table, hoping to put some distance between herself and whatever was making the noise. Her heart raced in her chest, and she felt every muscle in her body tense.

Another creak.

A clang.

Two clangs.

A footstep.

Two footsteps, faster than before.

Four footsteps.

Biddie began to feel faint; there were other people in the house. That could only mean one thing. Wellington was here. Her hands began to sweat and she desperately looked for a way out of the dining room.

The only exits she could think of were the door to the hallway, which seemed to be where the footsteps were coming from, or a window. Breaking a window would tell them where she was, though. She sank back against the wall and slid down it, crouching just behind the dining room table. Hiding seemed to be her only option.

The footsteps got louder and louder until she heard them in the hallway. Attached to them were two male voices. One deep and gruff, that she had not heard before, and another that made her skin crawl. *Wellington,* she determined.

She remained in her spot, trying to breathe quietly so as to not give herself up. To stay calm, she tried to think happy thoughts — her grandmother, the children, the moments that she had shared with Arch ... But the thought that two murderers were in the house with her was too much.

She could feel her heart racing in her chest. The two men walked around in the hallway for a moment, possibly trying to decide which room to look in, and then they stopped. She felt a lump rise in her throat. Words were exchanged in hushed tones, and then Biddie heard them walk into the dining room. She covered her mouth, clenching her eyes shut, and prayed that they wouldn't find her.

"Pretty little thing?" Wellington called. "I know you're here, come now, don't toy with me."

"We just want to talk ..." The other man called.

Biddie remained in her spot, crouched just low enough to be hidden by the large wooden table. The two men walked around the kitchen, yanking open the doors of cupboards, and Biddie listened to the clatter and clash of silverware and crockery.

After a few minutes, the noises stopped, and she heard them walk back toward the dining room table. They stopped just by it, and she held her breath. Opening one eye, she could see that they were standing opposite her. She slid further down the wall.

They exchanged whispers once again and then split up. She watched their feet as one walked one way around the dining table, and the other walked in the opposite direction. She clenched her eyes shut again.

There was no way out. They'd trapped her. She pushed herself up from the floor and let out a very shaky breath.

"Alright, fine," she said, falsifying confidence. "You two men are trespassing."

She looked from Wellington to the other man, whom she instantly identified as Monty. He was tall, slim, dressed in all black, and by the looks of it, Arch had managed to get at least one punch in before he was knocked down; Monty's jaw was purple and swollen. Wellington looked exactly as he had at the door, but, for some reason, he held a large cup in his hand.

The two men laughed loudly and grinned at her. She felt a tremor wash over her as they leered, and she felt her fake confidence fall away. Her lip began to quiver, and the men laughed even more. She cleared her throat in a desperate attempt to regain her bravado.

"You've not got so much attitude when he's not here to protect you, have you?" Wellington said. He walked over to where Biddie stood and placed the cup on the table in front of her. "I bought you a present," he said, his voice making the hair on her arms stand on end. She looked into the cup and saw a clear liquid with petals and berries crushed into it. Frowning, she looked from the cup to the men.

"What is it?" She asked. One sniff, though, and she instantly knew what it was. The berries smelt bitter, disgustingly so, but the color of them was fantastic — it was the plant that Angela had described. They were here to poison her.

"Pick it up," Wellington answered.

"Not until I know what it is," she said, shaking her head, pretending she had no clue. Before she knew it, Monty had pulled his gun from his holster and cocked it, and it was pointed directly at her.

"This isn't a request. Pick. It. Up." Monty walked closer, not moving the gun. Biddie's heart thumped in her chest and she shook her head again nervously.

"Why should I?" she asked, shaking where she was standing.

"Otherwise I'll shoot," Monty replied, frustration evident in his voice.

"I don't think that'll be conducive to getting Arch to give up the ranch," Biddie replied. Her heart was beating faster than a hummingbird's wings, but she knew that Arch would be back soon, and the children were not here. They could not make her drink it.

"Maybe, maybe not, but I'll enjoy myself all the same," Monty growled, moving closer until the gun was only an inch from Biddie's head.

"And I still wouldn't have drank it," Biddie continued. "So really, shooting me is your worst option."

"I wouldn't say worst. It'd get you to shut your pretty little face," Wellington said angrily. *I'm getting to them,* Biddie thought. If she could just keep this up a little while longer, she'd be saved by Rudy and Arch. All she had to do was ignore every fiber of her being that was telling her to break down and cry.

"No matter what happens to me, you won't get the ranch," she said matter-of-factly. "Arch will not sell."

"He might not sell, but maybe he'll move if he's heartbroken. Or maybe I'll just come after him next. And then those kids. Who knows …" Wellington grinned, and Biddie visibly shuddered.

"Don't you dare bring them into this," she hissed, turning to face Wellington. Monty pushed the gun into the back of her head, but her anger at Wellington had filled her with so much adrenaline that she did not care. "You will *not* touch a hair on their heads." She scowled up at the older man, her eyes full of rage.

"Oh, she is feisty, isn't she boss?" Monty laughed behind her. "If she won't drink it, maybe we should go upstairs to the kids?"

Good luck, Biddie thought to herself.

"Hmm, maybe ... Would you like that? If it was *your* fault that they had to deal with us?" Wellington replied, eyeing Biddie as he spoke.

"Go upstairs all you like," Biddie replied coolly. "I'm sure you won't be satisfied."

Wellington frowned and stared at her in confusion for a moment. He looked over her to Monty.

"Go and check to see if the children are upstairs," he demanded. Monty quickly reholstered his gun and dashed away, sprinting up the stairs. Biddie took the opportunity to step back, feeling a small amount of relief at the lack of a gun pressed into her skull. As she stepped back, Wellington grabbed her by the wrists.

"Oh no you don't," he hissed, pulling her closer to him. "We're just getting started."

She growled and tried to yank her arms away, but it was no use; he was much stronger than she was. Before long, Monty returned from upstairs, rushing back around to stand behind her.

"They're gone, boss," he stated.

Wellington growled and kicked the leg of the table, spilling some of the liquid from the cup onto the shining polished wood.

"You know, this is how I did it," he started. "This is how I killed Thomas and Sylvie, those pains in my backside. I snuck in late at night and gave them both a little drink. Told them if they didn't drink it that those cherubs upstairs would get a visit from Monty here ... Well, that was incentive enough," he laughed loudly, and Biddie's heart broke.

They died to save the children.

"Bizarre, really, how money didn't work as an incentive for them to give me what I wanted, but their dear little babies' lives did." He shook his head. "I'll never understand parenthood," he sighed and looked over at Biddie. "But since the children aren't here, you've kind of left me no choice. I can see that you're not going to willingly drink this, are you?"

Biddie shook her head, scowling up at Wellington. She debated headbutting him and running to escape, but she wouldn't know where to go. Besides, Arch would be back soon. She just had to keep reminding herself of that.

"Well then ..." Wellington sighed. He looked over her shoulder at Monty once again and gestured towards the table. Biddie eyed him confusedly, but before she could try and figure out what he was doing, Monty had pulled a chair out from the table and was forcing her into it by the shoulders. She fell against the hard wood with a thud, and groaned. He held her shoulders down, his fingers digging into the tender flesh either side of her neck. She looked up at him, her eyes full of panic, and he grinned.

"... We'll just have to make you," Wellington finished. He moved toward the chair, and with one hand, pushed her head back so that she was looking at the ceiling. Her spectacles went flying and crashed against the wall. Monty moved one of his hands to her forehead and placed it there, applying just enough force to stop her from moving. His skin was hard and calloused, and it rubbed against her forehead in a way that made her skin crawl. Wellington reached over to the glass and grabbed it, and Biddie's heart stopped in her chest.

She'd thought she'd managed to outsmart them. She thought that if she'd kept them talking, she'd live. But this was it. She was about to be poisoned, with no clue how soon Arch would return, and nobody around to help. Tears began to spring into her eyes, and Monty laughed at her, shaking his head.

"Aw, look," he said teasingly, as Wellington wrenched her mouth open with one finger. Before she could fight back, he slowly began to pour the liquid from the cup into her mouth, holding it open as he did. The hot water burned her tongue, and the bitterness made her squeeze her eyes shut in discomfort. It rushed down her throat, making its way to her gut, and she could feel every drop of it. She squirmed in her seat, and Monty's grip tightened. Wellington kept pouring until every drip was gone, and then placed the cup back on the table. Monty finally let go of her, and she doubled over instantly.

"We ought to move, she'll be sick in a few seconds," Wellington said to Monty. From where she sat, her head between her knees, she could hear their footsteps as they walked to the other side of the table. She tried desperately to lift her head to say something, but she just couldn't. Within seconds, she felt a lump rise in her throat, and a fountain of vomit barged its way out of her mouth.

"Not so pretty, now," Wellington laughed.

"With you gone, Archibald will be *inconsolable;* it'll be the heartbreak of his lifetime. He'll do anything to get away from the memory, and to keep those little ones safe." He beamed. "It's a small price to pay, really."

"Y-you're not going to get away with it," Biddie said, her hands grabbing her gut as the effects of the poison began to really take hold.

"Sweetheart, we already have." Monty rolled his eyes. "Haven't you realized? There's nobody around. The Sheriff is in town, your loverboy has rushed away … We're here to watch the poison do its job, and then we'll swan off. Nobody will know we were ever here in the first place."

"They'll figure i-it out," she replied, breathing out shakily as her throat began to burn. "I know they will."

She watched as Wellington rolled his eyes, and then suddenly her vision began to blur. She could feel the poison stripping her strength away, bit by bit. She was exhausted, and every few seconds her stomach would churn, jolting her awake as she felt her insides burning.

Chapter Twenty-Seven

The Sutton Ranch, Paddington, Texas

24th May 1885

Arch rode onto the ranch alongside Rudy, the pony he sat upon doing its very best to keep up with Rudy's stallion. The sound of the horseshoes beating on the ground matched the speed of his heart.

He'd hated leaving Biddie in the house alone when he knew those evil men were around, but he had little other choice. He just prayed that they'd left her alone. He'd only been gone an hour. As they neared the house, Arch's heart sank. There were two horses outside.

He directed his pony to a halt and all but threw himself down from its back. Rudy did the same, and the two of them barreled away from their horses and up the porch steps.

Arch barged the door down, not taking the time to unlock it - he could fix the door another time. All that mattered was that Biddie was safe. The door ripped from its hinges as Arch ran full force into it with his shoulder. Stepping up and over the wooden door, he raced into the house, Rudy not far behind.

As the two of them stepped into the hallway, Arch was hit with a bitter, fruity smell. It assaulted his nostrils, making his eyes water. He looked one way, into the lounge, and saw nothing.

Looking the other way, he spotted Biddie sitting in the dining room her eyes half-open and missing their glasses. Arch's breath caught in his throat. He couldn't tell if she was alive or dead.

"This way," he said quickly to Rudy, jogging from the front door to the dining room. His heart somehow quickened even further, and all he could think about was getting to Biddie's side and checking her pulse.

But as he and Rudy crossed through the doorway into the dining room, the two of them were knocked back onto the floor by two large men. Arch did not get a chance to see who before he was shoved hard in the shoulders. Arch groaned as his head hit the floor, and glanced to his right where Rudy had fallen. Then, looking up at the doorway, he identified Monty and Henry Wellington, standing shoulder to shoulder.

"You're too late," Monty said, a despicable grin across his face. "Shame you won't be able to get to her in time. You'll have to just watch," he snorted, locking eyes with Arch on the floor.

Arch grabbed the back of his head and then looked at his hand, checking for blood.

"Want me to take 'em outside, boss?" Monty asked. Wellington chuckled, and Arch watched as he shook his head.

"I think a fight would be more fun." He smirked. "At least make them think that they have a chance," he snorted. Monty smirked and stepped through the door, toward Arch and Rudy.

With a wince, Arch pushed himself up from the floor and then quickly turned to Rudy to offer a hand. Rudy took his hand happily and pulled himself up.

"There'll be no fight. Boys, you're under arrest." Rudy stepped forward, reaching for the cuffs on his belt. As he did, Monty balled his fist and swung for the sheriff. Arch pushed Rudy out of the way and punched Monty hard in the gut. Looking over Monty's shoulder, he spotted Biddie, bent doubled in a chair, her feet surrounded by a pool of vomit. His heart dropped, and rage filled him as he threw another punch, this time connecting his fist with Monty's face. He watched as Monty doubled over and groaned, spitting on the floor. Arch shot Rudy a look, and Rudy nodded, pulling Monty by the shirt away from the door to make room for Arch to pass. As Rudy wrestled with Monty, desperately trying to cuff him, Arch glanced over at Biddie. He watched as she blinked and tried to hold her head up, only to flop back down with a groan.

Angrily, he walked through the door, putting himself face-to-face with Wellington. Wellington reached up, pushing Arch by both his shoulders in an attempt to knock him down again, but it didn't work. Something in Arch had awoken, fueled by his anger and aching heart, and as Wellington pushed him he remained unmoved.

Instead, he clenched his fist and punched Wellington square in the nose. There was a small crunch, and Wellington yelped, his hands rushing up to his face as a small stream of blood began to dribble down onto his lip.

"Get out of my way," Arch growled. He punched Wellington once more, this time in the gut, and then shoved him against the doorframe. Wellington slammed into the wood with a thud, and Arch stormed past, rushing over to Biddie. He kneeled down next to her and slid his hand under her cheek, pushing her head upright.

"What have they done to you?" he whispered. Behind him, he heard handcuffs clink into place, and he let out a tiny sigh. Biddie opened her eyes a little and looked at him. Her emerald eyes were bloodshot and teary, and the green in them had faded. She looked him in the eyes, and her mouth moved, but no sound came out. He frowned and bit his lip, fighting off tears, and then turned behind him to ensure that the Sheriff had caught both the men.

He peered through the doorway and spotted Rudy holding Monty by the cuffs, his arms tied tightly behind his back, but he couldn't see Wellington. He scowled and looked at Biddie.

"I'll be right back, just hold on for me," he whispered, caressing her cheek gently. He leaned her back in the chair and then stood up, rushing out into the hall. He looked to Rudy for answers, his brows furrowed. Rudy gestured at the front door as he fought to keep Monty still, and Arch sprinted back out onto the porch. As he reached the stairs, he caught sight of Wellington riding away on one of the horses, laughing maniacally. Arch rushed back into the house.

"He's gone," he said, his voice full of anger. He growled and kicked the wall. "He's gone!" He yelled.

"We'll find him, I promise, Arch. We'll find him real soon," Rudy nodded as he spoke, clearly trying to reassure him. Arch nodded meagrely in response, but he couldn't help but question Rudy's words. Wellington was a well-off man. In a day, he could be halfway across the country. They'd be hard-pressed to get a hold of him before he used his considerable resources to skip town, and in the meantime, the woman who had stolen Arch's heart lay slumped over the kitchen table, fading before his very eyes.

Chapter Twenty-Eight

The Sutton Ranch, Paddington, Texas

24th May 1885

Monty writhed under Rudy's grip, still fighting for freedom. He growled and wriggled, pulling Rudy's arm and fighting with the handcuffs that he had been placed in.

"Pack that in," Rudy sighed.

"You don't control me," Monty huffed. He yanked on the handcuffs in an attempt to free himself, but Rudy's grip on them remained strong. He pulled the chain on the handcuffs backward, making Monty yelp in pain. Rudy smirked slightly and looked over to Arch.

Glad he's enjoying himself, Arch thought bitterly.

Monty tried his luck another time, this time trying to swing his and Rudy's arm. Having had enough of his shenanigans, Rudy delivered a swift kick in the calf, making Monty fall to the floor with a groan. Arch listened as his knees collided with the floor, a small creak echoing on impact. Monty panted for a moment; clearly the fall had hurt him.

"We don't have time for this," Arch grumbled. He needed to save Biddie, or catch the man responsible for her death. This little wrestling match was a waste of precious minutes. "We need to find him, and we need to save Biddie."

"Where might he have gone?" Rudy asked, holding the chain of the handcuffs and pulling it back to reveal Monty's face. Monty grinned up at Rudy maliciously and laughed, obviously trying to unnerve him. Arch wanted nothing more than to punch Monty in his stupid, cruel face, but that wouldn't get them anywhere. Rudy, oblivious to Monty's attempt to intimidate him, stared into Monty's eyes and raised an eyebrow. "Tell us, and maybe your punishment won't be quite as bad as his."

Monty snorted and shook his head. From where Arch was standing by the door, he could see a despicable grin on the criminal's face, even though he hung his head. Arch tensed his fists, shaking his head. Men like Monty filled him with disgust.

He was going to make sure that both Monty and Wellington were locked up for a very long time, even if it was the last thing he did. He was not going to let them get away with this. Not again. He eyed Monty suspiciously for a moment, waiting to see if he'd reply.

The grin on his face just got bigger, and Arch growled.

"He's not going to give us anything, Rudy," he lamented. "Even in his last moments of freedom, the man's nothing but wicked."

"Even if I did tell you anything," Monty laughed, "we've had the last laugh. You can't save her now. Ranch or no ranch, she's dying. Look at her, she's barely alive now," He peered around to his left, past Rudy, and through the dining room doorway. "I think that means we won."

Arch followed his gaze, looking over at Biddie. She was still sitting upright, like he'd left her a minute ago, but what little color remained in her cheeks was slowly fading, and her usually lustrous black hair was now hanging in limp strings, soaked with sweat.

Arch watched as she trembled, the muscles in her body seemingly fighting for their life. Her eyes flickered open, revealing two dull green irises ringed with red veins, and then fluttered shut again.

A wave of heat rippled over Arch, his vision blurring, and he rushed into the dining room, shoving Monty by the shoulder as he walked past. Arch used his full force, and Monty wobbled on his knees, almost falling face-first onto the wooden floor, only saved by Rudy's grip on the handcuffs.

"You're lucky that's all he's doin'," Rudy muttered to Monty as Arch walked over to Biddie. Monty chuckled in response, and Arch tried his best to block out the sound. There was nothing that man could say that would change what had happened, and if he was telling the truth, if Biddie was truly dying, he did not want to waste the last moments he may have with her fussing about some lowlife.

He'd rather be there for her. Besides, he could not bring himself to believe Monty, despite the state that Biddie was in. There had to be something he could do. He just needed to figure it out. He wasn't about to watch the love of his life go that easily.

"He can't be right," Arch said softly, falling to his knees beside Biddie. "I cannot lose you," he whispered. "I simply won't."

He reached for Biddie's hand and clasped it in his. Where he had once felt warm, soft skin, he now held a hand that was clammy and cool, a reminder that his Biddie was fading. Looking up at her from the floor, tears began to sting his eyes. He found himself thinking about the life that they could have had together, if only he had been here to save her. He would have given her everything she wanted.

The tears began to stream down his face.

He'd lost his opportunity to be happy in Atlanta. He'd lost the opportunity to have a good relationship with his brother. Now he was losing the chance at a life with the woman he loved. He lifted his hand to wipe the tears from his cheeks and then raised it up to Biddie's cheek. Gently, he cupped her face, stroking her cheek with the pad of his thumb.

"We could've had it all," he whispered. "I would've cared for you 'til the end of the Earth, Miss Edwards," he sniffed. Each moment he spent there with her ripped his heart further in two. She still looked like Biddie, *his* Biddie, but her wit, her charm, her kindness, all of it was fading away by the second.

He didn't even know what Wellington had done to her, so how on Earth was he supposed to fix it? He could see the life draining out of her by the second as the trembling got worse and she slumped further and further into her seat. Losing someone was hard enough, but watching them become a shell of themselves while you can do nothing but hold their hand … It was torture.

He wished he'd made her go to Angela's with the children. None of this would have happened. She'd be happy, safe … not barely conscious and in pain. He cursed himself; how could he have been so stupid? Of course leaving her here was going to lead to this. He should never have left her side.

Watching her, he cursed himself for not being kinder, for not telling her exactly how he felt. If he was being honest with himself, he'd known he would fall in love with her from the second he saw her. Her gorgeous black curls, her emerald eyes, and a smile that seemed to light up any room. He'd been head over heels for Biddie since day one — and he'd never told her.

He glanced over his shoulder at the men in the hallway, checking that they were preoccupied with one another. The two of them seemed to be bickering about something, and Monty was still on his knees on the floor.

They weren't listening. If Monty was telling the truth, and this *was* Arch's last chance to be with Biddie, to tell her how he felt, he had to tell her. He couldn't let her die not knowing, and part of him, deep down, thought that maybe she'd be able to hold on for longer if he gave her something to hold on for. It was the only idea he had.

"Biddie, I have to confess," he started. "I've been keeping this from you for a while, and, if I'm being honest, it was because I was scared. Nobody has ever made me feel the way you do. The only person in my life that I cared for was Thomas, and I failed him … " he sighed and took a deep breath. "I know that's not an excuse, and that I should've told you sooner, Biddie, but," he sniffed, tears continuing to stream down his cheeks. "Well, I-I-I … I love you. I'm in love with you," he looked up at her face, and her eyes opened slightly.

Up close, Arch could see that the whites of her eyes were beginning to turn yellow. He wasn't even sure that she had heard him, or that his Biddie was even still in there.

She looked like a shell of a person, drained and dreary, exhausted from fighting whatever was happening inside her body. He watched as her bloodshot eyes moved weakly to look into his. Even with the muted colors that had replaced her usual vibrancy, even when she was on the verge of death, looking into her eyes gave him a warmth in his chest. His heart ached.

This is all my fault.

He fought off a sob, and stood up. Carefully, he slid his arms under Biddie's legs and around her torso, pulling her up from the chair against his chest. She smelled like a mixture of her usual lavender with something else, something new, something bitter.

Arch could not quite place it. He began to walk through the kitchen and into the hallway, cradling her against him. She rested her cheek on his chest, and he could see small tears falling down her face. Whether it was from pain, or the realization that she was not going to come back from this, he didn't know.

"I'm going to take her to bed. If she's to pass, she can at least do so comfortably," he said quietly as he reached Rudy's side. Rudy looked at Biddie's face, and Arch saw his eyes fill with tears. He watched as the Sheriff nodded and sniffed away the tears.

"Very well," Rudy replied. "I'll take this piece of work down the station and get the manhunt for Wellington underway." He pulled Monty up from the floor by the handcuffs. "I'm real sorry, Arch," he added before turning away, dragging Monty with him before the man could say a word. Arch listened as Rudy rushed to his horse, the sound of strong footsteps on the ground outside echoed by Monty's half-dragged footsteps and groans. There was a grunt and a whinny, which Arch assumed was Rudy throwing Monty over the horse.

"Look after her, Arch!" Rudy called from outside. Shortly after, Arch heard a yell and then horse hooves running away from the house.

A small amount of relief came from knowing that Rudy was taking Monty to jail, but it did nothing to counteract the sadness he was feeling. The fact that even Rudy seemed to be saddened somehow made it worse. It hadn't occurred to him that Biddie had made such an impact on everyone. Even their neighbors had grown to love her. It provided him some comfort to know that he wasn't alone in his sorrow, but at the same time, it made him even angrier that somebody could have hurt her like this. He couldn't help but wonder what was wrong with Wellington. Something had to be for him to kill three decent people in cold blood.

He began to walk toward Biddie's bedroom, his eyes still red and stinging from tears, when he felt Biddie cough. She spluttered for a few moments, and then her eyes flickered open once more. His brows furrowed, and he looked down at her, their eyes locking.

Her face contorted into an expression of anguish, and she groaned, grabbing her stomach and clenching her eyes shut. He continued into the bedroom, pushing the door open with his shoulder. "It's okay," he said softly. "It'll be over soon," his voice was weak, and he moved to Biddie's bed. Rather than placing her down, he sat on the edge and continued to hold her.

I should've kissed her when I had the chance, Arch thought to himself. He stroked her hair back from her face. Even then, her hair maintained its curls, and the white stripe that sat right at her temple, which he'd once thought odd, was the most beautiful thing he had ever seen.

He'd never thought to ask her about it, he realized. Now he might never get the chance to. There was so much he had left to learn about her. So many stories that would go untold, adventures left undone.

"I'm sorry, Biddie," he said gently. "This was not your fight, and I should never have let you come anywhere near it." He watched her face closely, hoping for a response, but got nothing. "I shouldn't have listened to Angela. I should've let you go home ... At least then you'd be safe," he let out a soft, sad sigh. "I failed you, Biddie. I should've been here to save you."

He closed his eyes and rested his forehead on hers. For a moment, it was just them in the world again. *This is the last time it will feel like that,* Arch found himself thinking. He let out a shaky breath.

Out of nowhere, he felt Biddie shift beneath him, and his head shot up from hers. His eyes opened and he stared down at her. She wriggled slightly, then groaned. He relaxed — she wasn't going just yet. He leaned forward and placed a small kiss on her forehead, and her eyes opened ever so slightly.

"Biddie?" he asked, wondering whether or not she was conscious.

She strained, squinting her eyes as she looked up at him.

"A-a," she muttered. Her usual melodic voice had been replaced by a rough rasp. It sounded as if her throat had been burnt and her tongue had grown too big for her mouth.

"What is it, Biddie?" he asked again. He thought maybe she was trying to say his name. "I'm here. It's alright, I'm here."

"A-an," she groaned and let out a shaky breath. "A-a-angela," she breathed. "C-cure ... "

Arch's heart stopped.

She thinks Angela can cure her?

He still wasn't sure whether or not she knew what she was saying, but he tried to convince himself there was a chance she was right. After all, Biddie was a smart woman, even in the state that she was in. There had to be some reason that she thought Angela could cure her. Besides, at this point, he'd try anything.

If Angela knew anything about what had been done to her, or how to reverse it, he certainly wasn't going to just sit there and let Biddie go. She was worth fighting for. He just hoped that Biddie knew what she was on about and that Angela did know something about all of this.

He quickly tensed his arms around her and rushed out of the room, toward the door, doing his best to keep from jostling her about too much. His heart began to race in his chest.

Maybe this isn't the end.

He felt tears begin to gather in his eyes again and looked down at the woman he loved. She was still fading; she was barely able to open her eyes now. He stopped for a second at the bottom of the porch steps and looked up at the sky.

He hadn't prayed since arriving in Texas. In fact, he couldn't remember the last time that he had prayed. He'd been so busy back in Atlanta that he just hadn't had time. He'd done everything in his power to keep God in his heart, but this needed more than that. He closed his eyes, and squeezing Biddie close, whispered a prayer.

"Dear God, I am no noble or astute man. I am simply a man in love, that has done all he can to remain loyal to you as a man can be. I beg of you, please, do not take another life from me. Especially not her. I will pray more, I promise." He let out a small sigh. "I need her. She keeps me good. She is the love of my life. Keep her here with me, Lord." He opened his eyes and looked back down at Biddie. Placing another small kiss on her temple, he found himself with more hope than before.

She's going to be alright, he told himself. *You'll save her. You have to.*

Chapter Twenty-Nine

The Sutton Ranch, Paddington, Texas

24th May 1885

Arch looked across the yard, trying to come up with a way to get over to the Parkers' as quickly as possible. Standing outside of the house was his own pony, the one he'd ridden into town on, but the poor creature was barely able to manage taking him to town and back, let alone the two of them and in haste.

In the early morning sunlight, however, just behind the pony, Arch spotted a golden-brown horse — a mare by the looks of it — and he tried to rack his brain, seeing if he could remember the name of the horse, or whether it belonged to a ranch hand, but he came up empty. As far as he could remember, he'd never seen it.

It must be Monty's, he thought. *'Had the last laugh,' has he? Well, we'll see about that.*

He ran over to the horse's side, holding Biddie tight to ensure she wasn't being bounced around too much in his arms. As he reached the mare, she rolled her eye to look at him. He stopped still, careful not to spook the animal. Crouching ever so slightly, he did his best to project an aura of calm.

"Hey there," he said softly, approaching very slowly from the side, where she could see him. "I need your help, just for a short trip," he continued. The mare blinked at him, tossed her head, and then neighed gently. It felt like a sign, and Arch couldn't help but feel even more hopeful.

Thank you, Arch thought, glancing up at the sky. *This might just work.*

He rushed over to the horse's side. She was saddled up and everything was ready to go. Monty had clearly been in a rush to get in and get out. Arch eyed the mare nervously for a second, and then carefully began to place Biddie on the horse, leaning her on the beast's neck gently.

As if by instinct, Biddie's arms splayed out, holding either side of the horse's neck. The horse turned her head slightly to look at Biddie, clearly confused as to what was going on, then snorted and returned her attention to the fields ahead. Arch let out a small sigh of relief and quickly clambered up after Biddie, wrapping his arms around her and grabbing the reins.

"I hope to God that you're right, Biddie," he mumbled as he flicked the reins, ushering the horse into movement. As soon as they were on the go, he urged the mare straight into a gallop, racing through the crop fields. He tried his best to stick to the pathways that split the fields, but the route was winding, corner after corner, and the horse's gallop meant that both he and Biddie were being thrown around.

Arch did his best to hold Biddie as still as possible whilst directing the horse. In the early morning glow of the May sun, it was just bright enough to be able to focus on the house in the distance. As he fought to keep Biddie still and tried desperately to focus on the Parkers' house in the distance, Arch found himself losing hope. The stress of the night built up within him.

We can do this, he reminded himself.

His heart thumped away in his chest, and his mind raced almost as fast as the horse. As he fought off the thoughts of losing Biddie, he found himself wondering how Biddie knew that Angela might be able to help. *They must have discussed Thomas and Sylvie,* he thought. *Does that mean that Angela could have saved them? If they'd have just gone next door? Maybe if someone had been around ...*

He stopped the thought in its tracks. Instead, he tried to figure out exactly what Wellington had done. He clearly hadn't hurt her in any violent way. There were no bruises, nothing like that. Which meant that with Biddie's appearance, and her throwing up ... The only other option was that Wellington had poisoned her. At the very same second he realized this, he heard a gunshot echo behind him.

He ducked in a panic, uncertain where the shot had come from. His eyes darted around, looking left and right manically. He spotted the shooter; a few meters away, on a huge, black stallion. Squinting slightly, he identified the man. It was Wellington. He wore precisely what he had earlier; a three-piece suit with a bow-tie and sharply polished shoes.

A chain swung from his waistcoat that matched the smooth silver color of the pistol he held in one hand. In his other hand, he held his horse's reins. He stared at Arch and Biddie with a look that sent a cold shiver down Arch's spine.

"Oh no you don't," Arch growled. Tensing his arms around Biddie to keep her still, he sped the horse up. "I'm sorry about this, Biddie, I promise we'll be with Angela soon," he whispered as he took a dramatic right turn to get away from Wellington. With a few deep breaths, he slowed his heart down. *Focus,* he told himself. The horse whinnied, almost skidding as she followed Arch's directions, leading them into a field of growing wheat.

He whipped his head around; looking behind him, he couldn't immediately spot Wellington, but before he could turn back onto the right track, there was another gunshot, and his whole body tensed again. Moments later, he heard the thud of hooves approaching.

"Just leave us alone!" he yelled, turning his horse around once more. "Haven't you done enough?"

All he heard in reply was a chuckle, followed shortly by another gunshot. Arch jumped up, clear off of the saddle, as it narrowly missed him, skating past his leg and just barely missing the horse.

"You know I'll win," Wellington called from behind. "I won with Thomas. I won with his wife. Even if she lives — which she won't — I won't give up, Archibald. This ranch is mine!" he yelled, his tone full of malice.

"This ranch belongs to me, and my family. You will never, *ever,* get your dirty hands on it," Arch yelled back fiercely.

"We'll see about that!" Wellington retorted. Arch could hear the stallion catching up, and his palms began to sweat.

Just get to Angela. He told himself. Every part of him wanted to fight back, to knock Wellington off of his horse, to hurt him for what he did to Biddie, but that was not the priority right now. Biddie was the priority. Getting her to Angela could save her life.

With another flick of the reins, he pulled his horse back onto the dirt track between the fields. He gave the horse a gentle kick, hoping it still had a little speed left to accelerate them away from Wellington and onto the Parkers' property.

The race continued, and he felt Biddie weaken in his arms as they rode. Just as they crossed the threshold of the Parkers' ranch, he heard another gunshot from behind him. He growled and turned his head, checking to see whether the bullet had hit the horse.

In what little light the rising sun provided, he could see a small graze on the horse's rear, but it didn't seem to have bothered her. It felt as if he was being watched over — he was lucky that Wellington missed.

"That's it, good girl," he whispered, turning his attention back ahead. He could see the house clearly now. It wasn't far at all. He could still hear the sound of hooves hammering behind him as Wellington chased them, but as long as he could feel Biddie's weak breathing against his chest, he was not going to give up. He leaned forward, pushing Biddie over toward the neck of the horse, hoping to dodge any bullets from behind them, and kept the horse going at full speed.

"You will not win this," he muttered under his breath. In that moment, he promised himself that he'd not rest until he saw Wellington rotting in jail.

He steered the horse across Rudy's ranch, doing his best to avoid the crop fields. The sound of hooves beating on the compressed soil echoed around him, and quickly became the only thing he thought about as he closed the final distance between himself and Angela's house.

"Why the Sheriff's house, Sutton? You know he's not here," Wellington taunted. "There's nowhere to run!"

Arch clenched his jaw and continued riding; he was mere minutes away from the house now. From where he was, he could see two small figures standing on the porch, and his heart dropped.

Wellington had a gun.

The boys were in danger.

The whole reason he'd sent them away was to keep them safe and now he was taking the danger to them. Wellington was catching up to him. He could be about to lose everyone that he cared about. His body began to shake.

"No, no no no," he mumbled. He looked behind him at Wellington, and then ahead at the boys, hoping he hadn't noticed them. He thought about steering away or yelling for the boys to go inside, but before he could do either, the two of them began to launch rocks out from the porch. They flew past Arch as he slowed his horse down to a halt, and fell near Wellington. The boys threw one after the other, and Arch watched in consternation and awe.

He glanced back at Wellington as the mare pulled up next to the porch, and couldn't help but smirk. The boys' stones were hitting the horse, slowing it down. Wellington had been forced to holster his pistol, holding onto both reins instead in an attempt to balance himself out as his horse endeavored to dodge the flying debris.

His face was distorted in frustration and confusion as he held onto the leather straps for dear life. Arch watched, holding onto Biddie, as Fred threw a particularly large stone with a sharp point. The young boy grunted, launching the thing into the air, and let out a small cheer as it collided with Wellington's knee.

Whilst Wellington was distracted, Arch quickly jumped down from the horse and collected Biddie into his arms again. She groaned with the movement, and Arch's heart skipped a beat.

She's still with us. Dodging the rocks being launched rapidly at Wellington, Arch ran up the porch steps to the boys. He watched as their stones hit Wellington and his horse again and again. The stallion whinnied in annoyance, and Wellington growled.

He reached for his pistol, but before his hand could grab it, the horse turned, clearly thrown off by the assault of stones. The turn took Wellington by surprise, and he teetered on the saddle. Fred threw one more large rock, and it slammed into

Wellington's arm, destroying what little balance he had left and throwing him off of the saddle and into the mud.

He landed with a loud thud, and the two boys cheered. David threw one final rock, and then Arch beckoned them away from the steps to a safer space behind the railing.

With Biddie safely in his arms, Arch looked at the boys with a small smile. He'd never been so proud.

Chapter Thirty

The Sutton Ranch, Paddington, Texas

24th May 1885

Wellington remained on the ground, groaning and growling. He held onto his arm, wincing.

"Good job, boys," Arch said quickly.

"Thanks, Uncle Arch," Fred replied.

"What's wrong with Miss Biddie?" David asked, his eyes wide with panic.

"Nothing, don't worry," Arch replied. "She'll be alright, I just need Angela."

He was not going to let them panic. They'd lost so much so young, they did not need to worry about this too. He looked to the door, but before he could walk over or ask them where Angela was, she ran out, almost colliding with Arch. Looking around frantically, she spotted the boys and seemed to relax slightly. Her hair flowed down her back, and her face was paper white with panic. She'd clearly been awoken and rushed straight out of bed.

"I heard gunshots, and groaning," she spoke quickly, barely getting the words out on either side of ragged breaths. "What's going o–" She paused, looking down at Arch's arms. "Oh dear, no … " She shook her head, her hands rushing to her mouth. Arch could see tears filling her eyes and desperately wished he could reassure her somehow. He wasn't sure what to do, and decided just handing Biddie over and letting Angela take control was probably the best idea.

"Here, here," Arch said, lifting Biddie away from his chest carefully. She whimpered as he moved, and it made his heart ache. "Where should I put her?" he asked softly.

Angela looked him in the eyes, her face full of concern and confusion. Arch looked down at Biddie and watched as her eyes flickered open again; she looked up at Angela and squinted, smiled peacefully, and her eyes fell back shut. Arch let out a shaky breath. It was becoming clear that she didn't have long.

"What on earth happened?" Angela asked, her eyes wide.

"Wellington and Monty came by the house, they tricked us. Whilst I went to get Rudy, they did this ... I think they've poisoned her," he said quietly, hoping the boys couldn't hear. "She said your name and the word 'cure'. She might be just delirious, but I had to try," he looked at Angela, his eyes wide and pleading. "Can you help her?"

Angela watched him eagerly and then nodded. With a deep breath, she looked Biddie up and down, then looked over at the boys.

"I can certainly try," she replied. "I won't let her go. Not without a fight, Arch," she reassured him. "But it would help if I knew what she'd taken."

"I wasn't there, I-I'm ... I'm sorry, I don't know," Arch's breath hitched in his throat. Angela had to be able to cure her. That was their only option. If she couldn't, then Biddie was about to die.

"No, no," Angela shook her head. "It's alright, I'll sort something ... "

Arch nodded, letting out the breath that he had held and looked at Biddie. Her body was almost completely limp, and her face was still as pale as snow. He lifted his hand and caressed her face softly.

"You're with Angela now," he said sweetly. "She'll make you better. I promise we will fix this."

Biddie's eyes flickered open once more, and she looked from Angela to Arch. She moved her mouth, but no sound came out, and Arch eyed her with concern. She clenched her eyes shut, and coughed aggressively. Spluttering, she licked her lips and cleared her throat. Arch and Angela shared a confused look, and waited for a moment.

"Pretty... p-pretty flower," Biddie rasped. Arch's eyes widened. *She's trying to tell us what it was,* Arch realized. *What a brilliant woman. Even now, she's helping us.*

"Pretty flower ... Okay, what else, Biddie?" Angela asked, bowing her head to hear better.

"D-dark," Biddie let out a long, weak breath that sounded like it rattled her lungs. "Dark berry ... B-bitter," she sighed, and her mouth closed. Arch looked up at Angela expectantly. She wracked her brain for a moment, and then smacked her forehead.

"Spurge laurel! I should have known."

"Excuse me?" Arch asked.

"They used spurge laurel. I can cure her," she said excitedly, a look of determination on her face that Arch had not seen on Angela before. "I'll take the boys and Biddie, you go fix this mess."

"Are you sure?" Arch asked, looking from Biddie's face to Angela's. He didn't want to risk her dropping Biddie.

"I can handle it," Angela nodded to reassure him. She held out her arms and turned to the boys who were sitting behind the porch railing, watching the adults with confused and startled expressions.

"Let's go inside," Angela said sternly but softly. "Can you get the door?"

The boys nodded, jumping to their feet and rushing over to the door. Fred pushed it open, and he and David wandered in. With the boys safely inside, Arch gently placed Biddie in Angela's arms. She, much to Arch's surprise, held Biddie without much struggle. With a small nod, Angela turned and hauled Biddie over the threshold. "Arch?" she called back.

Arch peered around at Wellington, who was slowly starting to push himself up.

"Hm?" he replied, returning his attention to Angela and the front door.

"Rudy's safe, right?" she asked, her eyes wide and wary.

"He's headed to the station, with Monty," he replied, "he's safe, Angela, I promise." He'd seen Monty try to fight Rudy's grip. There was no way Rudy was letting that man go. They'd be at the station safely by now.

She nodded swiftly and then rushed into the house. He heard the handle click and then turned his attention back to the evil man on the ground, only to find that Wellington had moved. In his place was simply a dent in the mud.

"Not this time," Arch growled. He was *not* letting Wellington escape for the second time that day. He jogged down the steps and looked around, turning his back to the fields on the left. As he went to turn back around, Wellington tackled him to the ground, running full-speed. Arch went down instantly, falling before he'd even really processed what was happening. He landed on the mud with a thud. Looking up, he watched as Wellington reached for his gun, standing over Arch.

"This is over," Wellington said, cocking the gun and aiming it at Arch.

Arch's chest tightened, but with a glance over at the house, he remembered exactly what he was fighting for. With a small grin, he lifted his leg and kicked Wellington hard, firmly in the groin.

He wants a fight? He's getting one, Arch found himself thinking. He'd wrestled with Thomas a lot as a child, and while he may not have done much fighting since, he was sure he could beat an old man blinded by ambition. He was so full of anger about his brother, about Biddie, about Sylvie … He was going to show Wellington that he had made a grave mistake in trying to mess with the Suttons.

Wellington doubled over, a hand rushing to his groin. His face turned pink, and Arch felt a wave of confidence rush over him. Play-fighting with Thomas as a child was actually coming in handy, it seemed. Hastily, he pulled himself up from the ground and stepped away.

"You are done, Wellington," he hissed. "Your rampage, your evil acts, all of it — you're done!" He ran at Wellington, tackling the man to the ground. The two of them fell into the mud. Arch landed on top of Wellington with a groan. Wellington let out a small squeal as his injured arm hit the ground. He looked up at Arch and snorted, but his expression remained a clear sign that he was losing this fight. His jaw was clenched in pain, and his eyes were beginning to water.

"I don't think I am," he hissed. With his good arm, he swung for Arch, punching him in the jaw. Arch yelled and rolled off to the side. He moved his jaw and winced — Wellington was stronger than he looked.

Good, Arch thought. *Neither am I.* Standing up, he kicked Wellington in the side.

"Just. Let. It. Go!" he yelled as his toecap collided with Wellington's ribs with a crunch.

Wellington gasped. His eyes widened and he let out a breathless scream. Arch reached down and grabbed his shirt. With all of his strength, Arch pulled Wellington up from the ground by the fabric, and slammed the older man into one of the pillars of the Parkers' porch. Wellington winced and whined, and Arch felt the anger pour out of him as he slammed the man against the wood one more time.

"D-does this help?" Wellington asked, a small, almost smirk on his face. It filled Arch with rage, and he let go of Wellington's shirt, reaching instead for where he had kicked him. Carefully, he pressed his finger into Wellington's side, applying just enough pressure to hurt him, and to wipe that smirk off of his face, but not so much as to do any more damage. He wanted Wellington alive and well enough to suffer and spend the rest of his days in a cell. He wasn't getting away easily.

"No, but this does," he said simply. "This is for Thomas. For Sylvie. For the life that they will never get to live because of your *ridiculous* ambitions!" Arch yelled, his face only inches from Wellington's. "Now, I'm going to go and undo your actions. And you," he paused and gave Wellington a swift kick in the shin. The man fell in a heap on the floor, moaning, "well, you're going to stay right here until the Sheriff arrives. Move an inch, and I'll be sure you can't ever move again." He glared down at the quivering pile of a man by his feet and then turned away. He didn't want to have to hurt Wellington any further — he took no joy in the violence. He hoped that the damage he'd done so far was enough to encourage Wellington to remain where he was.

Arch walked over to the mare that he'd ridden in on, and tied her to the porch railing. With a small stroke of her nose in thanks for getting them there safely, he walked around the back of her to check her wounds.

The graze had not bled, luckily, so she'd be just fine. He smiled to himself and jogged back around to her front. Just as he went to wander up the stairs to the porch, he heard the barrel of a gun spin into place.

He jumped back and looked over to Wellington, who, from the ground, had pulled his pistol out and, with his one good arm, shakily pointed it directly at Arch's chest.

"Nothing in my way, if you're gone," Wellington breathed. "Sutton ranch will finally be mine," he grinned lopsidedly, and Arch's heart began to race. From where he was standing, there was nowhere to hide fast enough, and he definitely couldn't close the gap between the two of them. He eyed Wellington nervously, and, in a moment of desperation, he closed his eyes. *Please, God, let me live.*

"Pathetic," Wellington snorted. "J-just closing your eyes and accepting it? Even your woman put up more of a fight than that," he laughed a rattly, gaspy laugh of a man in serious pain.

There was a gunshot.

Arch's breath caught in his throat.

A second passed, then two, then three.

He felt nothing. No wound, no bullet, no blood. Not even the wind from a bullet flying past. He opened his eyes. His hands rushed to his chest, patting himself to be sure, and then his eyes landed on Wellington. Frozen in fear, the older man had aimed for Arch, but his hand had let him down.

His grip on the pistol had loosened just as he fired, it seemed, and the gun spun on his finger. The bullet had gone straight into his gut. At such close range, there was no coming back from a wound like that. Arch's heart dropped; *so much for rotting in jail*, he thought.

He watched as Wellington's arm fell, the pistol clattering onto the ground. His eyes began to droop, and the suit he wore slowly began to redden as the wound emptied onto it. Arch grimaced. As much as he'd wanted justice for Thomas and Sylvie, no man of sound mind wishes to watch another die. He turned away.

"Goodbye, Wellington," he said quietly, before slowly walking up the steps to the porch. With one last look over his shoulder, Arch took a shaky breath and walked over to Angela's front door. He turned the handle and stepped inside.

It was as if he'd entered another world. Where before there had been silence and death, the home was full of warmth and noise. Angela had the boys running around and grabbing her things. Through the hallway, in the lounge, he could see Pauline asleep in a cradle. Biddie lay on the dining room table, which Arch could see on the left of the front door, and Angela was bent over her, fussing about one thing and then another.

"Arch?" she asked quickly, without looking up.

"Yes?" he replied.

"Is he gone?" she asked. "I heard a gunshot."

Arch paused. He looked over his shoulder at the boys in the hallway. They'd stopped to hear his answer.

"He's gone. But it wasn't me. He did it to himself," he said simply. A second later, he heard the boys continue their rushed movements. Angela was silent for a moment and then nodded.

"Very well," she said quietly.

"How is she?" Arch asked, walking over to Biddie's side. At first glance, her face had regained some color, and her breathing seemed, at least to him, much stronger than it had been. His heart skipped a beat.

"She's stable," Angela answered. "I think we'll be alright. I just want her to wake up now," she said, looking up at Arch and then over at Biddie's face. Her eyes were shut as if she were peacefully asleep.

"When do you think she will?" he asked. He watched as Angela threw a handful of ingredients into a small ceramic bowl and began to mash them together.

"Anytime now," she answered quickly. "I've given her the cure, I'm just treating the effects now. She has some blisters in her mouth, and her temperature is all over the place … If I can keep a handle on those, she will be just fine."

For a moment, it felt as if time had stopped. Arch's heart swelled with relief and excitement. His Biddie was going to be alright. He'd done it. They'd gotten there in time. Angela had saved her. They'd done the impossible. He could not wait for her to wake up. Without warning, tears began to stream down his face. He quickly wiped them away and looked down at Biddie.

The sweat on her forehead had evaporated, and her hair had somehow become curlier as it had dried. He could see some blistering on the inside of her mouth and her lips were dry, but they were beginning to return to their usual pinkish tinge.

"Oh, Angela," he said gently. "You're an angel, truly."

Angela looked up from her pestle and mortar and smiled at him. "I wasn't going to lose another person," she said simply.

The two of them locked eyes. At that moment, his business, the ranch, none of it mattered. Together, he and Angela had saved Biddie. The children were safe. They were safe. That was all that mattered. He gave Angela a warm smile and reached over the table to clasp her hand.

"Really. Thank you," he said. "We won't be burdened with that vile man any longer."

"I'm glad," Angela replied. Arch withdrew his hand and returned his attention to Biddie. He watched carefully, taking in her beauty as the color returned to her cheeks. He looked at every freckle on her face, her eyelashes, her perfectly placed nose. He mapped out her face in his head as if it were something he might one day forget. Then, softly, her eyelids fluttered.

"Angela!" he whispered urgently. His heart raced with excitement and he gripped the edge of Angela's wooden table. Angela placed the pestle and mortar down and looked at Biddie's face. The two of them watched her eagerly. Sure enough, her eyelids fluttered again.

And again.

And again.

Then, slowly, they opened. Her green eyes were almost back to their vivid emerald, and the veins that had covered them were only a weak pink color. Arch's heart felt as if it was going to burst. She looked up at them, blinking slowly like a sleepy owlet. She lifted her hand to her head and rubbed her temple, wincing.

"Ah, yes, you're likely to have a headache for a few hours, hon," Angela said sweetly, a small laugh of disbelief following her words. "It's just a lingering effect of the poison."

Biddie looked at Angela for a moment, like she was processing what she'd said, and then nodded. She frowned slightly, passing a hand over her eyes.

"Blurry," she complained weakly, and Arch realized that her glasses were missing. He chuckled weakly. Looking back to Arch, her mouth slowly widened into a gentle smile.

"A-Archibald," she whispered. Her voice was hoarse and quiet, but somehow, it was the sweetest sound Arch had ever heard. A smile stretched across his face, and his eyes began to well with tears. He moved his hand, sliding it into hers, laid by her side.

"Hello, Biddie," he whispered. Glancing up at Angela, he noticed that she had tears in her eyes as well. He gave her a gentle smile and then returned his attention to Biddie. "You're safe now."

Biddie watched him intently, her focus unbreaking. Her eyes began to widen, returning to their usual soft almond shape as the two of them gazed at one another. Arch's heart fluttered in his chest, and he sniffed away the tears that were beginning to sting his eyes. Biddie shakily lifted her hand to his cheek and, using the pad of her thumb, wiped away a single tear that had escaped. A warmth spread across Arch's face. From the other side of the table, Angela cleared her throat.

"Don't mind me," she said half-jokingly. Arch chuckled and stepped back, looking across at Angela.

"Sorry, Angela," he replied. "So what now?"

"Well, the poison should be out of her system soon," Angela replied. She stepped closer to Biddie and pushed her unruly black hair back from her face. Placing the back of her hand on Biddie's forehead, she made a satisfied hum. "Very soon. Her temperature is almost normal already."

"W-wait, the poison is gone?" Biddie croaked from the table.

"Seems that way," Angela replied, a small, proud smile on her face.

"How? How did you know to get me here, Arch? I never told you about Angela's mother … " Biddie's brows furrowed again and she looked to Arch and then to Angela for an explanation.

"Don't you remember?" Arch asked.

"Remember what?" Biddie asked. "I remember being made to drink the poison, I remember … Not a whole lot, actually."

"Well, after you drank the poison, Rudy and I returned from town. We rushed into the house only to see you barely conscious in your seat. Rudy and I had to fight Monty and Wellington to get to you, and then I took you into the bedroom so that you could be comfortable. I was holding you when suddenly you just began to speak. You didn't say much, but it was enough to fill me with a shred of hope," Arch smiled down at her, and squeezed her hand before letting go. "So I flung you onto a horse, and here we are."

And we got shot at, I got beat up, and Wellington died, Arch thought to himself. He decided that was all information that he could share with Biddie when she was better, not the moment she woke up.

"So you saved me?" she asked.

"Technically you saved you," he replied.

"Excuse me, I think I had a part to play in that," Angela teased. "I think we all saved you, Biddie. Even the boys. They've been fetching ingredients and items to help me cure you," she gestured at the doorway, where Arch could see the two boys waiting to come in.

Biddie lifted herself up onto her elbows and followed Arch's gaze. At the sight of the children, her face lit up. She was still slightly pale, and it was clear that propping herself up was expending all of her energy, but Arch was glad to see her recovering so quickly.

"Hello boys," Biddie said sweetly. "You can come in."

Fred and David nodded and quickly walked into the room. They rushed over to Angela's side and she placed a hand on each of their shoulders.

"Now, boys, don't overwhelm Miss Biddie, she's just had a long nap," Angela said, raising a brow quizzically as if trying to figure out whether or not she'd said the right thing.

"Why did you have a long nap, Miss Biddie?" David asked. Arch felt a lump rise in his throat.

"O-oh, well." Biddie smiled. "I was a little bit sick, so I thought it best to sleep it off," she answered confidently. Her voice was still hoarse, and she had to pause after her sentence in order to regain her breath, but nonetheless, it looked like she'd be absolutely fine in no time at all.

"Do you feel better now?" Fred asked.

"I'm starting to," Biddie replied with a small nod.

"I think that's probably enough for now," Angela said gently. "I think we should let Biddie relax for a while. Boys, why don't you go and check on your sister?" she patted them both on the shoulder and they nodded quickly, disappearing out of the room to go and see Pauline.

"I'm going to go and clean up," Angela said simply. "I'll be back shortly." She gave Arch a quick nod, and then grabbed as many of her tools and ingredients as her arms could carry, and wandered out of the room. Biddie let herself lie back down and took a long, shaky breath.

"Take it easy," Arch said. "There'll be plenty of time to chat later. Rest now," he smiled at her, his heart full of warmth and happiness. She was back, Wellington was gone, and Monty was on his way to a cold jail cell.

The worries of the last few days were slowly starting to fade. "I'll leave you to it, and I'll be back soon," Arch added. He wanted to spend some time with the boys, to make sure they weren't too affected by what had just happened. Biddie nodded softly and gave him a warm smile before closing her eyes again.

Arch turned to leave, and as he went, Biddie's hand slipped into his, stopping him in his tracks.

"Arch?" she asked.

"Hm?" he turned, a tingle traveling up his arm from where their hands were clasped together.

"Thank you for saving me," she whispered, and with that, she let go of his hand. He smiled to himself and looked at her once more.

I'll always be there to save you, he promised her silently as he left the room.

Chapter Thirty-One

The Parker Ranch, Paddington, Texas

27th May 1885

Biddie slowly awoke in her makeshift room. The light shone through the panes of the windows and warmed her face, enticing her to open her eyes. With a small yawn, she stretched her arms above her head. Her muscles still ached from the events a few days earlier, but stretching them gave her a small amount of relief.

Carefully, she opened her eyes, covering them with her hand so as not to overwhelm her senses with brightness. Her eyes began to adapt slowly, and the room around her began to take shape. She looked around as the dust danced in the air around her and smiled. Slowly, she pulled herself into a sitting position.

Rudy and Angela had made her a bed in their lounge. They'd pulled an old mattress off of one of the beds upstairs — Angela insisted that Biddie was not well enough to climb stairs yet — and placed it across a frame made from their dining room chairs.

It was very sweet of them to do and surprisingly comfortable. Although Biddie imagined anything would be comfortable when recovering from a bout of poisoning. She was so tired all of the time, she'd be happy to sleep in the barn with the animals. She yawned again and rubbed her eyes with the heels of her hands.

Groping for the bent frame and cracked lenses of her eyeglasses on the small table beside her bed, she grimaced at them, then fit them to her head as best she could and squinted, looking at the clock on the wall opposite her.

After Wellington — or was it Monty? Well, whichever one it was had knocked her spectacles clear off her head and they'd hit the wall hard before sliding to the floor, denting the frames and sending tiny spider cracks through the glass.

Arch had found them and brought them over a couple days after the whole debacle. They were serviceable, but just barely, and she was counting the days until she was well enough so she could go into town to find someone to fix them.

She rubbed her eyes again and tried to focus. Thinking and concentrating had been incredibly difficult over the last few days, she'd noticed. She'd mentioned it to Angela and was told that it was a side effect of the poison. Angela reassured her it would pass. She stared at the clock a moment longer until she finally managed to see that it read eight minutes past eight.

As she continued to wake up, Biddie realized that she could smell eggs, and she could hear Angela rummaging around in the kitchen. A small smile appeared on her face and she started to push herself off of the bed. Swinging her legs around, she tapped her toes on the floor gently to make sure that her feet weren't asleep, and then pushed herself up from the mattress slowly.

Her legs trembled beneath her, and she balanced with the help of the makeshift bed frame. On wobbly legs, she wandered around the bed to the clothes that Arch had brought over for her. Rummaging through the fabrics, she spotted a dusty pink dress. She hadn't worn it since she moved, but it had been one of her favorites back home.

She carefully pulled the dress on and then used the looking glass that Angela had let her borrow. Her hair was still pinned back from the day before; her arms were too weak to hold above her head for long, so she'd had to have Angela help her.

Despite that, she was cheered by how much more color there was in her cheeks now than when she'd first been cured; she just wished her muscles would stop trembling.

One step at a time, she headed out of her bedroom and toward the kitchen. As she approached, she could hear Rudy and Angela chatting away, and smiled to herself. Eventually, she reached the kitchen. Stepping into the room, Biddie smiled warmly at her hosts. Angela stood by the stove, humming away as she cooked. Rudy, on the other hand, was sitting at the dining room table. He had a newspaper in one hand, and a cigar in the other.

"Good morning," she greeted, wandering over to one of the remaining seats at the table. Rudy instantly looked up from where he was sitting and smiled.

"Biddie! Morning," he said cheerfully. "How're you feeling today?"

"Well, thank you," she replied, sitting down. "My legs are a little shaky today, but I don't feel sick, I'm not coughing, and my mouth is starting to feel much less sore. All thanks to you, Angela." She looked past Rudy at Angela, who had turned her head to listen to Biddie's update.

"Well, I'm glad to hear it," Rudy replied, a big grin on his face. "We'll have you back up at the ranch and teachin' them boys in no time at all."

"Oh I hope so," Biddie replied with a small sigh. "Staying here is lovely, and recovering is important, I know, but I do so miss teaching them … " *And seeing Arch every day,* she thought to herself. Arch and the children had been visiting her whilst she stayed at Angela and Rudy's, but it wasn't the same. She missed waking up, wandering into the kitchen, and seeing Arch's not-quite-awake morning smile. Besides, ever since he saved her life, she was finding it even harder than before to get him out of her head. He was all she thought about.

"I bet you can't wait to get home, to your own bed, to your life. Everything can go back to normal," Rudy nodded. "I know we need normal after all of this … "

"Normal would be a welcome change of pace," Biddie agreed with a small chuckle. "But staying here's not too bad. Good company, for sure."

Rudy smiled back at her, and Angela turned around in the kitchen, a plate in each hand.

"And good food?" she asked slyly, walking over to the table and placing two plates of scrambled egg and bacon down in front of Biddie and Rudy. Biddie's stomach gurgled at the sight — she hadn't even realized she was hungry.

"Mhm, definitely," she smiled up at Angela. "Thank you."

"It's no problem, hon," Angela replied, winking. "So the Suttons are visiting today?" She asked as she returned to the kitchen to grab her own plate of food. Sitting down next to Rudy, she looked to Biddie for a response.

"Mm," Biddie nodded, her mouth full of food. She chewed quickly and swallowed. "Around midday."

"Wonderful," Angela beamed, tucking into her own food.

The three of them sat, eating in silence for a little while. The sun began to filter into the kitchen as it reached its morning height, and Biddie welcomed its heat on her back from the window behind her. She could feel her muscles relax as the sun warmed them, and had to stop herself from sighing with relief.

"So you said you don't feel sick anymore?" Angela asked as she finished her plate of food.

"Yeah, the urge and the lump in my throat are gone," Biddie replied. She was *very* grateful of the fact that her nausea was the first symptom to pass. She'd spent the whole day after being poisoned bent over a bucket. She never wanted to be sick again.

"And your mouth is better?" Angela asked, looking across at Biddie with her brows slightly furrowed across her forehead in thought.

"Mmhm," Biddie responded. She ran her tongue along the inside of her mouth, feeling for blisters. There were still two small ones on her left cheek, but for the most part, all she could feel was slightly tender tissue. "The pain is gone, and the blisters are almost entirely gone too. Only two left."

Angela nodded slowly. "I think you'll be back home before the month ends, then," she said with a smile. Biddie's heart felt as if it were about to burst. She grinned with excitement — she was almost fully recovered, for one, and she'd soon be back in the same house as Arch, whom she absolutely adored, and the children that she treasured.

"You really think?" she asked excitedly. "Oh, that would be brilliant!" she exclaimed.

"You still need to take it easy, but I don't think you'll need my watchful eye on you for much longer. It's not like I'm far away if you do need me, anyway," Angela replied. She smiled widely back at Biddie, and Rudy beamed at the two of them.

"We really did beat them," he said softly.

"It would seem so," Angela agreed.

Biddie felt a warmth spread across her chest. She had gone from feeling as if she had nobody, to having a real community, a real family, that had come together to fight for one another.

Moving to Texas was the best idea I've ever had, she thought to herself.

***

Biddie sat on the makeshift bed, her feet dangling off of the edge. In her hand, she held the mirror. She peered into it, checking her hair and making sure she looked as good as possible for someone who had just gone through what she had.

She'd made sure to clean her face after breakfast, and had borrowed some of Angela's perfume. She'd gone through exactly the same ritual two days earlier, when Arch visited her for the first time. She knew he would understand if she looked a little less than perfect, but she wanted to make the effort.

He always looked so wonderful, it seemed only fair that she tried to too. She may never be able to match up to his perfectly tousled golden hair, or his neatly shaved hay-colored beard, but she could do her best.

She wiped an eyelash away from her cheek, scowling momentarily at her beat-up spectacles, and ran a finger along each of her eyebrows, flattening them. She had tidied her hair as much as she could, tucking the wild curls into the pins that Angela had helped her put in the day before.

The white stripe that erupted from her temple was pinned into one curl at the side of her head. With a small smile, she followed the curl with her finger. Putting the mirror down, she stood up and fluffed out her skirt, then grabbed the edges of the dress and wiggled it into place, ensuring that the square neck sat flush against her pale skin.

The dress was much more lightly-colored than anything she usually wore, but she liked the way it looked. The blush pink color made her skin shine and her freckles stand out. It was the best she'd looked since recovering, easily. Once she was happy with the way the fabric was sitting, she walked to the door of the lounge, when she felt her heart flutter in her chest.

Am I nervous? Why am I nervous?

She shook her head and laughed lightly at herself. She had absolutely no reason to be nervous; it was just Arch and the children. The man had saved her life. They were past being nervous around one another, surely. She closed her eyes and took a deep breath.

Don't be ridiculous, she told herself.

Opening her eyes, she looked out the window of the living room. The room looked out across the ranch, and in the distance she could almost see the Sutton house. Her home. She let out a wistful sigh. Soon enough, she'd be back there with the children and the man she adored, and everything could get back on track.

She couldn't wait. As she watched out of the window, she spotted four silhouettes crossing the threshold. There were three smaller silhouettes and one larger one, and all of them were holding hands.

They're here! she exclaimed in her head.

A huge smile broke out across her face and she rushed to the front door. Swinging it open, she stepped out onto the porch. The warm May air rushed over her, and she had to brace herself on the porch railing whilst she adjusted and caught her breath. In the distance, she could see Arch and the children as they walked closer. She could make out their faces after a few moments.

The four of them were chattering away, smiling. It made her heart warm. Arch had grown so much as a parent since she had moved there; she was proud of him. He was really a role model for the boys now. She propped her elbows on the railing and watched them, waiting for them to be close enough to speak to.

The boys both wore smart clothes, outfits that she had only seen them wear for the fête or for church. Their hair was styled rather than just brushed haphazardly, and even Pauline was dressed in her Sunday best.

Looking over at Arch, Biddie noticed that he too had made an effort. He wore a pair of black linen trousers, an off-white shirt that was buttoned right up to his neck, and braces. She could just make out a bolo tie between the collar of his shirt, and there was a black jacket slung over his shoulder.

He looked exactly how she always thought of him. His outfit was smart, well-presented and neat, as was his perfectly groomed beard, and his artfully disheveled hair gave the whole look a bit of freedom. It was styled, but he did something to it to make it look as if he'd woken up like that. It was somehow messy and impeccable all at once. She loved it.

Within a few moments, the four of them were close enough to the porch to see her, and the children's faces lit up at the sight. She felt a warmth spread across her cheeks, only growing when she spotted Arch gazing at her with an intensity that sent a small chill down her spine. There was something in the look he gave her that made her feel at home, warm, and even more nervous than before.

"Biddie!" David yelled, letting go of his brother's and Arch's hand to rush over to the porch. He sprinted up the stairs and almost knocked Biddie over as he grabbed her skirt and squeezed. She desperately tried to regain her balance and patted his head gently before placing her hand between his shoulders and returning the embrace.

"Good morning, young man," she said softly. By the time David let go, the others had reached the porch. Arch picked Pauline up to carry her up the stairs, and Fred walked over to Biddie.

"You look much better than the other day," he said simply. David and Arch glared at him, and he furrowed his brows, looking up at them. "What? She does!" he exclaimed. Biddie giggled and nodded.

"It's true, I do," she said. "Thank you, Fred," she winked at the young boy, and his confused expression only deepened.

Arch is going to have to teach him how to charm, Biddie thought to herself.

"Good morning, Miss Edwards," Arch finally greeted her. He was standing behind the boys, and she couldn't help but notice what a good little family they all made. Placing Pauline down on the wooden porch, Arch extended his hand to Biddie.

She carefully placed her hand in his, her heart fluttering as his warm hand embraced her dainty fingers. Gently, he bowed down and brought her hand to his lips. Politely, and so, so softly, he placed a single kiss on the back of her hand. Biddie's heart felt as if it was going to give out!

She could feel warmth spreading across her cheeks and a tingle traveled down her spine. She smiled down at him, trying her absolute hardest to maintain her composure. He returned the smile, looking up at her through his blonde eyelashes, and then straightened back up.

"M-morning, Arch," she said weakly. Part of her wished he hadn't bought the children with him this time — then she could just tell him, right there, on the porch, that she wanted to be more than his employee.

"You do look well this morning," he said softly. The warmth Biddie felt on her face seemed to somehow worsen, and she looked down at the children to distract herself from Arch's incredible aquamarine eyes and the way his soft lips had felt on her hand.

"I feel well. How about you, how are you all this morning?"

She looked from Fred to David to Pauline, a large smile still on her face.

"We're good, Miss Biddie, but we miss reading with you," David replied, smiling up at her. His words filled her with joy. She'd often felt that her lessons were unwanted by the boys, but they actually missed her. She *was* making a difference after all.

"Well I'm glad to hear you're thinking about the book!" she said happily. "I'll be back soon and we can carry it on, I promise," she added. "How about you, Pauline?" she asked, raising her eyebrow. She wasn't sure that Pauline would reply, but she wanted to try anyway. The little girl looked at Biddie for a moment, and then up at Arch. He gave her a small nod, and Biddie watched with confusion.

"Hungry. And miss you," Pauline said quietly. She looked back up to Arch, who was beaming from ear to ear.

Did he teach her to say that for me? Biddie wondered.

"Well, if you're hungry, we best go see Angela and Rudy! I'm sure Angela will have something you can eat to keep that belly full," Biddie reached down and tickled Pauline's stomach with one hand. The young girl giggled and squirmed, then nodded enthusiastically.

Biddie straightened back up, pausing a moment to regain her breath, and then grinned. "Come on then," she said, stepping around the boys and leading the four of them into the house.

Biddie pushed the door open with a small groan, her muscles aching as her body moved, still desperate for her to rest. The door creaked open and the five of them piled inside. Angela appeared from the kitchen and smiled widely at the children and Arch. She wiped her hands on the apron covering her light green dress, and opened her arms for a cuddle. David rushed over, dragging Pauline by the hand, and Fred begrudgingly joined in a short embrace.

"I'm making pies," Angela said as she let go of the children. "For supper."

"That sounds wonderful," Arch replied. "When are you hoping to have supper?"

"Around 3 or 4, I think. Does that sound good to you?" she replied. "Rudy will be home by then."

Arch nodded, and Biddie smiled approvingly. She was just happy to have everyone there together. They could eat now, or never, for all she cared. So long as she got to spend time with Arch and with the children, she was not going to complain about anything.

"Perfect. Would you be able to keep an eye on the children for a while?" Arch asked. "I just need to speak to Biddie about some housekeeping stuff," he smiled at Biddie and then at

Angela. Biddie's heart stopped. *What does he want to talk about?*

Angela looked at Arch quizzically for a moment, and then glanced over at Biddie. Biddie gave her a small nod to show that she was happy to go and talk to Arch alone for a while. Quickly, Angela nodded back at Arch.

"Of course, you know I love looking after these little cherubs," she reached down and ruffled David's hair. "Beisdes, I could do with an extra pair of hands or three in the kitchen."

"Thanks so much, Angela. We won't be long," Arch said happily. He turned to Biddie and smiled delicately. "Where would you like to sit?"

"I'd love some fresh air," Biddie replied. She'd liked being at Angelas, but she had been so used to going outside with the children, to do laundry, to pick flowers ... she was really missing the great outdoors.

"The porch it is, then," Arch nodded. "See you all in a bit," he said to the children and Angela before turning around and walking back toward the front door. He opened it and stepped through, holding it open for Biddie. She spun around and stepped toward him. Looking over her shoulder, she watched as Angela led the three children away into the kitchen, giggling and chattering away about pies and fillings. Satisfied that they were all happy, Biddie walked through to the porch. She let Arch close the door, and then turned to face him.

"What's going on?" she asked.

"Let's take a seat," Arch said softly, taking Biddie's hand in his and leading her slowly to a bench on one side of the porch. Biddie felt the warmth spread across her face and a tingle down her spine at the feel of his hand on hers, and tried to ignore it. She let him lead her, then sat down carefully on the bench.

He sat next to her, angled so that his knees touched her leg and he was facing her rather than the fields in front of the house. Biddie could smell him, he was that close. A mixture of cinnamon and cloves, with a dash of something more summery. He smelt like a perfect autumn evening, and his hair was the color to match. She could feel herself melting into him a little, his warmth and charm distracting her from whatever it was they were actually outside for.

"What did you want to talk to me about?" Biddie asked, trying to keep her voice from wavering with nerves as she breathed in more of Arch's scent. She looked at him, but allowed her eyes to look past him rather than at his face for fear of distraction.

The last thing she wanted if he was going to talk to her about anything serious was to be swallowed up by the lakes of his eyes or stargazing at the constellations on his cheeks. Especially as, from the corner of her eye, she could see that Arch was gazing at her with the same look he'd given her when he arrived that morning.

"Well," he began, "first, I have something for you." His eyes sparkled and he smiled impishly as he pulled a small, rectangular package out of his coat pocket. Suddenly shy, he handed it to her. Her mouth formed a small 'O' as she realized what must be inside, and she hurried to free her present from its packaging.

A shiny new pair of spectacles rested in her lap, glinting in the gentle sunlight. The frames were cast, not wire like her old ones, and had a lovely pattern of vines and flowers down the sides. She didn't want to think about how much they must have cost. "Oh, Arch ..." she breathed, but he cut her off before she could say more.

"I need to confess something to you," he said quickly, as though he might lose his nerve. The words triggered something in Biddie's mind, and her memory shot back to the night she was poisoned. Arch had confessed something then, too. She'd just completely forgotten about it until now. Her heart began to race as she recalled what he had said as she had lain there, dying in his arms …

He told me he loved me. He said he wants a life together.

A smile broke out across her face, and she could feel tears stinging at her eyes. Suddenly, the nerves all dissipated. She knew the feeling was mutual. She just had to tell him. But first of all, she had to keep a lid on her feelings until he'd explained to her his new confession. She tapped her foot on the ground to try and expel some of the energy her memory had given her.

"I did something that I possibly should not have done, but … " He rubbed the back of his neck with his hand, and Biddie found herself struggling to keep her eyes off of him. "I looked in your room, for something with your old address on. I wanted to tell your grandmother that she should come and visit. We almost lost you and … well, I didn't tell her that but I just felt that she should see you. So I looked at your letters to her to find the address, and I-I-I," he paused, took a breath, and continued, "I wrote to her. To tell her to come. I paid for her ticket, too."

Biddie's eyes widened. He'd gone through her things? In any other circumstance she'd have been frustrated, but he'd clearly meant well. Plus he was obviously nervous; she'd only heard him stammer like that once before.

He'd just wanted her to see her grandmother and, in all honesty, she'd been missing her grandmother like crazy over the last few days. Arch had done a really, really sweet thing in contacting her, and to top it off, he'd paid for her ticket!

Biddie felt tears sting her eyes again as an overwhelming wave of gratitude washed over her.

"I, oh, Arch ... " she shook her head in disbelief. "You are such a wonderful man. Thank you, thank you so much," she smiled at him sincerely, her eyes full of tears. She was so full of emotion, she wasn't sure she could take any more! Arch watched her for a second, and then put his hand on her knee.

"You're not upset?" he asked.

"Not in the slightest," she replied, shaking her head. She ran her fingers under her eyes, dabbing away a few tears that had spilled over. "Thank you," she said softly. "Really." She placed her hand on his and for a moment, they were both silent. They looked into each other's eyes, and Biddie felt a rush of excitement and the hair on her arms stood on end. Biddie began to lose herself in Arch's eyes, just as she knew she would, and had to look away to bring herself back to the present. There was more to talk about.

"Since you confessed," Biddie said, causing Arch to blink and look away from her eyes. "I probably should, too."

"Confess what?" Arch asked. He tilted his head and raised an eyebrow. She giggled at his quizzical expression.

"The day I was poisoned," she started, and Arch's face quickly changed to a sorrowful expression. His brows knitted together in concern almost instantly. "No, no, no, it's nothing bad," she reassured him. His brows remained knotted, but they loosened slightly. "Well, when you were holding me, you ... you said some things. And I didn't remember them until today. But I can now recall them as clear as day," she spoke quickly, and her eyes could not decide where to settle. "You told me you loved me."

Arch froze. His brows relaxed, and he looked into Biddie's eyes. A small blush spread across his cheeks and Biddie eyed him eagerly, awaiting some kind of response. Moments passed, and Arch remained in his position. Eventually, he took a deep breath.

"Yes," he replied.

Yes? Yes, what? Seriously, that's the best reply you have right now? Biddie thought to herself.

"Yes?" she asked.

"Mhm." He nodded.

"Arch, what do you mean by yes?" she asked. "Did you mean it? What you said?" Biddie paused for a moment and looked across the fields, then back at Arch. "Do you love me?"

Slowly, a smile spread across Arch's face, and Biddie nervously awaited a reply.

"Bridget Edwards," Arch said softly, his voice sweet and thick like fresh, unfiltered honey. "I absolutely meant it. I have loved you since the second I laid eyes on you at the train station. I love your wild, beautiful curly hair, I love the way that your glasses sit on your nose ..." At that, he gently took her old spectacles and held up the new ones for her to try on, which she did. They fit perfectly, and Arch grinned as he continued.

"I love the way you smell, darn it. I love every single thing about you. You are incredible. The most incredible woman I have ever met," he spoke slowly, and his face had lit up as he listed off each thing he loved. Biddie felt a warmth in her chest, and couldn't help but beam. She felt tears streaming down her face as she looked Arch in the eyes.

"Arch ... " she said quietly, wiping the tears from her cheeks. "Oh, I love you too. I love you so much!" she exclaimed. "You are everything I want and more," she said. "I'm so glad you feel the same. So, so, so glad."

The two of them smiled at one another and Arch took Biddie's hand in his. He stroked the back of her hand with his thumb gently, and bit his lower lip. He looked at their hands for a moment, and then looked up at her through his eyelashes again. Slowly, he lifted himself from the bench and dropped down onto the floor, onto one knee.

"In fact," he said, "I love you so much, that, well, I was wondering ... "

Biddie's heart began to race in her chest. *Oh my goodness, it's really happening!*

"I was wondering if ... i-if you wanted to be Mrs. Sutton?" Arch asked, chewing his lip nervously as he held onto Biddie's hand. "Bridget, will you marry me?"

Biddie's entire body felt as if it were full of energy, and her hand began to tremble with excitement. She'd moved to Texas simply for a job, and yet she'd found the life that she had spent all of her years dreaming of. She looked Arch in the eyes, and, barely managing to get a word out, she nodded her head.

"Yes. Yes, a million times yes," she said excitedly, but in a hushed tone.

Arch stood up, a huge grin on his face, and pulled Biddie up by the hand. Breathless, she let herself be directed, and in one swift movement, Arch had wrapped his arms around her, squeezing her tight against him. His hands were on the small of her back, and his strong arms held her in place.

She could feel every muscle move under his shirt, and the warmth that he radiated. Up close, the smell of cinnamon was even stronger, and she could now determine that the lighter scent was lemon. His beard touched her forehead, and to her surprise, it was incredibly soft.

They stayed like that for a moment, and Biddie let herself melt into him. He was essentially holding her entire body weight after a few seconds. Slowly, the two of them began to separate, looking up at one another without really letting go.

Arch's face was bright pink, Biddie noticed, but she assumed hers was likely much the same. Before she could think any more on the matter, or look at Arch's face any longer, Arch leaned in. She felt him get closer and closer, until she could feel his breath on her lips and cheek. He paused there, for a moment.

"Is this okay, Biddie?" he asked. Biddie giggled — even after proposing to her, he was an absolute gentleman. *You can take the man out of Texas, but you can't take Texas out of the man,* she thought.

"Yes," she whispered.

If she had to wait any longer she thought she might combust. Luckily, as soon as he'd heard her, Arch pressed his lips against hers. Biddie felt her body scream with excitement; the hair on her arms stood up, tingles and shivers traveled down her back, and butterflies ran amok in her stomach. His lips were soft, but strong.

They guided her own, showing her how to move them. He moved one hand from her back to cup her face, and the warmth from his hand sent another shiver down her neck. She could have stayed in that moment forever, if it were possible.

It felt as if her life had finally begun, after all of these years. Senses were awoken that she didn't know she had, and feelings washed over her that she barely recognized. Their lips moved together perfectly, as if by design, and Biddie felt all of her worry, everything that had happened to her, and to them, fade away. It was just them in the world.

Eventually, their lips parted, and Arch moved his hand from her cheek, then frowned. "Oh, dear."

"What? What's the matter?" Biddie gasped.

Arch chuckled. "I think I've smudged your glasses.""

Epilogue

The Sutton Ranch, Paddington, Texas

3rd May 1887

The midday sun hit the living room window, filling the room with a soft yellow glow. It made the whole space feel warm. From where she was sitting, in the armchair opposite the window, Biddie could feel the sunlight on her face. The beams of light gave her a warm, relaxed feeling, and she sunk further into the armchair.

She held in her lap, cradled against her, her and Arch's firstborn child — Lily. The babe was almost five months old, and was the light of Biddie's life. She was fast asleep, snoring faintly as she cuddled into her mother's torso. Occasionally, when Biddie moved, Lily would coo and wriggle, trying to get comfortable and telling her mother off. Biddie smiled to herself and let out a soft sigh.

She turned her head to look at the couch next to her, where her beloved grandmother was sitting. Evangeline had come to visit two years ago when Arch and Biddie had gotten engaged, and shortly after, they moved her in. She slept in Biddie's old room, and helped to care for the children.

Biddie was glad to have her there and, whilst Evangeline often complained about the thickness of the air, she knew that her meemaw was happy to be by her side again. In Evangeline's lap sat Pauline, who was starting to grow quite fast. She was only four years old, and was already almost as tall as David had been at eight.

Evangeline bounced the young girl on her knee as she braided her hair and told her stories from her past. Biddie listened happily, even though she had heard many of the stories before, just enjoying the peace that had enveloped her life.

"And that's when I met my husband," Evangeline told Pauline. "He was a nice man. Wouldn't have harmed a fly. Unfortunately, I lost him when Biddie was very young. But he's still with me, in my heart," she smiled fondly at the memory of Biddie's grandfather. Biddie wondered if she had ever met George, Evangeline's husband. She had no memory of it, but perhaps she'd been just a baby, like Lily.

"He's in your heart like my mommy's in mine," Pauline replied with a confident nod. Biddie looked at her and nodded, a small smile on her face.

"That's exactly right," Evangeline replied. "And in your brothers' too."

"And papa is there," Pauline added.

"Your papa is definitely there," Evangeline agreed. "Watching over you like my George watches over me." She said with a small smile that filled her whole face. Pauline nodded again, and Evangeline went on telling her stories. Biddie leaned her head on the back of the armchair and closed her eyes, listening to her grandmother tell her tales.

From the kitchen, she could hear the two boys washing dishes. It was their job each day, in order to keep them busy when Biddie needed to rest with the baby. She could hear them laughing and talking, the clink of plates and silverware tapping each other almost creating a beat to which their conversations were the melody.

Without realizing, Biddie began to drift off, the noises around her acting as a lullaby as the warmth of the sun relaxed each of her muscles one by one.

When she awoke, her grandmother and Pauline had left the room, and the sun was no longer shining through the window. A shiver passed through her at the sudden lack of warmth. She yawned and looked around; Lily still slept peacefully at her bosom, and standing in the doorway, leaning on the wooden doorframe, was her husband.

He wore a pair of dark denim trousers, some brown leather boots, and a shirt that was only buttoned to his chest. On his head, he wore a Stetson which had once been his brothers. He'd been out on the ranch. Noticing that she had woken up, he took the hat from his head and bowed jokingly.

"Ma'am," he said, exaggerating the Texan accent that was gradually becoming prominent in his speech. His voice flowed like nectar, and it never failed to give her goosebumps, even after two years. "What's a woman like you doin' in a place like this?" he asked, walking over to her.

A warmth spread across Biddie's cheeks, and she bit her lower lip to stop from giggling, hoping to keep from waking the baby.

"Lookin' for a goodhearted man," she replied, attempting to mimic his accent but failing miserably. She let out a soft chuckle at her own bad attempt. Arch grinned and knelt down in front of her. He looked her in the eyes and winked, and then looked down at Lily. The way that he looked at their baby filled Biddie with so much happiness. Each and every time he saw Lily, he looked at her as if she were the sun, the moon and the stars all at once.

"Well then, ma'am, at your service," he whispered, looking back up at Biddie.

She giggled, unable to hold it in any longer, and a wide grin appeared on Arch's face. He leaned over to the baby, kissing her gently on the forehead, and then stretched up to Biddie. She bent forward, pressing her lips against his.

As their lips touched, she felt a tingle down her neck and spine, and her heart skipped a beat. Despite the fact that they were married and had a child, Arch still filled her with a nervous excitement that made her feel like a schoolgirl. Moments passed, and they pulled away from one another.

"Mm," Arch hummed, and Biddie blushed even more. "Uh oh." He grinned and held out a silk handkerchief, from a set he'd gifted her with on their wedding day. He called them her "glass-kercheifs" because he'd gotten them for her to wipe the smudges off her spectacles.

She chuckled, remembering their first kiss and the way he'd left an awful smudge on the new glasses he'd given her, and allowed him to gently rub the lenses before returning them to her face.

"How're you feeling today?" he asked once her vision was no longer obscured, however slightly.

"I'm feeling good," she replied. "Sleepy, though, apparently ... How about you? How was the ranch?"

"It was alright; the men showed me their system for crop rotation and we went through what to do when to yield the most corn. A visitor came, from downtown. He owns a ranch just outside of Paddington and the union helped him to secure water. He came to thank us," Arch smiled. "It was nice."

"That's sweet of him. I'm so proud of you for doing all of this. The ranch was never your thing. For you to take it on, and to delve straight in," she said softly. "Everything that you've done for the ranch, for the town ... It's incredible."

After they got engaged, Arch decided to let the accounting business take a back seat for a while. He'd been struggling to drum up any custom in Texas. He and Biddie spoke about it at length; He always included her in his business decisions. It was unorthodox, but she appreciated it. She felt like he trusted her.

He explained that the business was suffering because he was new in town, so few people trusted him. After a few weeks, they decided that Arch should throw himself into ranch work for a while to take his mind off of it. The ranch workers took a while to warm to him, but as soon as they realized that he really did want to learn, and that he wanted to help, they quickly taught him the ways of the work.

He remembered very little from when he used to help his father, so much of it he had to be taught from scratch. Biddie watched from the porch in the early days, and she always giggled when Arch did something wrong and the other men rushed to correct him. He'd get all flustered and embarrassed; it was sweet. Some days, he'd take the boys out with him and they'd work too.

Before long, he very much felt like one of the workers, and they all became good friends. They worked long hours together, but Arch never acted like it was a chore.

He enjoyed being out there. As their friendships grew, Arch would always come home after a day on the ranch and tell Biddie everything. She loved hearing about it all.

The two of them quickly learned that, while they were allowing all of the neighboring ranches and everyone else in Paddington who needed it access to the water which he controlled, that wasn't the case everywhere. There were still ranches that went without, and families that were struggling because of it.

So Arch and the ranch men got to work. They contacted other ranch owners that owned water rights all over the county, and persuaded them to come together to form a kind of union.

They combined their water rights, and each owned a share, and agreed to let others use them in exchange for the support and goods provided by the other owners. Soon, more ranches were prospering, trade increased, and Paddington had never been busier. The Sutton Ranch in particular was the most successful it had ever been. Biddie was so incredibly warmed by what he'd done, everytime she thought about it she remembered exactly why she fell in love with him.

Arch looked up at her and blushed. The pink tinge of his cheeks made his eyes shine brighter, and Biddie caught herself getting lost in them, like she often did.

"Thank you," he replied. "I'm sure someone would've come up with the idea eventually," he said sheepishly.

"I wouldn't be so sure. It takes a real selfless man to allow people access to what is his without the promise of anything in return," Biddie said, shaking her head. "Besides, you had to campaign really hard to convince those other ranch owners to come together. I can guarantee you that some of them would much rather have kept their water rights to themselves."

"I suppose so," he replied.

"You and the ranchmen worked tirelessly — you should give yourself more credit. This entire town's ranch success is down to you all. There are families eating at night because you helped them gct their business back off the ground by giving them access to water!" she spoke excitedly, her voice full of pride and love. "Not only that, Arch, but you've given the boys a real role model.

Their uncle beat the town villain and proceeded to change the entire economics and structure of the town to make it more fair for everyone ..." She beamed at him. "Your brother made the right choice, making you their guardian."

"Oh, Biddie," he said, his voice shaky. She could see tears in his eyes. As much as he was a strong, intelligent businessman and ranch owner, he was always, deep down inside, her gentle, loving Arch.

"I am proud of what I did. It's led to more trade for us, for all the ranches, and it's even led to people moving here. I never thought it'd have such an impact; I just wanted to help people," he said plainly. "It bewilders me that something I did could possibly have done so much for so many. I never even thought I'd work on a ranch again, let alone change the way every ranch in the country worked," he chuckled as he spoke.

"But, whilst I am proud of that, I'm more proud of what we've achieved together," he added. He looked down at Lily again, who was just starting to wake up.

"You did an amazing thing," Biddie said finally, before following his gaze. Lily wriggled and waved her tiny arms in the air, grabbing at nothing in particular. Slowly, she opened her eyes. She had Biddie's eyes, without a shadow of a doubt. They were big, so big that they took up much of her tiny face. But her hair, or what little she had of it, was definitely her father's: it was golden, and shone in the light like a star. "She's so beautiful," Biddie said in agreement. "We are so lucky."

"I'm so lucky," Arch said in response. "I have the two most beautiful ladies on the planet, and they're both mine," he shook his head. "I could never have dreamed that this would happen."

"I dreamed about it," Biddie admitted. "Every day until I moved here, I imagined a man just like you, whisking me away to start a family," she blushed and looked down at Lily, who was now staring up at her parents with her bright green eyes. "And here I am."

"And here you are," Arch agreed. "And here she is," he said, reaching to grab Lily and picking her up. Biddie adjusted herself, enjoying the freedom of not having a sleeping baby on her lap. Arch stood up, holding Lily under the arms. He brought her close, kissed on the forehead, and then thrust his arms in the air. Biddie watched, her stomach turning with nerves. Almost instantly, Lily began to giggle excitedly, waving her arms around as Arch dipped and raised her.

"She will be sick," Biddie warned.

"No she won't, she's got a gut of steel, just like her father," he grinned up at Lily, who was still in a world of her own.

"Hmm, don't ask me to take her when she spews on your shirt," Biddie joked, standing up from her seat. "How long were we asleep?"

"About two hours," Arch replied, pulling Lily back down and holding her against his chest. He stroked her back gently, and she let out a small burp.

"Oh, okay, not too long, then," Biddie replied. She hadn't actually been planning to sleep at all, they were having the Parkers over for supper that afternoon and she'd hoped to help set up. "Where are Meemaw and the children?"

"They're out picking vegetables and flowers for tonight," Arch replied with a smile. He walked over to where Biddie was standing and wrapped one arm around her, pulling him against his chest. "Don't worry, we've set everything up. You just relax. You've only just gone back to housework and teaching, and it's clearly taking it out of you.

Let yourself unwind this evening, okay?" he asked, kissing her head as she nuzzled closer into his chest. He still smelled like cinnamon, lemon, and cloves, and she'd grown to associate the scent with home. She'd smell it and instantly any worries would begin to fly away. She nodded in response and let out a deep breath.

"It's just, it's the first time that Angela and Rudy are coming over for dinner since we had Lily, and I want to make sure it's perfect," she said. The Parkers had come over since they'd had Lily, but only ever for a short visit. Rudy had his hands full at work, with people coming forward with more complaints about Wellington and his gaggle of misfits, and Biddie had just been so tired it hadn't been feasible.

"Biddie, it's Angela and Rudy," Arch said, leaning back from her to look her in the eyes. "They are our friends. As long as we're all dressed and there's food, they'll be happy."

"B-but … " Biddie went to argue. She knew that Arch was right. Angela had literally saved her life, and Rudy had seen her when she was at death's door. There was very little either party could do to shock or upset the other at this point; they were bonded for life. But she wanted to put the effort in.

"But nothing. Trust me, alright? Your meemaw was in charge of everything. She knows what she's doing. We've got chicken pies ready to cook, everything is clean, and when they get back from the gardens the boys and Pauline are going to go and wash up and get dressed — you don't need to intervene," he raised his eyebrows, and Lily cooed on his chest as if to punctuate his point. "See, even she agrees, don't you Lils?"

Biddie put her hands up in a jovial surrender and stepped away from Arch.

"Alright, alright," she said. "I suppose I will go and get washed up, then. Can you hold onto her for me?" she lifted her hand toward Lily's face and wiggled her finger. The little girl giggled and reached to grab it. She wrapped her entire tiny fist around Biddie's finger and squeezed.

"Of course," Arch replied. "We'll do some storytime."

"Perfect, thank you," Biddie whispered. She wiggled her finger to freedom, and then kissed Lily on the cheek. Lifting herself up on the tips of her toes, she planted a peck on Arch's lips and then disappeared out of the room.

***

By the time Biddie walked downstairs, she could hear Angela and Rudy's voices in the kitchen. As usual, Angela was fussing over Lily, and Rudy was playing with the boys. Biddie stopped at the bottom of the stairs and straightened her dress out.

It was a dark blue dress that her grandmother had adjusted for her during her pregnancy, and the stomach was still large enough to allow for her recovering body, but tight enough that it complemented her shape. Her hair was worn in a large curled bun at the back of her head, and she had attempted to make herself look at least a little bit less tired. With a deep breath, she walked from the stairs into the kitchen.

As she stepped into the room, she was taken aback by how wonderful it looked. The table had been made, with a runner down the center, two candles in the middle, and a bouquet of fresh flowers in between. There were candles dotted around the room, and jugs of iced tea, lemonade, and cider collecting condensation on the kitchen counter.

Each place had been set perfectly, and the silverware glimmered in the candlelight. From the doorway, she could smell the chicken and the pastry cooking away in the oven, and could hear the vegetables boiling on the stove. Looking around, she saw that everyone had dressed wonderfully.

Her grandmother wore a high-necked yellow day dress with a large skirt, and had dressed Pauline in a similar outfit. The two boys both wore suits, although David's was beginning to get too small for his growing body. Angela had a square-necked lilac dress on, with a golden necklace draped across her collarbones.

Rudy wore his sheriff's uniform, but with cleaner, newer-looking boots than usual, and Arch had changed into a suit to match the boys. He'd even put little Lily in a tiny pink dress.

Biddie's eyes began to well up; they all looked so wonderful. This was exactly the life that she had imagined for herself back in St. John, and had never thought that she'd actually achieve. Her grandmother smiled at her from across the room, where she was standing pouring drinks.

"What would you like to drink, Biddie?" she asked.

"The iced tea is divine," Angela piped up.

"I'll go for that, then," Biddie smiled over at her meemaw, and then stepped over to Angela and Rudy to say hello. As soon as she reached them, Rudy enveloped her in a large bear hug. Biddie gasped, and Angela chuckled as the three of them embraced one another.

"Afternoon, Mrs. Sutton," he greeted her as he let go, a huge smile on his face. Biddie beamed up at him. Something about Rudy just made everyone smile. He was like a big ray of sunshine.

"Hello Rudy," she replied. "Afternoon Angela."

"Hello hon," Angela smiled. Biddie turned back to the table and walked over to her seat. Despite her nap earlier that day, she was already exhausted. Pulling the seat out from under the table, she sat down.

"How was your day, boys?" she asked David and Fred, who were sitting opposite her.

"It was good. We got to help Evangeline cook," David answered quickly.

"And I got to help Arch on the ranch," Fred answered, his voice breaking midway through the sentence. He looked away, his cheeks bright red.

Arch walked over and placed a kiss on the top of Biddie's head, and then sat down beside her. Angela and Rudy followed suit, sitting next to the boys, leaving the head of the table for Evangeline, and a seat next to Arch for Pauline.

One after the other, everyone except Evangeline took their seats, and began to chat away. Biddie let herself just observe. Arch had been right, going back to teaching and cleaning had wiped her out. She was so tired, but, sitting there at that table, she was so full of peace and happiness that it didn't matter one bit.

She looked over at Lily, whom Arch was holding against his chest, and smiled at her. Lily returned a toothless grin, cooing as she did.

"When will she talk?" Fred asked, breaking away from the conversation he had been having with David.

"Well, we don't know," Arch answered. "Usually, babies talk when they are around a year old. But some take longer, some talk sooner. Think about Pauline, for instance," he turned to smile at Pauline who looked up at the mention of her name. "She spoke really young, but then stopped for a few months," he explained.

"And now she doesn't shut up," David joked. Pauline frowned and stuck her tongue out at him.

"Hey, be nice," Rudy said, staring at David. Begrudgingly, David nodded and kept his mouth shut.

"I think she'll talk soon," Fred said. "She's Biddie's baby, and Biddie is super smart."

Biddie blushed and beamed at Fred.

"Thank you, Fred," she replied, and Fred nodded in response.

"More importantly than when will Lily speak, when will the pies be done, Mrs. Edwards?" Rudy licked his lips and turned in his chair to face Evangeline in the kitchen.

"They're just coming out now," Biddie's meemaw replied as she disappeared behind the counter to pull the pies out of the stove.

Suddenly, the room was filled with the scent of cooked pastry and chicken, and a warmth spread from across the kitchen toward the dining table. Biddie inhaled deeply, the smell of her childhood filling her with an even deeper peace than she already felt.

Shortly after, Evangeline wandered through with plates of food, placing them down in front of each person. Looking around the table, Biddie couldn't help but smile at everybody's responses. The two young boys shared an excited look, and she even saw David lick his lips excitedly.

Rudy stared at the plate, his eyes like saucers, and Angela had a small, delicate smile on her face that Biddie had come to learn meant that she was excited. Even Pauline looked thrilled. She'd always known that her grandmother was a good cook, but it warmed her heart to see other people appreciate her too.

"Who wants to say grace?" Evangeline asked as she sat down with her own plate. There was a moment of silence, and Biddie looked around the table, willing someone to speak up so that they could tuck into the steaming pie and vegetables. She hadn't realized how hungry she was. A few seconds of silence passed, when eventually Fred rose from his seat.

"I'll do it," he said simply. Biddie smiled at him proudly. He wasn't a very talkative boy, and especially as he was going through the changes, his voice was wavering a lot lately, and she knew he was a little insecure about it. For him to say grace in front of all of them was quite a big deal.

"Great job," she said softly. "Take it away, Fred."

"Thank you, Biddie," he said with a small nod. "*Heavenly Father, bless us and the food which we are about to enjoy. Bless Miss Evangeline for making such a wonderful meal, and for serving us so graciously. Lord, bless our family and keep us safe from harm. Keep us in your heart as we keep you in ours, Lord,*" Fred said, his eyes closed and his head tilted down. "*We thank you for bringing Biddie and Evangeline to us, as part of our family, and for saving Biddie when we needed her. We thank you for giving us Uncle Arch to care for us, and for watching over us always,*" he added. "*Thank you Lord. Amen.*"

"Amen," the table echoed, all with their eyes shut and heads tilted down. As soon as the word was uttered, they opened their eyes again. Biddie looked to Fred, her ears filling with tears. He'd never before suggested for a second that he was grateful for her presence, or for Arch's. She felt an overwhelming sense of love, and a few tears began to spring from her eyes.

"Fred that was lovely," she said, wiping the tears away.

"It was wonderful, boy," Arch nodded. "Thank you for saying that."

"We are so lucky to look after such a wonderful gentleman like you," Biddie added. "And your brother, of course," she looked to David. "In fact, I am so lucky to have all of you … " she smiled and reached for her glass, raising it in the air. "I am so grateful for each and every face at this table. For being here for myself, and for Arch and I as we enter this new chapter of our lives. For raising me," she looked to her meemaw, who smiled at her with a sincere warmth. "For saving me," she smiled at Angela who nodded with a gentle smile on her face. "And for caring for us, even when we were new to all of this. Arch and I did not expect our lives to pan out this way, but, I hope I speak for both of us when I say that I am so incredibly glad that it did. I love each of you, and I dreamt of a life like this every night for a very long time," Biddie smiled.

Angela, Rudy, Arch and her meemaw all looked at her, pride and love across their faces. She looked across at the children. Pauline smiled vacantly at her, as if she was a little unsure as to what was happening, and Fred smiled warmly across the table. She turned to look at Arch, and he leaned forward and kissed her on the cheek.

This is it, she thought to herself. This is the life I deserve. This is the life all of us deserve.

"Can we eat yet?" David said, his voice high-pitched and whiny, interrupting her moment of satisfaction. Turning to look at him, she smiled, and Arch laughed loudly beside her. "Well, that's not an answer … Can I eat or not?" David huffed.

Biting her lip to stop herself from giggling, Biddie nodded at David, and the young boy quickly picked up his silverware and dug into the still-steaming pie in front of him. Quickly, everyone else followed suit, cutting into the pies and devouring them in silence.

Biddie tucked into her own food, taking small bites and bigger breaths as she continued to take in everything around her. It might have been the leftover sensitivities from her pregnancy, but she just couldn't stop feeling so thankful for everyone in the room, and the life that she had somehow managed to cultivate.

She felt so full of love that she genuinely thought she might burst at any given moment.

"This is delicious, Mrs. Edwards," Rudy said from across the table.

"Mm, truly," Angela agreed. "You know, the first thing Biddie ever told me about you was that you were a wonder in the kitchen. Now I see exactly what she meant."

"Biddie told you about me?" Evangeline said softly.

"She told us lots about you!" Angela nodded, taking another bite of her pie.

"I missed you, meemaw," Biddie reminded her grandmother. "And I'm so glad I don't have to anymore."

"Yeah, we're a real family now," Arch smiled, looking between Evangeline and Biddie.

"Our little makeshift family," Biddie nodded, beaming. "The best family there is."

From beside her, little Lily cooed against Arch's chest.

"She agrees," Arch said jokingly.

"Well, why wouldn't she?" Biddie laughed.

The others chuckled, and they continued to eat their supper. Biddie remained quiet, sitting back as they all joked and ate. Once the food was done, the boys jumped to their feet, taking everyone's plates and piling them away.

Rudy and Arch helped them to wipe down the table, and then David dashed away upstairs to fetch the dominoes. He ran back into the room excitedly and placed them on the table.

"Can we play?" he asked, grinning from ear to ear.

"I don't see why not," Angela replied.

"You might need to remind me of the rules," Evangeline said. "I'm a little forgetful in my old age," she joked.

"Dominoes isn't hard!" David exclaimed.

"He's right," Arch nodded, teasing Evangeline. "I'm sure even Pauline will be able to keep up."

Pauline scowled up at Arch, and the rest of them laughed. Quickly, David tried to explain the rules of the game, missing out several important ones that Rudy had to interrupt and add in. Before long, David was setting the game up, and the eight of them began to play.

Biddie held little Lily against her chest, letting Arch drink and rest, and smiled happily to herself. There was nothing in the world that could change how good that evening felt to her. She felt like her life had just begun, and she could not wait to see what it held.

With her beloved husband by her side, their gorgeous little child, the boys, Pauline, and her grandmother, she could finally begin to make up for all of those years that she felt alone. In her new life, she'd never have to feel like that again.

I've made it, she thought to herself, placing a domino down on the table. Who'd have thought that my life's dream would culminate in a game of dominoes? She giggled to herself, and Arch looked over at her.

"You alright there?" he asked.

"Better than I've ever been," she replied.

THE END

Also by Ava Winters

Thank you for reading "**An Unexpected Governess to Tame his Wild Heart**"!

I hope you enjoyed it! If you did, here are some of my other books!

My latest Best-Selling Books

#1 An Uninvited Bride on his Doorstep

#2 Once upon an Unlikely Marriage of Convenience

#3 Their Unlikely Marriage of Convenience

#4 An Orphaned Bride to Love Him Unconditionally

#5 An Unexpected Bride for the Lonely Cowboy

Also, if you liked this book, you can also check out **my full Amazon Book Catalogue at:**
https://go.avawinters.com/bc-authorpage

Thank you for allowing me to keep doing what I love! ♥

Printed in Great Britain
by Amazon